Fate Succumbs

Fate Succumbs

Timber Wolves Trilogy :
Book 3

A novel by
Tammy Blackwell

Cover Design: Victoria Faye (www.victoriafaye.com)

Cataloging Information

Blackwell, Tammy
    Fate Succumbs/ Tammy Blackwell. - 1st ed.
    286 p. ; 22 cm.
    Summary : Having narrowly escaped an unjust death sentence,
Scout Donovan is on the run. But the more she discovers about the Alpha Pack
and herself, the more she realizes she can't run forever. Destiny is propelling her
towards an unavoidable battle. Can Scout survive, or will she finally succumb to
fate?
    ISBN 978-1479101764
    [1. Werewolves - Fiction. 2. Kentucky - Fiction. 3. Supernatural.]

For the Beta Fish.
You make me better.

Chapter 1

"I can't do push-ups." Sweat slid down my neck, clinging to the top of my shirt. It was only eight in the morning, but it was also August in Kansas's Cimarron National Grassland. "In case you forgot, my hand hasn't been fully functional since I jerked it through a pair of handcuffs."

"Of course you can," Liam said, pouring a bottle of water over his head. "You're a Shifter."

"Which means I'll have use of my hand tomorrow."

"Fine. If you can't handle it, do them one-handed."

For two weeks I had been roaming across the United States in a car with Liam Cole. During our road trip from Hades, he only spoke to inquire on the state of my bladder (which is exactly how he phrased it); offer up some more Tylenol or Advil (the only medicine I was taking for my shattered hand); or ask me what I wanted from the latest drive-thru window (where he always ordered a cheeseless triple cheeseburger). Now, the morning before the full moon, he was suddenly a chatterbox, with every single word used solely to antagonize me. I could tell I was being baited, and it should have stopped me from trying to do them two-handed. Unfortunately, I've never met a challenge I didn't like.

There was a chance the residents of Timber, Kentucky, heard my scream.

As if the physical torture and snide comments weren't enough, Liam also felt the need to enrich my brain with a tedious lesson in Shifter Basics.

1

"And how do you react if you run into a member of the Chase Pack tonight?"

I willed my eyes not to roll. "I drop my head and expose my throat in submission since this is their territory and I have no desire to take it over," I said for the fifth time.

"It's not going to be easy," he assured me, also for the fifth time. "You're going to have to override your instinctive response to exert your dominance."

"I know."

"But if you don't, it could get ugly. You might be able to take another Shifter in a one-on-one match, but if you Challenge someone, the whole pack will come."

"I know."

"The Chase Pack normally doesn't come over to this side of the park, but you need to be prepared just in case."

"*I know.*"

And to think, just weeks ago I wanted to learn more about the Shifter world.

"We've been over this," I said, grabbing yet another granola bar from the backseat of the car. It was the last one in our third box of the day. "I promise I'll follow your lead, stay on this side of the park, and treat any other Shifter I come across with the utmost respect. Seriously, Liam, I'm not going to flake out on you. I don't want someone snitching my location to the Alpha Pack any more than you do." Because God only knew what they would do to me when they found me. Well, I guess God wasn't the only one. I mean, I had it pretty much figured out since they tried to chop off my head with an actual guillotine.

"Good," he said. "Now let's go over the landmarks you need to be on the lookout for again."

There were oh-so-many reasons to be excited as the light of day began to fade from the sky.

2

In the Cimarron, there aren't a whole lot of places to strip naked and wait for your body to rip itself apart so it can reform in the shape of a wolf, but we found a large turtle-shaped rock which would offer up a reasonable amount of privacy. As we were heading over Liam said, "Remember to pull the energy from the ground as you Change."

I stopped at the edge of the rock. "What?"

"Make a conscious effort to pull the energy from the ground. It'll make the Change quicker."

"What are you talking about?"

"Energy transference."

I thought about it, searched the recesses of my memory, and... "I have no idea what that is."

Liam looked towards the setting sun with obvious annoyance. "I thought you said you understood the science behind the Change."

"I do, but Dr. Smith's book never said anything about energy transference or pulling stuff from the ground."

"Dr. Smith..." Realization flashed in Liam's eyes. "You have Dad's book?"

This was not going to be a comfortable conversation.

"Alex gave it to me," I said. It had been a Christmas present. Alex knew I would have a million questions about the whole Shifter thing once I discovered he was a werewolf, so he gave me the one book in the world that explained the science of what happened to the body during the Change. It talked about bone reconstruction, cellular regeneration, and nerve remapping, but never delved into the stimulus for those transformations. "I was going to give it back, but then..." But then Alex died in my arms after a horrible accident. It still caused me physical pain to think about, and I knew it couldn't be any easier for his brother to hear, so I just shrugged off the end of the sentence. "I've been taking really good care of it. You can have it back."

Liam did a kind of head bob thing which could have been interpreted in a myriad of ways. "When you're Changing," he said, switching back to the original subject, "imagine you're pulling strength from the ground and air into your body. We steal energy from our surroundings during the transformation. Mentally opening yourself up to those energies relaxes your body and makes the Change easier."

As far as logic went, it was pretty sound. "Thanks," I said as I stepped around to my side of the rock.

"Scout." I stopped, if for no other reason than it was the first time he ever called me by my name. "Good luck."

* * *

A year ago, I was a normal girl living what I thought was a normal life. That all changed when Liam and Alex Cole moved to my hometown of Timber, Kentucky. Alex, Liam's younger brother, was the living embodiment of perfection - smart, funny, and so hot you worried about spontaneously combusting in his presence. It took me all of five seconds to fall head-over-heels, which wasn't surprising. Everyone loved Alex. The shocker was that he loved me back.

Alex was the one to introduce me to the world of Shifters and Seers, but I soon realized I had been living smack dab in the middle of it my whole life. Thanks to skills I learned from watching too much *Veronica Mars*, I discovered Jase, my step-brother, and Charlie, his cousin who I'd loved since my idea of quality TV included a singing purple dinosaur, were also also Shifters. Not only that, but my best friend, Talley, was a Seer who could See a person's thoughts and feelings with a touch.

Finding out everyone I trusted made it a daily practice to keep elephant-sized secrets from me wasn't one of my better moments. I may have done a bit of property damage as a result.

In April, Alex died in a horrible accident. I was devastated and heartbroken, not to mention sporting some major injuries of my own. I thought things couldn't get any more complicated.

I thought wrong.

Thirty days after Alex's death my world changed again. That night I became a Shifter, Changing into a wolf under the light of the full moon.

It shouldn't have been possible. For one thing, I'm a girl. For another, my father isn't a Shifter. Since the ability to Change is passed from father to son, my newfound abilities were met with some not so pleasant feelings, most of which came from me.

At that moment, crouched down in Middle of Nowhere, Kansas, I welcomed the Change for the first time. It wasn't just because I was going to get the use of my hand back thanks to the Change's tendency to heal injuries - although that was a big, shiny gold star bonus - but I yearned to be wild and free. I was tired of being pinned in with only the crappy thoughts in my head to keep me company. Human Scout was more than ready to hand over the reins to Wolf Scout.

Maybe that's why the Change went more quickly than ever before. Or maybe it's just one of those things that gets better with practice. It could have been that Liam was right and the whole pulling energy out of the ground thing worked, but I didn't want to jump to any crazy conclusions.

Once I emerged from behind the rock I found myself staring into the eyes of a gray wolf. Not just any gray wolf, *my* gray wolf.

Being trapped in a car with his scent for hours on end hadn't dulled its impact on Wolf Scout. Her nose kept nuzzling into his neck, confirming he was really there. There was a period of time when Human Scout had questioned the gray wolf's existence, but Wolf Scout never doubted. But she had never seen more than a glimpse, had never been able to actually touch him.

The part of my brain that was still human, the part that used logic instead of instinct, knew this was the same Liam who hated cheese and was completely unfamiliar with the concept of smiling. Wolf Scout didn't care. She only knew him as the friend who had always been there for her when she was in need, as the one who came to her rescue time and time again.

Liam nipped at me, and I nipped back. Then, he was off. I caught up with him quickly, but only because he let me. We ran together, our sides rubbing against one another as we went. Eventually, Human Scout faded out completely; leaving Wolf Scout at peace with the one person on earth she trusted above all others.

Chapter 2

Before, when I was just a naive teenage girl who knew
nothing of the real world where magic was possible, I paid little
attention to dreams. I rarely had any and thought people who
wanted to analyze them or believed they were passageways to
something mystical were idiotic. That all changed once I became
involved with Alex.

Although he was a Shifter and male, Alex had a few Seer
abilities. While he couldn't do the whole non-verbal, in-the-brain
communication thing Seers are capable of, he could Dream Walk.
He had developed the ability as a child, although it only ever
showed him one thing: Me. Once we finally connected in the real
world, I started participating in those dreams. For months I
dreamt of a place on the lake with a rocky patch of beach
shadowed by a cliff. In April, I found myself at that very spot. It
was the place where Alex and I had our first date, and where we
were attacked by my brother and Charlie.

It was the place where Alex died.

After that night, I continued to dream of our spot on the lake.
In those dreams, Alex was there. I could see him, feel him, and
taste him; he could hold me in his arms and help me sort out my
plethora of problems. Those dreams kept me going when my
heart was in shambles and during my incarceration by the Alpha
Pack. But since my escape those beautiful dreams were gone, just
like everything else in my life.

That, however, didn't mean my nights were dreamless. I slept very little those first few weeks, but when I did I was rarely alone.

Most nights featured Jase, my step-brother, who I loved like the twin people believed him to be. Those sleep-induced mini-movies weren't dreams so much as memories. He would stand in front of the Alphas, head held high, and testify against me. The next morning I would wake with the words, *"She's not my sister,"* echoing in my ears. It would take hours for the betrayal and pain to loosen their hold on my lungs enough for me to breathe normally. On the other nights, I found myself with Travis, a now dead member of the Alpha Pack. The most disturbing of those dreams were the ones where everything seemed normal. I would be sitting in class or trolling the aisles of Wal-Mart and there he would be. He would walk towards me, his mouth curved up slightly as if to say, "Oh, hello friend." I would try to get away, to run, but he was always just around the corner, or blocking my way.

The day after the full moon, my dream took me to a restaurant. It was the fancy kind with actual cloth table cloths and napkins. I could hear and feel other people, but I couldn't see them. All I could see was the Texan with blue eyes and dishwater blond hair who sat across from me.

"Scout," he said by way of greeting.

I didn't respond. I couldn't. I tried to open my mouth, but it wouldn't budge. An attempt to get up and leave was also unsuccessful. I was trapped.

"It's been a while. I haven't seen you since..." A quirk of the lips. "Well, you know."

Tears were hot against my cheeks. I wanted to sob, but none of my muscles worked.

"How does it feel to kill someone?" He leaned closer, no more false amusement on his face. His eyes were hard and accusing. "Did you like it? Did you like the feel of the gun in your hand? Did you enjoy watching me die?"

I tried to shake my head, but it still wouldn't move.

"You did, didn't you? You murdered me, and you liked it." He wasn't yelling or raging, which made it worse. The calm accusations, the absolute certainty he was right in his voice. I wanted to tell him he was wrong, that I was truly sorry. That I would take it all back if I could.

When I woke it wasn't sudden, although my heart did pound frantically in my chest. The guilt weighed heavy in my stomach and clogged up my throat.

No wonder Charlie zombied out on me, I thought. When I shot Travis it was a situation of kill or be killed. There is no doubt in my mind I did the right thing, the only thing that could be done, and yet I couldn't shake these dreams or mend the rip in my soul that ending another life caused. How much worse had it been for Charlie who didn't have the small comfort of knowing it was self-defense? How much worse would I feel if I thought I killed Travis in a fit of rage?

I found Liam sprawled across the other bed when I finally sat upright. Of course, an argument could be made he was actually comatose instead of merely asleep. The motel was one of those places which had been standing since 1950 and hadn't found the need or money for any updates since. I tried to be quiet as I went about my business, but with ancient plumbing and doors in dire need of WD40, it was basically impossible. Yet, when I emerged from the bathroom, as clean as one can be when the water smells of rust and they only own three outfits, Liam was still in the same position, his eyes closed against the afternoon sun.

I rummaged through the multiple fast food bags littering the room, feeling more than a little like a victorious hunter when I discovered an uneaten sausage biscuit hidden in their depths.

With nothing else to do, I sat down, devoured my kill, and watched Liam.

There was a time when I thought Liam was just a bigger, angrier version of Alex. Upon closer inspection, I realized they looked quite different. I mean, anyone who saw them would know without a doubt they were brothers, but they could hardly pass as twins. Liam's hair was starting to grow out, making the red tint absent in Alex's shaggy brown mane, more evident. Their bone structure was similar, but Liam's jaw was more pronounced and boasted a line of stubble. And while their eyes were the exact same shade, Liam's were shaped differently and his lashes, while not as thick, were much longer.

Alex was beautiful. Liam could never be called beautiful. It was much too tame a word. Handsome didn't seem right either. Arresting. That was the word to describe Liam's look. He was arresting.

He was also awake.

"Scout?"

I'm not sure when I got up out of the chair and moved onto the edge of his bed, but that was where I was. And that was certainly my now unbroken hand stretched out, frozen just inches from his face.

"I'm hungry," I said, as if it made the whole Creeper Scout thing okay.

Liam sat up, rubbing his face. I found my way back to the chair as quickly as possible, which for a Shifter the day after the full moon means really freaking fast.

"Want to order some pizzas?"

"Sounds perfect!" I was doing that really fast, high-pitched talking thing girls do. I wanted to slap myself. Liam looked as if he might volunteer to do the deed for me.

After much discussion, some of it actually done in a normal, non-spastic voice, we ordered two large pizzas, an order of breadsticks, two orders of wings, and something they called a s'mores pizza, which I had reservations about. Liam sat some cash on the dresser once the order was placed and disappeared into the shower.

I gleefully passed the time by watching the Cartoon Network. When Liam had control of the TV, which was anytime he was around a TV, we watched The Weather Channel nonstop. An obsession with weather patterns was apparently a Cole thing, because Alex was always Johnny-on-the-spot with the forecast, although, it could have just been because he spent so much time with his brother. I can't even pretend to care about high pressure systems or rotating storms, but after a couple of days with Liam I was able to talk dew points with the best of them.

I was watching a new show - the premise had something to do with talking appliances and a suicidal microwave oven - when the pizza guy came knocking.

"That'll be fifty-seven even," the guy said without looking up. He was really overweight and somehow managed to balance all the food on a fat roll with one hand while he held the receipt in the other. I wasn't sure what the proper etiquette was when it came to grabbing your dinner off a guy's stomach. I started to reach for it, but chickened out at the last minute when it became obvious I might have to actually touch some part of him. He apparently saw me going in, thought I had it, and let go.

If I was a normal girl, the food would have hit the floor.

If I was thinking, the food would have hit the floor.

No food hit the floor.

"Holy shit!" Pizza Guy exclaimed. "How did you do that? You were like The Flash, dude."

"Ummm... I work out?" I straightened back up slowly, as if the action would somehow negate the super-human swiftness I exhibited saving my pizza from a tragic end. I looked up, hoping my somewhat embarrassed smile would keep Pizza Guy from

11

asking any more questions. Once I met his eyes, I realized that wasn't going to be a problem. He was too busy doing the open-mouthed-staring-at-Scout thing people tend to do.

Unfortunately, I wasn't in the mood to deal with it. "Yes, I'm pale. Yes, this is my real eye color. No, I don't dye or bleach my hair to make it look like this." I shoved the money towards him. "No change needed. Thanks."

He didn't take the hint.

"You're her." His eyes had grown huge behind the tops of his cheeks. "You're her. That girl." He waved his hand impatiently in front of him. "What's your name?"

I relaxed my face and willed it not to flush. "Elizabeth," I said, giving the response Liam had drilled into me.

"No, that's not it."

"Ummm... I think I know my own name." My heart was going all kinds of crazy in my chest. Who was this guy? He didn't smell like a Shifter, and Liam said we were at least a hundred miles from the Chase Pack's den.

"No, really." He was clearly getting very frustrated. "You're that chick on TV."

I laughed. It was just one loud burst, more of a squawk than a laugh really, but it was the first one to escape in longer than I could remember. "Nope. That's not me." I looked over my shoulder at the motel room with its stained once-was-shag-but-is-now-matted carpet and mismatched bedspreads. "I mean, would I be standing here in this room if I was?"

He didn't seem convinced. "I can help you," he stage whispered. "I'll get you out of here."

He didn't reek of pot, so he hadn't been smoking. My money was on pills. Lots and lots of pills.

"It's alright," I assured him. "You've mistaken me for someone else."

He still didn't budge. I thought I was going to have to literally push him out the door when Liam stepped out of the bathroom.

"Who are you?" Liam asked in his oh-so-friendly manner.

"Pizza Guy," I answered since Pizza Guy seemed frozen to the spot and incapable of speech. I suppose a six and a half foot tall glowering muscle man probably has that effect on some people. "He was just leaving."

Liam came up behind me and put one hand on the top of the door. "Thanks. See ya," he said, nudging Pizza Guy out with the door. Once we heard him shuffle back to his car, which was several long minutes later, Liam turned his glare on me. "What were you doing?"

"Getting our dinner?"

That, apparently, was the wrong answer.

"What part of 'in hiding' don't you understand?"

"The part where I hide from Pizza Guy?" Was he seriously yelling at me for getting our food? "What was I supposed to do there, Oh Wise One?"

"Hand him the money, take the boxes, and shut the door. There was no need for discussion."

In a move of utmost maturity, I rolled my eyes. "Oh, for the love of all things shiny, not all of us can survive in the real world with glares and few well placed grunts. We have to rely on speech and social norms."

He turned the normal Liam glare up a few notches so it appeared laser beams were about to shoot out of his eyes. I've spent my whole life dealing with bullies - when you look like an escapee from the circus freak show they're pretty much a staple in your life - so he didn't scare me... much.

"Come on, Liam." I used my talking-to-a-two-year-old voice. "Use your words."

"How about these words? You. Screwed. Up."

I wanted to throw something, but since my arms were loaded with the food I fully intended on eating, I restrained myself. I did, however, growl and stomp my foot.

"What? You think Pizza Guy is a spy for the Alpha Pack? That Sarvarna and her army is going to descend on the motel while we sleep?"

A much more impressive growl escaped from Liam's throat. "I told you not to talk to anyone."

"You're not the boss of me," I said, borrowing a phrase from my seven year old sister.

Liam leaned forward, his nose hovering just inches from mine. I could feel the Dominance leaking off him, charging the air with feral energy. "Yes, I am."

I rose up on my tip-toes, as if that would make me seem bigger and more intimidating. "No, you're not." I flashed my teeth, a sure sign Wolf Scout was in control. "I'm not going to come to heel like some whipped puppy just because you've got your panties in a bunch." My hands flexed as if my claws were trying to make a reappearance. "He was just a guy delivering pizza. It's no big deal."

"And if you're wrong?"

"Then I'll get down on my knees and kiss your feet while begging for forgiveness."

He pulled back, and the energy in the room calmed. "Food," he said, holding out a hand. Since there was no cheese to hold the "double all the meat" on his pizza, I made sure to give the box a good shake as I passed it over.

Chapter 3

The knock at the door sounded like gunfire to my super-sensitive ears. My nostrils flared, trying to decipher who it could be, as Liam pulled back the edge of the curtain.

Hide! he mouthed, looking back at me in alarm.

We were still in the world's oldest and dirtiest motel somewhere just past the the Colorado border. The beds were the kind with wood panels along the edges, blocking the obvious hiding spot. *Where?* I mouthed back. Not like it would matter where I hid if it was a member of the Alpha Pack, but my nose was telling me it was just a normal human. I could smell a manly smell - a mixture of Old Spice and natural eau de boy - along with coffee, fried food and sugar. There was no hint of a wolf scent underneath, nor the tickle of power other Shifters and Seers give off.

Liam looked around for a second before nodding at the paneled ceiling above the sink alcove. Lycan strength made it possible for me to hop onto the vanity, slide back the tile, and hoist my body up in a matter of seconds. I was just sliding the tile back home when the pounding on the door started up a second time.

"Can I help you, Officer?" Liam's voice drifted through the ceiling where I was folded up like a burrito. There wasn't a lot of space between the the little drop down ceiling and the actual roof. Added onto the burden of having roughly a three foot by four foot by one foot space to squeeze in my five foot eight inch frame into, I had to be careful where I put my weight. I'm thinking even the most clueless of police officers could find me if I came crashing down through the ceiling.

I fastidiously ignored the inch of dust and grime covering every inch of the crawlspace and the scampering noises.

"I'm following up on a tip we received this morning," came the voice of a man who sounded to be older than dad age, but not quite grandfather age. "Mind if I come in?"

The door hissed against the carpet and the smell of coffee and donuts got stronger.

Seriously? The cop smells of coffee and donuts? I had to bite my lip to keep from laughing out loud.

"Are you here alone?" Cliché Cop asked.

"Yes, sir."

"Were you last night?"

There was a pause and the sound of something rubbing together. It must have been Liam rubbing the back of head, a habit of his, because his smell momentarily intensified.

"I...ummm..." A gulp. "I had company last night."

"I see." The cop was moving around in the tiny motel room. I heard him slide open a drawer. Did he think I was hiding in the dresser? "Don't suppose it was your sister or something like that."

Liam made a sound which might have be a laugh, although it couldn't have been since he didn't know how. "No. Definitely not a sister."

"A friend?"

"Just a girl I met in the bar last night."

The cop was now standing directly below me. I made a conscious effort to breath more quietly, which of course made it sound like an elephant was panting for breath.

"Don't suppose you got her name and number?"

"Beth. Or Elizabeth. Yeah, Elizabeth. That's what she said her name was." Liam sat down on the bed. "Listen, man, she told me she was nineteen. She said she went to college. I swear. I mean, I met her at a bar."

The cop ignored Liam's extremely well done panic attack. "Was this the girl you were with last night?"

The silence seemed to stretch on forever. Finally, Liam said, "No. I mean, that Elizabeth chick was a blonde and looked a little bit like this girl in the face, but she didn't look this... weird." My face flushed with embarrassment and hurt, which was just ridiculous. Of course Liam thought I was weird looking. I *am* weird looking. Somehow, though, hearing that didn't help.

"Are you sure?"

"Man, I was a little buzzed last night, but not drunk enough to forget that." Yop, definitely not helping. "Is this Photoshopped? Or is this chick for real?"

"You don't know who this is?"

The bed springs creaked. "I'm telling you, I've never seen her before in my life."

"That's interesting," the cop said in a way that said he found it to be something a bit more than interesting. "Haven't you been watching the news lately?"

"The news? No. I can't really afford cable at home, been laid off from the plant for six months now. I'm actually on my way up to Denver to see about a job my cousin thinks he can get me." Liam shifted on the bed again. "Has something happened to this girl? Is she missing or something?"

"Or something," the cop said. The sound of paper on paper and then, "Here's my card. If you change your mind, decide maybe this is the girl you were with last night, give me a call."

"Of course." Liam stood up and moved towards the door. "Sorry I couldn't be more helpful. I hope they find this girl, and she's okay and everything."

The cop snorted. "Don't count on it."

I was going to wait until Liam gave me the all clear before coming down, but then I felt something on the back of my neck. Something hairy and crunchy.

I rolled out of the ceiling and onto the vanity, pulling chunks of hair out in my attempt to get the hell spawn off of me.

Liam was completely unaffected by my hysterics. While I frantically searched my body for creepy-crawlies, he turned the TV to CNN. After a story about yet another celebrity entering rehab after making a complete and total idiot out of themselves within twenty feet of someone with a video camera, which is to say "in public", my face appeared on the screen.

"The search still continues for Harper Donovan, granddaughter of Senate Majority Leader William Harper," the anchor woman said as I stared at my senior yearbook picture. "Donovan has been missing since a car crash over two weeks ago. The crash occurred just miles from her home, and according to the Senator's spokespeople, was the work of a radical militant group known as God's Army of Defenders."

The screen changed to show a video of people examining a crash site in what appeared to be the Land Between the Lakes National Forest near my home in Lake County. It was hard to see past all the emergency response vehicles, but the cameraman finally got an angle clearly showing the car my grandfather gave me for graduation wrapped around the trunk of a tree.

"The crash occurred around 3:00 a.m. on the morning of August third. According to a statement given to police by the girl's parents, Donovan had been camping with her brother and some friends that night. One of the crash survivors, Talley Matthews, said a large, unmarked black SUV began following them as soon as they left their campsite to head into town for provisions. When Donovan, who was driving, tried to lose the vehicle, they began nudging the smaller Toyota. Eventually,

Donovan lost control, crashing into a tree at what experts believe to be about forty miles per hour."

The screen cut back to the studio where a stone-faced anchor woman relayed the lies of the night I went missing. "In a press conference given two nights ago, local police stated that after the crash three men in masks approached the car. Two of the men held guns on the other occupants as a third lifted an unconscious Donovan out of the vehicle and carried her back to their SUV.

"Four people were in the car when it crashed. Matthews and Jase Donovan, Harper Donovan's step-brother, both escaped with minor injuries. Charles Hagan, the third passenger, is still in critical condition due to both injuries sustained in the crash and a bullet wound inflicted when he attempted to stop the abduction of the senator's granddaughter. Although his wounds are extensive, Hagan is expected to make a full recovery.

"Another unidentified man who came to assist when he heard the car crash is also in critical condition due to a gunshot wound inflicted during the incident. He is reported to be on life sustaining equipment and doctors are not hopeful about his prognosis."

I sucked in a breath and then couldn't let it out again thanks to my throat, which decided to close itself off.

"The incident was kept under wraps until just three days ago when Senator Donovan released a statement to the press stating he had received a ransom demand from known members of God's Army of Defenders. The letter was received by his office on August fifteenth and verified by government intelligence officials as legitimate twenty-four hours later. In the letter, of which CNN has been able to obtain an exclusive copy, a member known as Michael Avett asks for several members of both his organization and the Secret Brotherhood be released from government holding facilities by the end of the month if the senator wants to see his granddaughter alive again.

"As you may remember, Senator Harper has been very outspoken--"

"Turn it off," I choked out through the tiny opening that was once my throat.

"--Many experts believe his vote on Senate Bill--"

"Turn it off!"

The screen went black, and I concentrated on pulling air into my lungs.

"Charlie..." Oh God. I had left him standing there in the middle of all that carnage knowing the rest of the Alpha Pack was closing in. What did they mean critical condition? Two weeks in critical condition was bad, right? I mean, if he was going to get better, he would have by now. And a gunshot wound? I had heard the gun go off, and I kept running. I chose my life, my freedom, over Charlie's. What the hell was wrong with me? "What will they do to him when he recovers?"

"Depends on what happens to Stefan." Liam began moving around the room, shoving the few things we had back into the two duffel bags that had been in the trunk of the car when we made our escape. "If he lives, he will be under the protection of the Alpha Male, putting him on the exact same level as any children Stefan and Sarvarna might have. Even if he dies, Charlie will probably be offered a position in the Alpha Pack."

I opened my mouth, shut it, and then tried again. "Charlie shot Stefan."

Raising a single eyebrow, Liam said, "You shot Stefan."

"No, I'm pretty sure it was Charlie." There may be many things wrong with me, but memory loss isn't one of them. It was the night of my trial, after the Alphas delivered the guilty verdict. Not one to keep an innocent girl wasting away on death row, the Stratego led me out in the woods to dutifully remove my head from my shoulders. My arms were handcuffed behind my back.

Charlie had hugged me, a last goodbye, and then pulled a gun. He shot Stefan in the chest before the Stratego tackled him.

Charlie shot Stefan and killed Mandla. Liam killed Hashim. I killed Travis.

"How do you explain Charlie's gunshot wound?"

"Bob? Cory? Rocco?" I named off the three Taxiarho, the Shifters in the Alpha Pack stationed just below the Stratego who also oversaw my care.

"No, it was you. You managed to get out of your handcuffs and attacked the guards. Because of the life debt, Charlie was forced to protect you in the battle, although he tried very hard not to actually inflict any true damage to any member of the Alpha Pack. Once they were all dead by your hand, you shot Charlie, knowing he would bring you back to face your rightful punishment. He had, after all, shown the strictest of adherence to Shifter rules and traditions."

"What are you talking about? That isn't what happened at all."

Liam walked over the sink and began to gather up strands of hair. "Makes more sense than Charlie turning on the Alpha Pack, who considered him a friend, and then shooting himself."

My butt slammed down onto the corner of the mattress when my knees finally gave out. "I... What...?" I shook my head, hoping to clear some of the confusion but only jumbled my thoughts further. "I don't understand."

"Charlie worked for two weeks to gain the confidence of the Alpha Pack. He claimed the life debt, which gave him an excuse to be near you, but it also gave him the appearance of someone who followed the old traditions. The Alpha Pack likes the old traditions. It's what gives them absolute rule." Liam's hair scavenging duties took him to the bed where I slept. "By the time your trial rolled around, he was highly regarded by Stefan. I even heard the Alpha Male offer him a position in the Alpha Pack as they walked to your execution sight."

I nodded. I had heard that too.

"When the Taxiarho finally made it to the clearing after hearing the first shots fired, they found three dead Stratego, a mortally wounded Alpha Male, and Charlie with what was supposed to be an *almost* life-threatening gunshot wound." He rubbed the back of his head. "I told him to watch the artery. Dammit. I should have Changed back and done it myself."

With nothing else to do for two weeks, I had plenty of time to think about what happened that night. It was obvious Charlie and Talley had been working with Liam. I mean, they both knew where the truck would be, and Talley had shown me through our more-special-than-most Seer-Shifter link where to go. Since the clothes found in the trunk of the get-away car were made for Liam's hulking body as opposed to Charlie's much shorter and more lithe frame, I knew Liam had been a part of the plan from the beginning, not just a guardian wolf who happened to show up at the right time. But hearing the plan aloud, realizing that it was more complicated than just asking Liam to take me away and hide me, seeing it was Liam's plan all along... There was an actual threat that I might go catatonic from information overload. My brain was in serious danger of completely shorting out on me.

"Do you think..." God, I couldn't even complete sentences. "Will he live?"

Liam ducked his head even lower. Even though we didn't spend a whole lot of time having face-to-face conversations, I knew this was purposeful avoidance. "The news said he was expected to make a full recovery."

"That's the exact same moron who said it was surprising an actress the size of a broom handle and has more nervous twitches than a squirrel on caffeine has a drug problem. I'm not putting my faith in her opinion."

Liam looked up and met my eyes. "But you'll put it in me?"

"You saw him. You know where he shot himself. This was *your* plan." I gave him a second to correct me on that point, and when he didn't, I continued on. "So, tell me, Liam. Is Charlie going to be okay?"

I wouldn't be able to live with myself if he wasn't. I knew that with absolute certainty. Charlie would never be the love I dreamed of for so many years, but he was still mine in every way that mattered. We parted as friends, but friend didn't seem the right word to encompass what Charlie was to me. He was a part of me, the good part. If he died, he would take that part with him. I would still exist, I would still live, but I wouldn't be me.

Liam grabbed what appeared to be a container of Clorox wipes out of his bag and started scrubbing down all the surfaces in the room. "I would say the injuries from the fight are probably causing more problems than the gunshot wound." He disappeared into the bathroom, but kept talking. "I'm surprised the doctors haven't said anything about how they're not consistent with a car wreck. He had scratches from human fingernails down his face for God's sake." Liam trailed off, talking to himself more than me. "Of course, Sarvarna could've called in the Alpha Pack's doctor, probably pulled some strings to make it appear he was called in by the Senator's office. Or maybe she did get the Senator's office to call him in. Who knows what kind of connections she's got her claws into."

When I questioned that statement, Liam explained how far the power of the Alpha Pack reached. There aren't exactly a ton of Shifters in the world, but there are enough in positions of power throughout the world to make the Alphas major players in world politics. According to Liam, the Den - the Alpha Pack headquarters located in Romania - operated like a small but powerful country. In addition to the strongest fighters and most gifted Seers, it was home to the smartest and most skilled of us from all over the world. I hadn't touched a computer or cell phone since our escape on Liam's insistence that the Alpha Pack could trace a call, text, or Facebook message in seconds. Like Liam, I didn't doubt her ability to make sure a well-respected Washington politician called in the doctor she wanted to attend to a person hurt while trying to save his granddaughter. What I doubted was my grandfather's desire to call in anyone, Alpha Pack doctor or not. Sure, he would play up the whole granddaughter kidnapping story for press coverage and polling points, but to actually care enough to do something about it? We didn't have that kind of relationship.

"Why the car crash/terrorist story?" I asked as Liam got down on his hands and knees and started combing the carpet I didn't even want to have my feet on. "And what on earth are you doing?"

He plucked a long silvery strand of hair off the floor. "Being cautious. The police most likely won't come back here, but if they do, I don't want them to find your DNA conveniently lying around." Not for the first time, I questioned his sanity. "And the news story was a way to flush you out using the best resources available. You and I might have been able to slip around the country unnoticed for years before, but now that the whole world knows the granddaughter of Senator Harper is missing? Every person who sees you will be calling 9-1-1."

He was right. Of course he was right. I let out a frustrated roar, flopped back onto the bed, realized what I was doing, and hopped back up and began looking for any hairs that may have landed on the comforter.

"I should turn myself in," I said, thinking aloud. "The Alpha Pack can't do anything to me with the world watching. Their plan will backfire. I'll get to go home to my family, and they can't touch me without attracting unwanted attention."

Liam's voice was bland when he said, "They'll kill you before you ever see your parents again. And not only you, but anyone they see as collateral damage. Police officers. FBI agents. It doesn't matter. None of them stand a chance against well-trained Shifters."

"Then what are the options? It's not like I can blend into the masses." He had to realize that. After all, he was the one who pointed out less than an hour ago how someone couldn't forget my weird face.

"I've got a plan."

"Care to clue me in?"

Liam looked around the room with a critical eye. "No."

Chapter 4

I kept a steady stream of curses aimed at Liam going as I climbed out the tiny window whose width was exactly the same measurement as my hips. *Just climb on the back of the toilet and hoist yourself through,* I mimicked his voice in my head. *Be sure you don't make any noise or scratch yourself on that metal. Someone might notice the blood. Oh? What? You wanted me to be concerned about it hurting you? Sorry, no. I don't care if you get cut by rusty metal, except the resulting infection might slow us down as we carefully execute this elaborate plan I have but won't tell you because you're so far below my notice I can't be bothered.*

If I didn't rip out his throat with my bare human teeth it would put us even for him saving my life, right?

We drove on to Denver that day since there was the chance the police were keeping an eye on Liam. Or, I guess I should say *Liam* drove to Denver. I had to stay crouched down in the back seat the entire journey. My legs hurt from staying scrunched up and I was getting claustrophobic from sitting in the floorboard, but it was better than Liam's idea, which had me riding in the trunk.

The motel in Denver was a bit better than the other one, but still somewhere my family would have never considered staying on our vacations. At least I got to walk in the front door instead of shimmying through a window or vent.

I should have known something was up when Liam left his bag in the car and then decided he needed to "run some errands". In two weeks he hadn't left me alone any longer than it took for me to go to the bathroom. After sitting in the Denver motel room for four hours, I finally accepted he wasn't coming back.

"I don't blame him," I told the anchorman on the TV screen. Despite knowing it was a bad idea, I had been flipping between all the news stations since Liam left, watching the fictional account of my disappearance over and over again. My parents declined to comment, which Fox News found suspicious, and Charlie's medical records weren't being released to the media, which caused some ire from the good folks at CNN. I refused to watch MSNBC after I realized they were using the school picture from my sophomore year, which was possibly the least flattering photo of me ever taken. "He doesn't owe me anything. Heck, I owe him more than I could possibly ever repay. At least he got me somewhere where I can make a decent run for it."

And yet, I felt abandoned and kind of hopeless. Not exactly shiny new emotions in my world, but they sucked all the same, especially for Wolf Scout who trusted Wolf Liam so explicitly. But I wasn't going to let it break me. I had already been through hell and back and was still in one piece. Sure, I might have thought about throwing myself on the proverbial sword for a few minutes earlier in the evening, but then one of the news stations showed a shot of my family walking into our house. My parents both hurried inside, heads down, as if not looking at the crews camped out in our front yard would make them disappear. Angel, on the other hand, stopped at the front door, turned around, and looked directly at the camera. And even though she didn't say or do anything, I knew what she was thinking.

You promised.

It had been an attempt to soothe my little sister after I almost died when Jase accidentally ripped out my stomach last

April, but it turned into something more. I wasn't going to die, at least not easily. If for no other reason, it was my way to ensure Sarvarna and the rest of the Alpha Pack didn't win. If she wanted me dead she was going to have to work for it. I wasn't giving up.

Of course, that meant coming up with some sort of plan. I couldn't exactly eke out the rest of my existence in a cheap motel room. For starters, I didn't have any money, which left me with the same overwhelming problem that made Liam bolt: Disappearing into the crowd despite my freakish face, which every person in America knew.

I pulled myself off the super-uncomfortable motel bed and ambled over to the sink. The mirror hanging on the wall was one of those really old dull things with the actual shiny reflective stuff peeling off around the edges. It made me look like a ghost, which caused me to giggle. Scout Donovan, the girl who came back from the dead. Twice.

I don't know how long I stood there, but eventually I stopped looking like myself. That's not exactly right. I still looked like me - it's not like my face suddenly morphed into the wolf's or anything - but I became a collection of features instead of just Scout. And those features? They're not so bad. It's not like I have a hook nose, crossed eyes, and bologna-like flesh. If it wasn't for my hair, skin, and eyes being pretty much the exact same color, I could pass for any other normal teenage girl on the street.

All I had to do was change the coloring issue, right? Except, it's not as easy as you would think. For one, I can't just get a suntan and look different. My skin doesn't understand that whole browning process. It pretty much operates on two settings: pale white and painful, blistered red. Eye color can be changed with contacts, but where was I going to find those? Maybe if I had an optometrist or Internet connection, but I was lacking both. Hair dye was also out of the question. I tried it once before, even had it professionally done. At first it looked great, but then I took a shower and most of the color washed down the drain despite being permanent. By the third day my hair was a really unpleasant grey color. My hairdresser refused to put anything else on it, and I was too chicken to try again.

I fingered the strands hanging down to the middle of my back. Even if I did manage to get some contacts and develop a tan, the hair was a dead giveaway. The color is a silvery white, much the same as my fur when in wolf form. Sometimes you'll see a little kid with my hair color, but never anyone over the age of five. My hair is the first thing people notice about me.

So what if I didn't have any?

As soon as the thought hit, a plan started formulating. I could shave my head and then wrap it up in a scarf. My skin tone already screamed "sickly," and thanks to the trauma of the past few months, my bones were a bit sharper than looked healthy. What better way to avoid notice than passing as a cancer patient? No one wants to look too closely at sick people, and if I coughed every once in a while, everyone would keep their distance.

Liam had one of those fancy electric razor things in his bag, but all I had was some cheap disposables, which meant I was going to have to cut it all off before shaving my head. Fortunately, Talley had been the one to pack my escape bag, a fact I realized the moment I opened it up to discover everything organized neatly into individual freezer bags. I dug through what was now a random assorted mess until I found the travel sewing kit. Inside was a tiny pair of scissors, but a test of the ends proved they would cut as long as I did it strand by strand.

I pulled the first strand out from my head and positioned the scissors an inch from my scalp.

Snip.

I had about a fourth of it done with my arms started getting tired. Halfway through I got so bored I thought I might scream. At three-fourths of the way through the door swung open.

"What are you doing?" Liam asked, setting some bags on the dresser.

I couldn't even say anything I was so shocked. I just sat there on the vanity, my feet in the sink, with microscopic scissors in my hand and a pile of hair scattered about me.

"Did you cut off your hair? With those?" He looked at me as if I was completely nuts. "Why?"

"I need to be incognito." I sounded like a little kid who just got caught doing something stupid, which pissed me off. What was it to him anyhow?

Liam reached in a bag and pulled out a brown wig. He cocked his head and lifted his eyebrows as if to say, *what do you think this is for?* I looked back at the mirror, actually saw what I had done to myself, and burst into tears.

If the little kid voice had made me angry at myself then the tears pushed me firmly into the livid camp. I hadn't cried in weeks. I didn't cry when Talley's mom, the woman who took care of me when I was a kid, turned me over to the Alphas, or when my brother chose a mateless, Taxiarho-in-Training existence over my life. I hadn't shed a tear when I saw the guillotine that was to kill me, when Charlie hugged me goodbye, or when I saw the devastation wrought from my escape. But now I was in full waterworks mode over *my hair*. Yet, no matter how furious I was with myself, I couldn't stop. It was like a dam had broken.

"You're crying," Liam observed with more than a hint of horror.

I answered with a gasp for breath.

Since I buried my face in my hands so I didn't have to look at the tragedy of my hair any longer, I didn't see Liam move up behind me. But I smelled him. And I felt him tug the scissors from my hand and then begin lifting up strands of the remaining hair.

"I used to cut Alex's hair," he said. "We never really had the money to go somewhere to get it done. The first few times I cut it, it was horrible. I think I may have even given him a mullet on accident, but he somehow pulled it off."

I looked up and watched in the mirror as the remainder of my hair started falling away. "I bet half the guys at school were sporting mullets by the end of the year."

Liam smiled. It was the first time I'd ever seen him do it, and until that moment, I would have thought him incapable. He didn't have Alex's dimples, but his cheeks folded up in a way that was equally boyish. Because of his Dominance, it was easy to forget that Liam was just a few years older than me, but when he smiled he actually looked like the college-age guy he was. I found the corners of my mouth twitching upwards in response.

"You know, he didn't even notice. The whole town started looking like a Billy Ray Cyrus convention, but he had no idea it was because he started a new hair fad." He tilted my head forward and started trimming the hair at the base. "To be such a smart kid, he was pretty oblivious when it came to how other people saw him."

"That was part of the charm," I said, somewhat surprised I was willing to talk about him with Liam. "He was beautiful and smart and funny without being even the littlest bit arrogant." And he had loved me, which was the most amazing part of all.

Liam's hands paused. "You made him happy," he said. "I'm glad he found you before he died."

He didn't mention how if it wasn't for me Alex would still be alive, which both amped up my guilt and made me feel oddly affectionate towards Liam. Would I have been so generous if the roles had been somehow reversed? If it had been Alex who killed Jase over something Liam had done? Could I have stood there talking to Liam as if everything was okay? Would I have risked myself to save his life?

"Okay, turn around so I can do the front."

I swung my legs around so they would dangle off the edge. The vanity was high enough that Liam and I were right at eye level as he began doing something with what would have been bangs if I had enough hair left. I didn't know what to do. Looking at his face seemed too intimate, so I kept trying to stare at my hands, but that tucked my head down, which caused him to lift it back up, which meant he would touch me. And that was just all kinds of awkward. Because while Wolf Liam and I were cool, and Wolf Liam and Wolf Scout were BFFs, Human Scout and Human Liam were merely two people forced into a strange alliance. Touching was not part of that alliance.

"Well, that should do it," he said, brushing stray hairs from my shoulders. "Sorry, but there were some patches I couldn't do much with."

Those patches were the places where I had snipped a little too close to my head. And while Liam was probably a better barber than most twenty year old guys, he wasn't exactly a trained hair stylist. The result left me looking like an unsupervised three year old.

"Thank you," I said, meaning it.

He shrugged and looked anywhere but at me. I tried not to laugh at his obvious embarrassment. "No problem. It'll probably make the wig fit better, so that's good."

The wig! How could I have forgotten there was a wig to cover up this mess? I leapt from the counter and raced the three steps it took to get from the sink to the bed where Liam had dropped it.

There were lots of layers, but eventually I figured out the front from the back. I slid it on, turned towards the mirror, and...

"Did you beat up some old lady and take her wig?" It even smelled faintly of mothballs and Chanel No. 5.

Liam scowled. "It's not that bad."

"All four of my grandmothers have better hair than this."

Liam stalked over to the other bags and pulled out a second wig. This one was definitely not granny hair.

"That's awesome!" I said as I made gimme hands. "I'll look like a rock star!" This wig was also layered, but not in short puffs. This one had the whole razor cut edges thing going on, some trendy hipster bangs, and the coloring was a dark brown shot through with streaks of the deepest purple I ever saw.

"You'll draw attention."

I ripped off the monstrosity on my head and replaced it with the new wig. I just barely suppressed the urge to bounce up and down as I looked over the results. "Too bad my eyes aren't a really light green instead of blue," I said squinting at my face. "I think the coloring of the wig would have made them darken up a bit." As it was, my eyes were still way too Scout-like.

Liam mumbled something under his breath about me being a girl, which I ignored as he went back to his bags. This time he produced a small plastic case. I opened it to discover a pair of turquoise colored contact lenses.

"Where did you get these?" The last thing our extended road trip needed was for me to get some sort of bacteria that would rot my eyeballs out of my head.

"Stole them from a girl at the park. I think she had to take them out because of a nasty eye infection," he said as if he could read my mind. I offered him the sight of my newly healed middle finger, fully extended. "They're new, hence the safety seal you just broke."

They were a little difficult to put in. My eyesight has always been perfect, so there was never any reason for me to stick little discs of plastic in my eyes before. It probably would have gone a lot quicker if I hadn't automatically squeezed my eyelids shut every time my finger got anywhere near my face.

"What do you think?" I asked, turning away from the mirror once I got everything adjusted.

Liam had stretched himself across one of the beds and turned the TV to The Weather Channel while I was ineffectually jabbing myself in the eye over and over again. His glance lasted less than a second. "You still look like you."

"What do you mean I look like me?" I leaned back over the sink. Thanks to my bloodshot eyes, I looked more like a strung-out coke head than Scout Donovan, Granddaughter to the Senate Majority Leader. The eye color didn't look one hundred percent natural, but only if you looked real close. It was much less distracting than my normal shade. The hair was obviously not natural, but it was an expensive wig, not one of those things you buy at the Halloween shop for ten bucks, so it looked like real hair with an extreme dye job. I didn't see that as a problem since at least half of American women color their hair. I thought I could easily walk into a mall and not be rushed by the FBI.

"I mean..." Liam did some sort of wave thing with his hand that I think was supposed to indicate my general appearance. Or maybe there was a fly. "You look like Scout in a wig. It's not exactly going to keep someone from recognizing you."

We were going to have to agree to disagree on this one, except... "I'm not riding in the trunk."

I think he might have considered it, but finally relented. "It's probably good enough that as long as you don't talk to anyone or draw attention to yourself, no one will look close enough to notice."

Oh yay! An existence of only talking to Liam. Maybe I should revisit that *I want to live* thing.

Liam went back to his magical bags of treats and tricks and fished out a pair of Jackie O sunglasses. "Here," he said, tossing them my way. "Wear these at all times."

"What is the point of the contacts if I'm going to keep half my face covered with sunglasses?"

"The contacts are the backup plan."

Of course he had multiple plans for keeping my identity concealed. Liam was a man just filled with plans. Plans on how to save me from the Alphas without implicating Charlie. Plans to go out and buy me some snazzy costume supplies while I sat in a motel room thinking he was never coming back. Plans for where we would go next. Problem was, he never saw fit to inform *me* of any of these plans.

Chapter 5

"Let me see if I've got this right." I rubbed my eyes underneath the sunglasses I was forced to wear. "There are more Stratego than the three we killed?"

The sun was just starting to stream through Liam's window as we headed south. Today was a backroads day, which made me happy. I liked looking at all the tiny towns, seeing something other than the side of an interstate.

"Nine more, although they've probably already promoted some of the Taxiarho so there's a full twelve again."

Dots appeared on the horizon. I zeroed in on them without turning my head so I wouldn't draw Liam's attention.

"Is there always twelve Stratego?" The dots solidified into animals. "And those are my ten cows."

Liam looked around until he finally spotted them in the field. His cuss word was said from between clenched teeth.

"That's forty-seven cows for me, and only three for you."

"This is the stupidest game I ever-- My cows!"

"Five for you."

Liam gave his head a good frustrated rub. "Stratego," he said, getting us back on topic. "Always twelve, same goes for the Taxiahro. Sometimes it will take them a while to decide who will fill the spots, but they never let them stay open long. That's why they tap so many Potentials."

"A Potential being someone who may one day join the Alphas as a Taxiarho or Stratego?" Not for the first time, I longed for a handbook.

Liam was just as frustrated by my lack of knowledge. "Do you know anything about Shifter culture?"

"Let me see…" I tapped my bottom lip with my finger. "They treat all girls except for the Alpha Female like crap and like to kill anyone they consider different or annoying."

"And…"

"And nothing. I think that about covers everything I know about you guys."

Thus began a long, long, loooong lecture on all things Shifter (included how it was "us" instead of "you guys") by Professor Liam Dry-As-Burnt-Toast Cole. By the time we pulled into a parking lot of a garage on the outskirts of Houston I was contemplating fashioning a noose out of the seatbelt.

"I don't think they're open," I said as he cut off the engine.

Liam just glared and told me to stay put. Curiously, he seemed nervous as he knocked on the office door. Even more curious, someone actually answered it. I couldn't really tell much because the light bombarding the darkness was blinding, but I thought there were several someones inside. Four minutes later, he came to get me.

"Keep your head down and don't say anything," he said under his breath as we walked towards the building. "Nothing, Scout. No words of wisdom. No questions. Just keep your mouth shut. Got it?"

"I don't know. Do you think you could explain it to me in more detail? Maybe give me some examples?"

I'm not sure where the ability to actually snip back at Liam was coming from. Either I was finally growing comfortable with him after so much time together, or Wolf Scout was still close to the surface. Then again, it could be that what my mom referred to as my "Good Sense Filter" was broken again.

Liam led me into an office, which was indeed filled with people. There was a guy either asleep or passed out on an old ratty couch in the corner. His skin and hair were dark, and his arms were covered in tattoos, several of them written in Spanish. A woman sat next to his feet, eyes glued to the phone in her hand. Another guy, who looked like he was maybe a brother to the unconscious guy, sat at a desk. His gaze was critical and assessing. A third guy sat on the edge of the desk, tossing a ball in the air. He was the only white guy in the room, so of course he was the one to greet me with a "Hey, Chica." None of them seemed to notice the toddler crying in the middle of the floor.

"So, this is your girl?" the guy behind the desk asked.

Liam wrapped an arm around my shoulders and tucked me into his side. It took some effort to override my instinct to stomp on his foot. "Elizabeth, this is Diaz, a friend of mine from way back. He might be able to help us find a place to stay for a little while."

Since I wasn't allowed to speak, I just kind of shook my head a little bit. I was really more concerned about the poor kid, who had graduated from full-on tantrum to tiny defeated sobs. My hand itched to grab a tissue and wipe the snot off his face.

"Turn around for me, Beth."

Since the guy reminded me of a Mexican Shawn Michaels from Dad's Monday night wrestling show, I complied.

"Not bad," Diaz said. "Tight, young body. Average face. You'll need to get some new clothes, but Trina can help you out."

I was still confused, but apparently Liam had caught on because he was well beyond pissed. "No," he ground out. "She's with me. She's not working the streets."

Working the streets? What...?

Oh. My. God.

"You want me to be a hooker?" I completely forgot my orders to keep my mouth shut. "Are you insane?"

White Guy laughed. "Ooooh... She's all sweet and innocent, too. That'll definitely jack up the price the first few times."

I buried an elbow in Liam's hip to keep him in place, although I really wanted to stab White Boy in the eye with an ice pick myself.

Diaz leaned back in his office chair and stretched his beefy arms over his head. "I thought you needed money," he said to Liam.

"I do, but I'll work for it." His arm tightened around my shoulders. "Leave her out of it."

The kid on the floor started screaming again.

"I don't know, friend." Diaz sat back up and shrugged as if he somehow regretted what he was saying. "Around here, everyone contributes. That's how a family operates, everyone pulling their weight. Now, either your girl here is part of our family and has a place to stay for a while, or she's not."

Liam's body tensed. For a guy who was usually so closed off and stoic, his internal conflict was amazingly obvious on his face. He wanted to tell Diaz to go and do inappropriate things to himself, but he was counting on whatever arrangement this was working out. I knew we needed the money. The roll of bills I found obscenely huge when we first started our journey was getting rather small. How much more did we have? How long would we survive on it? And for the love of all things shiny, would someone please shut that kid up so I could actually think?

And just like that, inspiration struck. "I can babysit," I said. To prove my point, I shrugged off Liam's arm so I could go scoop the kid off the ground. He kept crying, and looked more than a little frightened, but I bounced him up and down a few times while making shushing noises until he calmed. "See? He likes me."

"She's a girl, genius," White Boy said.

"She's not crying," I countered.

Diaz laughed. "She's got you there, Fists." He stood up, which meant I got to see how he wasn't even as tall as I was. His muscles might have had muscles, but he was kind of a shrimp. Liam completely dwarfed him as Diaz walked over and stuck out a hand. "Welcome to the family."

"We're glad to be here," Liam answered for the both of us.

***

"Here" ended up being a tiny ancient camper. Once Diaz and Trina, the iPhone girl, left, we tried to make ourselves at home. Liam claimed the bed that ran along the back wall, which meant I was left to sleep on the one that folded out of the wall above the kitchen area. The microwave didn't work, but the miniature fridge did. The bathroom was small and disgusting, but sadly that was the sort of thing I had grown accustomed to during our tour of the nation's crappiest motels.

"Not to alarm you or anything, but I think you just made a deal with a Mexican gang." I've read Simone Elkeles's books. I know how this whole garage as a front thing works.

"Don't worry about it. Just keep your head down and your mouth shut from now on." I thought about suggesting he get that tattooed somewhere on his body, but decided he might think it was a better idea to tattoo it on me instead.

"So, what's the plan?" I asked as I sat down at the table not really big enough for two.

Liam grabbed my bag and tossed it onto the table. "First we unpack, and then I expect to see you on your knees."

After the exchange with Diaz my brain automatically went somewhere very, very bad.

"W-w-what?" I could feel the blush stretching over every inch of my body. Seriously, I think my feet were even embarrassed and angry. "I'm not... I won't..."

I knew the moment Liam realized what I was thinking because his face also shot up in flames.

"No! Not... *That*." He looked as though he was having some sort of episode, like maybe an aneurysm. "You were supposed to get down on your knees and beg me for forgiveness because you were wrong about the pizza guy. I don't want... I mean, I wasn't asking you to--"

I held up a hand. "Please don't say it. I think we've both been traumatized enough."

He gave a quick jerk of the head in agreement before quickly turning away. This would normally be the point where I disappeared into another room and not show my face again until the awkwardness had passed. Unfortunately, we were stuck in a space about half the size of my bedroom back home.

"I was actually talking about more of a long term plan," I said because the silence just wasn't doing it for me. "How long are we staying? A couple of weeks? Months? As long as we can?"

Liam tossed a handful of individually wrapped toothbrushes in one of the drawers in the bathroom. "Six weeks, max."

"And then?"

"And then I'll tell you what you need to know."

"Or you could tell me now," I said, leaving off the "*instead of being an arrogant bossy control freak.*" Did he appreciate the gesture? Of course not. He actually pretended I hadn't spoken at all. "Come on," I said nearly five minutes later. "What is it going to hurt? Maybe I could be helpful if I was actually in on the plan instead of bouncing around like an uninformed idiot." Which is exactly what I had been doing for the past year. I didn't know about Shifters until I saw Alex in his wolf form. I hadn't known Jase and Charlie turned into coyotes during the full moon or my best friend could See people's thought and emotions just by touching them until I discovered it on my own by accident. Once I became a Shifter myself, I was still kept in the dark. I didn't know the traditions and customs, yet I was expected to abide by them. I didn't know what a Thaumaturgic was, yet I was put on trial for being one. And no one ever cared to inform me of the Free Scout plan, which may have worked a bit better if I had been clued in.

I was sick and tired of being kept in the dark.

"It's need to know information, and you don't need to know."

"Why the Hades not? It is my life we're talking about here, right?"

I've developed an immunity for most of Liam's looks, but the one he shot me made my gut clench. He wasn't angry or annoyed or even exasperated. He was disgusted. "You think this is all about you?" He balanced his hands on the table and leaned in until we were face to face. "This is so far beyond you that you couldn't see it with a telescope. It's about time you stopped with the princess routine and realized you're nothing more than a pawn."

Chapter 6

Whatever progress Liam and I had made was immediately undone. Thankfully, we saw each other very little during our tenure as part of the Diaz family. My babysitting gig turned out to be an on-call twenty-four hours a day thing. Trina and Diaz, who were married, had three kids. Sophie was the baby, Eddie was three, and Lili was four. I was also expected to watch Diaz's nephew, Xavier, who was seven, the same age as my little sister. I spent almost all of my waking hours with the four of them. Babysitting isn't really one of my strong suits, especially not when there are diapers involved, but after a few weeks I started getting the hang of it. At least, that's when I stopped feeling like I was going to burst into tears at least once every hour.

Liam worked just as many hours as I did, usually stumbling back to our tin can living quarters in the wee hours of the morning. I had been half joking when I told him I thought the garage was a front for a Mexican gang, but I realized I might have been right. Sure, Liam worked in the garage on cars, but most of those cars came in looking a lot better than when they left. I'm not exactly sure what a Chop Shop is, but I think Diaz runs one.

My salvation from the monotony and loneliness finally came the night before the full moon.

"It's you." My grin was so big my cheeks hurt. "You're back."

"In the flesh." Alex bowed. "Or not, as the case may be."

I launched myself at him, and he caught me in his arms as Nicole, the wolf pup, danced around our feet. They certainly felt like flesh - well, flesh and fur - but I knew it was impossible. I still wasn't completely convinced these dreams were real, that he was somehow reaching out to me beyond the grave, but I was opening myself to the possibility.

"Where have you been? I've missed you." Nicole yelped. "Both of you," I amended, reaching down to scratch the top of her adorable little head.

The last time I saw Alex was the night before my trial with the Alphas. I had been convinced they would find me guilty and impose a death sentence that very night. Alex was convinced I would live, that it was my destiny to keep going. In the end we were both basically right.

Alex shrugged, a wry grin on his face. "Turns out dying doesn't prevent you from getting grounded. My spirit guide status was yanked after I broke a few rules the last time."

"Don't tell me they," whoever *"they"* might be, "were mad because you finally told me something about Thaumaturgy. Because really, it wasn't all that helpful."

"No, I think they took issue with my parting words."

"This is real, and I didn't leave you alone. I have always loved you, and I will always love you until the end of time. Now, wake up and live."

Not that I had it memorized and recited it to myself on a regular basis or anything.

"Which part did they take exception to?"

He raised his eyebrows and batted his lashes. "I'm sorry, but I must answer that in the vaguest and most obtuse manner possible so you continue to question the validity of these dreams you're having. Because they are just dreams." He leaned in, a smile spread across his face. "Or are they?"

"You are so going to get grounded again."

Alex threw both hands over his heart. "Who? Me? But I'm an angel."

I knew he was just teasing, but my curiosity was piqued. "Are you really?"

"Am I really what?"

"An angel."

Alex craned his neck over one shoulder and then the other. "I don't see any wings..."

I kicked some rocks in his general direction. "Don't be a smarty pants." I felt a little stupid for asking. After all, when I was here, he just felt like Alex. The idea of him hanging out on white fluffy clouds, wearing hippie sandals, and playing a harp was beyond stupid. But what were the other options? He's dead. Really, truly dead. There may have been some doubt in my mind in the beginning, especially when I thought the wolf stalking me was Alex instead of Liam, but even then I think a part of me knew he was really gone. So, when a dead boy is still having conversations with living folks he's either an angel or a ghost, right? "I just don't understand how this can happen. Are you in heaven now? Is this heaven? Or is it like some in between place where the living and dead can coexist?"

Alex plopped down on the ground. "You ask too many questions."

I sat down beside him, although in a slightly more dignified fashion. "You don't answer nearly enough." It must be a genetics thing. He and Liam were certainly two peas in a pod when it came to telling me stuff.

Since he couldn't really argue the point, he just smiled and plated a tiny kiss on my temple. We sat there, side by side, for a long time, not saying anything as we watched Nicole chase butterflies.

"How have you been?" he asked after a while.

I lifted my face up to the sun whose warmth I shouldn't have been able to feel. "What? You don't get to spy down on me from your lofty perch? No crystal balls wherever it is you go when you're not here?"

"You know how sometimes your parents will ground you from your phone, and sometimes they ground you from going out with your friends, and sometimes you're so grounded you're not allowed to even think about leaving your bedroom?"

"Never happened to me, but I remember those things happening to Jase."

"I was so grounded I couldn't even think about thinking about leaving my bedroom. No contact with anyone. No one told me what was going on. They let me know you survived the Alphas, but that was it. I don't know where you've been or what's happened since the last time I saw you."

"I've been spending a lot of time with your brother." I picked up a pebble and rolled it through my fingers. "Remember when you told me that if we got to know each other we would end up being friends?"

"I remember saying something to that effect."

I let the pebble fall back to the ground. "You were so remarkably wrong it's not even funny."

Alex's eyebrows knitted together. "What happened?"

I ended up telling him all of it. I told him about the trial, and the one-two punch of having both Mrs. Matthews and Jase turn on me. I told him about the epic battle to get me free. I even tried to outline our entire road trip, though I couldn't quite remember everywhere we went or the order in which we got there. "And now we're part of the Latino Bloods or Mexican Crypts or whatever gang Diaz is running." I took a deep breath and looked out over the lake, keeping Alex's face in my peripheral view. "Liam is carrying on the Cole tradition and won't tell me what is going on. He told me it's none of my business, that I'm just a pawn."

"You are not a pawn." When I kept my focus on the lake where the sun was both rising and setting, Alex took my chin in his fingers and turned my face to his. "You're not a pawn, Scout. Yes, this is something big. It's bigger than you or me or Liam, but that doesn't mean you're not important. You're hugely important, and not just for the part you're supposed to play. To me, Talley, Charlie, your family, and tons of other people, Liam included, you're important because you're Scout. We care about you and believe in you. We're putting our faith and the future in your hands."

I looked down at the hands in question. Half my nails were broken and there were stains from making the kids Jell-O, "I'm pretty sure you screwed up there."

His smile was radiant. "Not possible."

"Your devotion borders on insanity. You know that, right?"

He just kept smiling. "Give Liam a chance, okay? He carries the weight of the world on his shoulders and has some trust issues. It'll take time."

It would take a miracle. "I'll try."

"That's all anyone can do." He squinted at the sun. The day had already turned into morning, something only possible in this crazy place. "You're going to wake up soon."

"I know."

"But I'll be back."

It was my turn to smile and surrender to faith. "I know."

***

When I woke up, I felt light and happy. I smiled throughout the day, even when the baby's diaper exploded all over her clothes. Okay, maybe I didn't exactly smile during that horrific experience, but I didn't scream or panic, so there was a definite improvement.

As the full moon started approaching again, I found myself drifting back towards Liam. I was still frustrated, angry, and confused, but Wolf Scout missed her friend. I think the same must have held true for Wolf Liam, because in the days leading up to the full moon he began showing something that could've been mistaken for kindness. By the time we were in a borrowed car driving out to find a place to run, I could actually stand to be around him for more than five minute at a time.

That night was much like the first time we ran together. Wolf Scout took over almost completely without Talley there to rein her in, and food being of the kill it and eat it variety. Liam and I spent the majority of the night alternating between pouncing on one another in surprise attacks and nuzzling our noses into each other's necks. The most amazing part of the night was I somehow slept through part of the Change. Liam and I had curled ourselves into a miniature wolf pile after we ate our fill of squirrels for the night. I thought I would just lay there and rest up a bit, but I found myself waking up in immense pain. It took a few moments for my brain to process what was happening, but once I realized I was Changing back, it was almost over.

Liam was waiting for me once I got my clothes back on.

"I have donuts, breakfast sandwiches, and two boxes of Pop-Tarts," he said as I made my way towards the car.

"Seriously? When did you get that?"

He shrugged. "I Changed about an hour ago."

An hour ago the sun hadn't been anywhere near up.

"What flavor of Pop-Tarts?"

A box came flying towards my head. I snatched it out of the air and looked at the label. "Hot Fudge Sundae? That isn't a Pop-Tart flavor, it's an ice cream treat." I grabbed the already open box sitting on the hood of the car. "What's this one?" I looked down at the words "Hot Fudge Sundae". I knew my glare was nowhere near as impressive as one of his, especially since I couldn't keep the corners of my mouth from lifting at the sight of his guilty expression. "Some of those donuts better have jelly on the inside," I said, leaning back against the car, so close to him our sides grazed.

"A full dozen," he assured me as I opened up the box emitting a sweet raspberry scent. "And there is even a half dozen of sprinkles."

"But I don't like sprinkles."

"Oh yeah." His grin was both shocking and breath-taking. "It's me that likes those, isn't it?"

This time I couldn't even pretend to glare. "Let me guess, almost all those breakfast sandwiches you spoke of are cheese free?"

His grin grew and for the first time ever I was able to see a resemblance to Alex that went beyond physical appearances. "If you wanted cheese you should've Changed earlier and went with me instead of being a lazy sleeping wolf."

"Sorry, Super Shifter, that isn't in my nifty bag of supernatural tricks."

"It could be."

"Is this going to be another lecture--?"

"You know, if you would put a little more effort into getting control--"

We argued the entire way back. He was obnoxious and self-righteous. I was resolute and snarky. As the Houston skyline formed on the horizon, Liam made some ridiculous assertion, and I realized I was laughing for the first time in a long, long time.

Chapter 7

We arrived in Texas in a nice, respectable Honda Civic. We left in an asphalt-colored car the size of a modest yacht. I'm not sure, but I think the aim was to blend into the road, Invisible Jet style.

"The kids are going to miss you," Diaz said as we were loading up.

"I'll miss them, too." The little demons had used the dark powers of cuteness to worm their way into my heart.

Diaz reached in his back pocket and pulled out an overstuffed envelope. When he passed it to me I noticed the bills were hundreds, not tens or twenties.

"What is this?" I asked, afraid I was getting ready to be asked to deliver a package filled with cocaine or semi-automatic weapons disguised as Elmo dolls.

"You think I don't pay my nannies? You did good work for us. The kids love you. Xavier even says he's going to marry you." Diaz grinned as if we were old friends. "His mama has been using it to get him to eat his vegetables. She tells him he's going to have to get big and strong if he's ever going to take you from your man."

My man...? Oh. Yeah. Good thing we're hermits. I would've totally blown that *cover in less than twenty-four hours.*

"Tell him I'm keeping my options open."

As surprised as I was to actually get paid for a job I didn't think was optional, Liam seemed more surprised when I added it to the stack of bills he got for what I chose to believe was changing tires and air filters. He tried to give it back, telling me I earned it, but I argued that he'd been my sugar daddy for months. The least I could do was throw what I had into the general finances.

Like before, our route held no rhyme or reason. I'm not sure Liam even knew exactly which direction to head each time we left a gas station or motel. Then again, maybe he did, since three days after leaving Texas we found ourselves in Cincinnati, crossing the bridge into Kentucky.

"Oh the sun shines bright on my Old Kentucky Home..." I sang under my breath, but had to stop when my throat closed up. It was stupid, really. Northern Kentucky is nothing like Lake County, but the *Welcome to Kentucky* sign might as well have said "Welcome Home, Scout!" for all my heart knew.

We pulled off once we got to the famous "Florence Y'All" water tower and found a gas station. I was forced to stay in the car, despite my overly full bladder, while Liam ran inside. When he returned he had a University of Kentucky knit hat and a map.

"Put this on," he said, tossing the hat in my lap. "And you've been getting lax with the sunglasses. Don't take them off again."

I did as he asked, but pouted the whole time. The threat of being recognized had dropped drastically over the last few weeks. No one involved in the case was optimistic about my recovery, and with no new leads, the media moved on to the next big story. Currently they were all about some lady who tried to kill her husband because, according to her, he was an alien sent to destroy the earth.

"I look ridiculous. It's a cloudy October day. No need for a hat or sunglasses."

He didn't respond, just studied his map.

"Where are we going? I can probably help." When Jase and I were kids, Dad's idea of a fun game was to memorize the location and county seats of all the counties in Kentucky. This is the sort of thing that happens when an educator is allowed to raise children. I found it ridiculous at the time, but now I can pretty much navigate my way across the state with just a few road signs as guides.

Of course, Liam didn't think he needed my help, which meant we had to pull onto the side of the road to check his map more than once. We took back roads through Pendleton County (county seat Falmouth); Harrison County (Cynthiana); and Nicholas County (Carlisle). Once we passed into Bath County, I started getting nervous.

"Listen, I know I'm not always up-to-date with my Shifter knowledge, but I think we're closing in on Matthews Pack Territory," I said, referring to Talley's father's pack, who lived in the hills of Eastern Kentucky. "Unless you're not telling me something about how they're really on our side, I think you should reconsider trespassing. Those guys pretty much hate me."

Liam, being Liam, only grunted in response. Over the next forty minutes I laid out several very reasonable arguments for why we should turn around, but he was either deaf or ignoring me. He didn't say another word until we pulled into a packed-to-capacity parking lot somewhere in Red River Gorge.

"Ummm... What are we doing here?" I asked, not really expecting a response.

"Going for a hike."

"Hiking?"

"Yes, hiking. We're going to walk around on trails through the mountains and enjoy nature." He looked towards where the well-worn path met the parking lot. A family in full outdoorsy regalia stood arguing, the dad emphatically pointing towards a map while the woman hooked her thumb back towards the trail. "Or maybe we'll make our own trails. We are Shifters after all."

It was a good thing we were in excellent shape, because it took some creativity and effort to avoid the crowds. The clouds had given way to a wonderfully sunny autumn day, and the trees towering up to the sky boasted leaves of brilliant reds and oranges. It was a perfect day for hiking, hence the overwhelming number of people.

"Come on," Liam said, offering me a hand. My legs were just a few inches too short to scale the jagged outcropping of rocks where he stood. "We're almost there."

"There's a there?" I asked between grunts. Good grief, rock climbing was so not my thing. "I thought we were hiking. You know, walking through the woods. Enjoying nature."

His response was the predictable glare.

Once we reached the mouth of a cave sitting atop a 400 foot drop-off, Liam stopped dragging me over the mountain. He paced about, exploring the inside as far as the sunlight would allow and looking over the edge of the cliff it opened up onto. After thirty minutes, I couldn't take it any longer. I wasn't so much afraid of the cave as the things I could hear moving around inside, and the sight of Liam so close to a life-ending plummet made me slightly ill.

Leaving Liam at the Bat Cave, I went off to do some exploring of my own. I didn't go far before I found a tree with a bench-like branch. It looked funny and inviting. The sun warmed me as I stretched across it like a lazy cat. Usually, I don't find lounging across trees super-comfortable, but something about the way the light played through the leaves and the way the breeze kissed my skin lulled me into complacency, allowing my heavy eyelids to get their way and slam shut.

But when a familiar scent came floating through the air, they flew back open, and it wasn't Human Scout peering out from their depths.

I was nearly silent as I lowered myself to the ground and slunk through the trees. He wasn't alone. A girl trailed behind him, her hand clasped in his. It wasn't the Alpha, but she was a Seer. I could feel it.

He didn't know I was there until I sprung, and by then he only had time to turn halfway before impact. Since we were on the side of a mountain, we rolled several feet before stopping with him on top. He didn't stay there long. I flipped him back over, a primal roar leaving my throat. I pinned his lower body with my legs and then, with absolutely no finesse, started swinging.

"Scout! Stop!" The voice was familiar, but I refused to listen.

Betrayer! Wolf Scout bellowed inside me.

"Scout, it's Jase!" She was standing too close. My elbow caught her in the stomach, but still I didn't stop until I was grabbed from behind, two arms of steel trapping my arms by my side as they lifted me off the ground.

"Breathe," he whispered in my ear, breaking through the rage. "Deep breaths. In and out. Relax." And I did. I closed my eyes, pulled air slowly into my lungs, and relaxed against the broad chest I was hoisted against. When I was back to something that could pass as normal, Liam dropped me.

"You okay?" he asked, standing above Jase. "Anything broken?"

"Just my entire face." My brother took Liam's hand and pulled himself up. Talley was immediately there, her fingers tracing over his nose, cheeks, and chin.

"I think your nose is broken again," she said once she finished her physical assessment. "You're not having any trouble talking, so your jaws are okay. Of course, I don't really know how to diagnose a brain injury." She held up three fingers. "How many fingers do you see?"

"I don't think I'm the one you need to be testing for a brain injury." He looked over Talley's shoulders and met my eyes. "Hey, Sis. Nice to see you, too." He rubbed his jaw, which was already starting to swell. "Out of curiosity, what the hell was that?"

"You helped them." The fight was completely gone out of me. My words were laced with weakness, a feeling of defeat overwhelming me. "They were going to kill me, and you helped them." I blinked back the tears, refusing to let them fall. "You were going to let me die."

Jase's fury, which was growing instead waning, focused on Liam. "What is she talking about?"

"You should know," I answered. "You were there. Maybe it didn't stick out in your mind like it did mine, but there was this trial..." I took another of those deep breaths, this time to calm the human instead of the beast. "You know, I can't do this. I'm done."

I stood up and started back towards where I thought the trail might be. I made it about three steps before a hulking behemoth stepped into my path. I took a step to the right. He mirrored my movement. I took a step to the left. Once again, he moved with me.

"What's wrong with you?" Liam honestly looked a little lost.

"He told them..." Yet another deep breath. "Jase's testimony was one of the things that helped the Alphas convict me. He sold me out to join the Alpha Pack and become Sarvarna's boy toy. Now, please let me by so I can get the hell away before I succeed in ripping his pretty face from his head."

"You didn't tell her?" Talley appeared at my elbow. I could see why Wolf Scout didn't immediately recognize her. She looked different. Her hair was different. The way she held herself was different. Even the way she dressed was different. "You've been with her for two months and didn't tell her Jase was a mole? You let her believe her brother was actually on the same side as the Alphas?"

She was standing up to Liam? Maybe this wasn't the real Talley after all.

"You thought...?" The look Liam gave me made me feel a bit like a two-headed cockroach. "He's your brother. How could you think that?"

Wait. I was the bad guy here? No. Nuh-uh. I don't think so.

"You knew?" Righteous indignation laced my words. "Let me guess, it was all part of the Liam Cole Plan. Was letting me feel betrayed and broken down part of that plan, too? Did it make me more malleable? Did I bend easier to your will since I had so little left to fight for?" I am a trained martial arts fighter. I have a black belt in four different disciplines. Yet, when my fist pounded against his stupid arrogant chest, it was the same inconsequential swat women have been giving larger, stronger men since the dawn of time. "You.... You... You *ass!*"

I put both hands on his chest and shoved with all my might. He staggered back a few steps, though more out of shock than my brute strength. Liam's jaw clenched as he shifted his weight slightly, and I could see in his eyes that the gloves were off. I put my weight on the balls of my feet and brought up my hands.

Things were about to get interesting.

"Jase! Do something!" Talley demanded.

"No need," he replied. "I've got a pretty good view right here."

"Jase!"

"Come on, Tal. He deserves it."

Showing the utmost confidence in me, Talley said, "He'll hurt her."

"Well, maybe she deserves it, too."

I weighed my options. Liam was bigger, stronger, and possibly even faster. I had to be smarter. He would expect stealth and misdirection, but if I went straight at him? Would I catch him off-guard enough to have the advantage? There was only one way to find out--

"Are you sure there is a cave up here?" Came a giggling voice from about halfway down the mountain.

Crap.

"I promise. It's called Murder Cave because --"

"We have company," Liam announced. I thought about adding a "No, duh," on there, but realized he was probably saying it for Talley's benefit.

"Seriously?" Make that Talley and Jase's benefit.

Liam shot me a look and said, "We can discuss this late, but we need to move now. It's too risky for us all to be seen together."

"We're parked near Chimney Rock," Talley said. "You?"

"Princess Arch," Liam answered. Jase made a valiant effort to not laugh, but was unsuccessful.

"Okay, Jase will go with you and guide you back to the house, and Scout will come with me."

"You'll never find your way down the mountain," Jase said exactly at the same time as Liam declared, "It's too risky for you to be seen with her."

The look of annoyance Talley shot the both of them was priceless. "One, I grew up hiking these trails, Jase. In case you've forgotten, I'm the one who guided us here." She turned towards Liam, who had the sense not to glare back. "And two, what risk? Who is going to recognize her? I'm her best friend and it took me a while to realize the person behind the wig and color contacts was Scout."

"Sunglasses," was all he said in response.

Delighted over Talley's ability to put the boys in their place, I slipped the sunglasses back on with a smile.

Chapter 8

"How are my parents? How is Angel?" The questions came spewing out the moment Talley put the key in the ignition. "Charlie?"

"Everyone is fine." She turned her palm up so she could squeeze my hand in hers. Through our bond she sent a shot of reassurance. "They're fine, Scout."

I took a deep breath, trusting her unlike I would anyone else. She may have looked different, but she was still my Talley. I could feel her goodness in every cell of my body, and if Talley said they were okay, then they were okay. But still...

"Details. Lots of them, please."

Talley backed the car out of the parking spot before fulfilling my request. "It's been a bit tricky with your parents. Jase is playing the part of Sarvarna's lapdog, and she's keeping a pretty close eye on anything he does, so he can't just out and tell them what is going on. Luckily, I have a bit more leeway. They keep me around because my skills are valuable, but they all think I'm too much of an emotional basket case and way too devoted to you to be of any real use. So, I've been the one to talk to your parents mainly. I keep it vague so as not to get the Alpha Pack nosing around and to keep your folks from freaking out, but they know you're alive and in hiding. Your dad wanted to go out and find you, thinking he could protect you from whatever you need protecting from, but Jase managed to stop him."

She tapped her finger on the steering wheel. "And...?" I prompted, knowing there was something there she wasn't so keen on sharing.

"And, well, they're currently not speaking to each other, but don't worry. It'll work itself out."

I sighed as I slid back against the seat. Dad and Jase weren't speaking to each other? Great. Add that to the list of things I've royally screwed up just by being me.

"Angel?"

Talley smiled, which made me nervous. Things other people found amusing about my little sister usually aren't that funny to me. "Well, of course she has no clue about what is really going on and thinks the whole car crash story is true..."

"Oh God." Somehow that seemed worse. "The news is implying I'm dead." Poor Angel. My poor, sweet, innocent little--

"...So she called CNN to set them straight. She left a message telling Nancy Grace to shut her stupid mouth and quit saying her sister is dead, because she's not."

"She did not. She's only seven, for pity's sake. Where would she even get the phone number?"

Talley was really going to have to stop smiling like that. My peace of mind was in serious jeopardy. "She may have been under the influence of Jase."

"This is the reason they really should be kept apart as much as possible." Although, I found I was actually grinning a little bit myself. "Did Nancy Grace reply?"

"Oh yes. She played the voicemail on air. The whole world got to hear Angel call her a lying wicked witch."

"Nuh-uh."

"She did!"

Talley slowed down to a virtual crawl, letting a red pickup pass. I glanced in the rearview mirror and saw a familiar blue-grey car.

"She's sorta kinda grounded from now until she's thirty, but that's probably for the best. Angel isn't exactly the kind of kid who needs access to computers and phones. There's no limit to the amount of havoc she could cause."

"True," I admitted. "And if she's grounded, that means Mom and Dad will be keeping an extra-close eye on her. That makes me feel a little better."

Talley reached over and gave me another reassuring hand squeeze. "Everyone is fine."

"Everyone?" I bit the inside of my lip so hard I tasted blood. "The news said he was in critical condition."

We were at a stop light, so Talley was able to turn to look at me. After some consideration she said, "Can you promise to not make a single sound?"

I shook my head, but was truly confused where this was heading until she punched some buttons on the console. After a few seconds the pop music, which had been pouring through the speakers, ceased and a trilling filled the car.

He answered on the third ring.

"Hello?"

"Hey, Chuck! How are you feeling?" To my knowledge Talley never called Charlie Chuck. In fact, as far as I knew, I was the only person given that honor.

"Talley?" He sounded weak. Not zombified or sad, just not strong. Like maybe he wasn't really used to talking and needed a nap.

"Yep. It's me. Jase and I decided to head into Eastern Kentucky for the weekend. He needed some air, and I wanted to look for bears."

Bears...?

"Did you find one?"

"Two actually."

There was a rush of air over the speakers and when Charlie spoke his voice was clenched. "And how were they?"

"Good." Talley spared me a glance which I really wished she wouldn't do since she was navigating an overly curvy road. "Really good. A little tired and cranky, but they're bears. They're supposed to be tired and cranky, right?"

"Cranky is exactly how I like my bears."

With considerable effort, I swallowed my giggle.

"Speaking of cranky bears," Talley said, "how is your therapy going? You're not still giving the physical therapists a hard time, are you?"

Charlie was giving the physical therapists a hard time? That didn't sound like Charlie. Jase? Yes. I've actually seen him go head-to-head with a trainer over a basketball injury, but Charlie is usually more laid back.

"I'm not giving them a hard time. I just don't understand why we can't go ahead and increase what I'm doing if I'm ready. Anyway, they should *want* to push me harder. The sooner I can walk, the sooner I can go home and get out of their hair."

I gasped before I realized what I was doing, causing Talley to shoot me a shut-the-heck-up look.

"Well, surely someone is there to keep you in line," she said, more for my benefit I think than Charlie's.

"Yes, Mama Talley. Bob and Cory have been very good babysitters in your absence." It sounded patronizing and sarcastic, but both Talley and I knew he secretly loved Talley's overprotective, Mother Hen-like tendencies. "Actually, Cory is waving hello to you right now."

If Cory the Canadian, an Alpha Pack Taxiarho, was still around, either Liam was right about that whole Charlie-is-beloved-by-the-Alpha-Pack thing, or he was being treated to the same around-the-clock attention I enjoyed back in July. If it was the second, I wondered how they kept the gun trained on Charlie's head without the nurses and doctors saying anything.

"Hey, Tal. You remember that girl who quit high school and became a truck stop waitress? I think her name was Flo?" Talley raised her eyebrows at me, and I nodded. Leave it to Charlie to remember a random rant from a year ago. "If you see her, tell her I miss her. A lot. Is she still living with that guy?"

"I don't think they're getting along too well, but yeah, they're still together."

"Tell Flo to lay off him. He's a good guy. He'll take care of her."

He'll forget to tell her that her brother didn't really betray her and let her walk around with a shattered heart for no good reason. That's what he will do. Not a good guy. Not someone I want to take care of me.

Talley must have been able to see my thoughts etched across my face. "You know, I can imagine what Flo would say to that. I can't tell you though, because I think it would involve a lot of cuss words."

Charlie laughed and it was one of the single most beautiful sounds in the whole world. "I'm sure it would. But she needs to believe me on this one. I know what I'm talking about, and she should trust him, one hundred percent."

I shook my head in denial, but Talley said, "I'll tell her."

There was some commotion in the background, an IV pole beeping and a female voice.

"I've got to go, but thanks, Tal. Thanks for calling me."

"Get some rest, Charlie."

"I love you."

Her hand reached out and grabbed mine. "Love you, too."

Then the connection was cut, and I burst into tears.

Chapter 9

"It's not that bad," Talley said, her fingers trying to fluff out my natural hair in vain. "It's pixie-like."

"Remember Thomas Bardwell? That weird kid who was only around for the third and fourth grade?"

"The guy who told us he had to move to Timber because a dragon ate his other house?"

"Yeah." He was also the kid who got a piece of corn stuck up his nose and didn't tell anyone for three months. "I have his haircut."

Talley chuckled, throwing her arms around me for the tenth time in thirty minutes. "I've missed you so much," she said for the twentieth time.

"I've missed you, too," I told the top of her shiny black hair. "It's been lonely."

We were sitting on the porch swing of an old clapboard house watching the boys as they did something underneath the hood of our car. The place belonged to Talley's Aunt Della, her mother's non-Seeing sister, who was at a bluegrass festival in Virginia. Talley assured us her father's pack wouldn't come around due to some bad blood and hurt feelings, and Liam decided it was remote enough for us to stay the night. The house was located in a literal hole in the ground, accessible only by driving to the end of the world and hanging a right onto a single-lane serpentine road whose pavement had more cracks and chunks missing than could possibly be considered safe. The driveway was all but hidden and cut down at such an angle I may have left fingerprints in the dashboard of the CRV Talley was driving. The house itself looked like something out of a Depression era picture on the outside and a ceramic doll museum on the inside.

That's right. Ceramic dolls. Hundreds of them staring at you from every available surface.

There was a reason Talley and I chose to sit on the porch instead of inside on the couch.

"I really should do the selfless thing and leave, but I can't seem to make myself do it," I said. Even though the house was seriously isolated and Talley assured me no one other than her trusted Aunt Della would ever know we were there, I kept thinking about what would happen if someone found Jase and Talley with me. I was a dangerous person to be around.

Talley patted my leg. "Stop worrying so much. Liam wouldn't have brought you to the meet-up point if he thought there was any chance of danger. He's had every contingency planned out for this meeting since July."

My teeth ground together. "Of course he has."

"How is life with Liam?" She asked cautiously. She was still cuddled against my chest, so there is no way she missed my growl.

"Stubborn, self-important ass." I was taking what Charlie said into consideration, but trusting Liam didn't mean I had to like him.

Talley jerked up, scandalized. "Scout! You shouldn't say that."

"I'm just stating facts, Tal. Honestly, this is the watered down, if-you-can't-say-something-nice-don't-say-anything-at-all version. Would you like to hear what I really think of him?"

"He's not that bad."

At that moment he was telling Jase how to hold a wrench, and even more annoying than that, Jase was *letting* Liam tell him how to hold a wrench.

"Oh, you're right, Tal. He's a peach. Always so happy and warm to be near. And the way he's so open and honest, and how he never tries to boss anyone around. A diamond in the rough, that one."

"Shhh! Library voices," Talley said, digging an elbow into my ribs.

"Why?" I said a little too loudly. "I don't care what he thinks."

"Scout, please don't provoke the extremely Dominant Shifter who is very angry with you at the moment."

"The moment? Try 'the life'." I scowled towards where the boys were now removing some part of the car which was probably necessary for it to operate. I hoped they knew what they were doing. "And I'm the one who has a right to be angry here. How could he not tell me that Jase was only following his orders? Do you have idea what it was like for me to stand there and hear him say those things? To think that he didn't care they were going to kill me?" I wanted to cry so I screamed instead. "And your mother. God, Talley. I mean, it was like she hated me."

Talley's head jerked down and her fingers immediately went to her hair.

"Talley, your mom was just putting on a show, right? Like Jase? It's all part of Liam's *Let's Torture Scout* Plan?"

"You have to understand," Talley said in a small voice, "my mother was raised with some very strong beliefs. And with my dad being so close, close enough to prod and provoke..."

"She wasn't acting."

"She was doing what she thought was right--"

Betrayal hurts just as much the second time around. "How could she? She's your mom. She taught me how to skip and play hop-scotch..."

Talley's eyes were overflowing. "I know. I *know*. I've tried to talk to her, but I've got to play the part of a good little Alpha Potential, and..." A sniffle and lots of rubbing of the cheeks. "I'm sorry, Scout. So, so sorry."

I wasn't going to cry again. I refused. Anyway, Talley was shedding enough tears for the two of us.

"It's not your fault," I said, meaning it. Like we have any control over our parents. I mean, mine are pretty great most of the time, but when your dad is the superintendent for the school? There are lots of times you have to apologize to your friends for things he does. Sure, he never tried to get any of them killed, but he did make us switch to a schedule that made our summers super-short. When you're thirteen, two weeks less summer vacation feels like someone is trying to kill you. "I don't blame you. I would never blame you."

A wrench or socket or some such thing landed with a thunk on the porch. "Just me, right?" Jase said, squinting against the afternoon sun.

"What are you talking about? I don't blame you for Mrs. Matthews' turning me over to the Alphas."

His jaw muscles twitched. "You sure? I mean, why not? You believed I would willingly stand there and let them take you."

Well, it looked like we were going to do this now.

"I overheard you talking to Sarvarna," I said, sounding way more aloof than I actually felt. "She offered you a way out of being mated and a position in the Pack. It was a good bargain."

"A good bargain?" Jase's voice was about two notches louder than necessary. "Seriously? My sister's life in exchange for a place in their corrupt ranks? You thought I would want that?"

There may have been a time when I would have apologized, quelled at his anger. Jase always had the stronger personality of the two of us. He led, I followed. But no more. Things had changed. *I* had changed.

"How was I supposed to know any different? Did you send me a message?" I turned to Talley. "Or you? Did you try to send me a brain note saying, 'Don't worry about Jase. We have a plan.'?" Now I was getting loud.

"Do *not* yell at Talley."

"You let me sit in that cell and think you didn't care."

"I was trying to save you!"

"You didn't come to see me!"

"I had a role to play!"

"But you didn't come see me! You left me! Alone!" I swiped away a single escaped tear. "What kind of brother doesn't even come and say goodbye? Even Sarvarna would have understood the need for closure. But you didn't come. It could have all went wrong. I could have died, and you would have never said goodbye."

"How could I?" He was practically whispering now. "How could I go down there, look at you in that cage, knowing you might die, and not show them how much I love you? You've been my best friend since I was six months old. Almost every single one of my happiest memories has you at its center. Just the thought of losing you makes me literally sick to my stomach. How could you not know that?"

Emotional conversations are not commonplace in my family. Yes, we love each other, but we don't normally feel the need to say it. Maybe we should more often, though, because hearing how much my brother cared for me was enough to start repairing some of the fissures in my soul.

I bolted towards him, arms wide, and he caught me in a bear hug. I squeezed back with all I was worth. He saw it as a personal

67

challenge, and squeezed harder, making my ribs scream in protest.

"I love you, too, you know?"

"Damn straight you do."

I rested my cheek on his shoulder. "Now that we've got this settled, can we kick Liam's ass?"

Jase laughed. "Doubt it. Have you sparred with him yet?"

I shook my head. "He's too busy making me run around in circles and do push-ups to actually let me do something fun."

"Dude, I have, and I promise 'fun' is not a word I would use."

I tried not to be annoyed at Jase and Liam's obviously close relationship, but failed miserably.

"You've never sparred?" Talley asked.

"Nope."

"No physical altercations of any sort?"

"Since you stopped me earlier today, no."

Jase was working on something in his head. I could tell by his scrunched-up face and the way his finger hovered in the air, periodically following an imaginary trail.

"No punching?" he asked.

"No."

"No kicking?"

"No."

"How about arm wrestling?"

"No. And before you ask, we've avoided Slug Bug, Slap Bets, and any and all Dance-Offs."

Jase rubbed his chin. "And in wolf form?"

I shrugged. "We rolled around a bit." My cheeks heated slightly as I said it. For some reason, talking about it felt akin to divulging intimate details I would rather not share with my brother. "So, what's the deal here? You seemed surprised that one of us hasn't tried to kill the other yet."

Actually, once I thought about it, it was kind of miraculous.

"It's just not normal for two Shifters to not try to determine a hierarchy," Talley said. "Usually, when two Dominant Shifters like you and Liam are around each other, it takes less than an hour for a brawl to break out."

"Maybe it's because I'm a girl," I pontificated. "There really isn't much use in getting into a pissing contest since I have to sit down to pee anyway."

Jase made a choking noise. "Wow, Scout, that was unbelievably crass."

"And a lie," Liam said as he walked up the porch steps. "If she would have sat down to pee at half the places we've been to lately, she would have gotten a disease or worse by now."

"And that," Jase said, "was unbelievably crass *and* gross."

Liam collapsed into an old rocking chair, which considered giving way under his weight. "Sorry, man. I didn't mean to offend your mate."

I was about to correct him over the whole "mate" thing when something caught my attention. I don't know how I missed it up until that moment.

Jase and Talley were holding hands.

"Wait. What?" I couldn't seem to pull my eyes off their clasped hands. "Okay, someone needs to start talking now, and I choose..." I looked from one to the other. Jase was smiling at Talley who was looking at her bellybutton and flushing bright red. "Jase. Spill it."

"The ceremony hasn't been completed yet, but we plan to do it in the spring."

"You're getting married. In the spring. To Talley." The world officially no longer made sense.

"Not married," Talley said. "We're just completing the mating ceremony then. We're going to wait until we finish school to get married."

69

Very sensible and Talley-like. Only one problem... "You guys don't want to be mates and get married."

Jase finally looked away from Talley and at me. "Says who?"

"You. There was yelling involved. Yelling and pouting and lots of anger. All of it directed at me."

"Did I ever actually say I didn't want Talley to be my mate?"

"You know, quite a bit has happened between then and now--"

"No. I never said I didn't want her."

"But there was yelling."

Jase brought Talley's hand, which was still entwined with his, up to his mouth and gently kissed her knuckles. The look on Talley's face said she was imagining little frolicking birds and butterflies dancing around their heads.

My brain was beginning to hurt from trying to wrap itself around this new development.

"I was angry at you for forcing Talley into being with me when she deserves so much better." His smile was all Jase. "Now she's made that decision for herself, I'm more comfortable with the situation."

"So you like Talley? Like, *like* like Talley?"

"I love Talley."

I looked at my best friend, who was still seeing those animated critters. "And you?"

"Head over heels," she replied.

Liam watched the entire exchange with amusement. "How long have you known this?" I asked him.

"Me? May."

"May?" I narrowed my eyes at the traitorous couple. "You confided in *Liam* and not me? What the Hades is up with that!"

Jase's hands flew up in a defensive pose. "Calm down, Anger Monkey. I don't know what he's talking about. Tal and I didn't figure it out until September."

I took a deep breath to calm my nerves and reminded myself that everything wasn't about me. What I really needed to focus on here was Talley. I love my best friend, but she's one of those people who only see the sunshine and rainbows. The problem was, Jase can be a lot like sunshine and rainbows. When he's shining, there is truly nothing better. When all of his smiles and attention are just for you, the world is a brighter, happier place. But like sunshine and rainbows, he has a tendency to disappear without warning and stay gone for a very long time. Being his sister shielded me from a lot of his darker days, but I've seen him drop girlfriends and friends on a whim and never so much as think about looking back. It's not that he's cruel; he just doesn't realize what he's doing. When it comes to relationships, he's got a bit of an AD/HD problem.

Sure, he seemed genuinely into Talley at the moment, but what about next week or next month? What would happen when the cute girl in his English 101 asks him to a party? Or when things started getting complicated with Talley? How would Talley, who never put anything less than her whole heart into anything, survive the aftermath?

The cold, simple truth of it was she wouldn't.

"Have you guys really thought about this?"

"What's to think about?" Jase said. "It's just a lifelong commitment. We decided to jump into it all willy-nilly like. What's the worst that could happen?"

Talley rolled her eyes, which was proof enough she was spending too much time with him. "Of course we've thought about it." She looked me straight in the eye. "This is what we both want. Promise."

"Are you sure? I mean, you might *think* this is what you both want *now*..."

71

Talley's gaze didn't waver. "I love him, Scout. And he loves me." She held up their linked hands. "Trust me. It's not exactly like he can lie or hide his true feelings from me."

"But it's *Jase*."

"It's Jase," she smiled. "My mate."

Chapter 10

I couldn't sleep that night. The day had been a revelation-filled piñata. Jase hadn't betrayed me. Mrs. Matthews had. Charlie was hurt and under constant Alpha Pack supervision, but he was alive and healing. Jase and Talley were dating, or whatever it is you call a pre-mated relationship, and they both seemed really happy about it. The small part of my brain not obsessing over those new developments was busy coming up with new and inventive ways to kick Liam in the head.

When I finally couldn't lay there with all those creepy dolls staring at me any longer, I got up and wandered through the house. Jase and Talley were sleeping in the living room. Jase was on the couch and Talley had an inflatable mattress. As I snuck towards the front door I noticed Jase's hand was dangling off the couch and onto the air mattress, where it was interlaced with Talley's. It might have been sweet and cute if it wasn't so bizarre and creepy.

Liam said he wanted to sleep on the extra couch on the screened-in back porch, but that wasn't where I found him. As I stepped through the back yard, keeping a wary eye out for the assorted vermin running about, he had to have heard me, but he just sat on the fence and stared off into the mountains.

I climbed up on the other side of the post. Balancing on top of a fence is a bit more difficult and uncomfortable than all those cowboy pictures would have you believe. After a bit of awkward maneuvering I finally found a position that didn't make it feel as though the slat of wood was going to leave bruises on my butt.

"It looks like a John Denver song out here," I said, breaking the stillness of the night. There was no moon, but the stars gave enough illumination for my sensitive Shifter eyes. Eastern Kentucky might get a lot of flack because of its economy, but it really is one of the most beautiful places in the world. "You know, life really isn't anything other than a funny, funny riddle, and I do thank God I'm a country girl."

Liam didn't so much as roll his eyes.

I shifted ever so slightly so I was somewhat facing him. "This isn't working."

"Try leaning forward," he said. "Put more pressure on your feet and less on your backside."

"Not what I meant." Although, he was right, it did help. "This arrangement of ours, the one where I trust that you know what in the Hades you're doing and don't ask too many questions. I can't do it any more." Not after he let me suffer when all it would have taken was one lousy sentence to tell me Jase actually cared if I lived or died. "If you want me to play whatever part it is you have planned for me, you're going to have to talk."

"And if I don't?"

I took a deep breath. "Then I walk."

"You really think you have any chance of surviving without me?"

"I don't have a chance of surviving period." I knew the truth, had Seen it in one of the visions of the future Talley claimed she didn't have. "The question is, does your mysterious plan have a chance of working without me?"

He didn't answer immediately. We both sat there, staring out into the distance. My super-senses were at their weakest, so I couldn't pick up on much other than the area immediately surrounding us. Most everything was sleeping, although there

74

were some mice in the barn having a grand old time. If I concentrated hard enough, I could just make out the sound of Talley's snoring.

"What do you want to know?" he asked just when I had made up my mind to go back inside.

"Everything."

"That all?"

I thought about all the unanswered questions, all the mysteries crowding my thinking space. "Start with your real name."

That seemed to actually catch him off-guard. "What do you mean?"

"After Alex's funeral Stefan approached me. He said Alex's real name was Christopher, but that you both changed your names after running away. So, what is it?"

There was another long lull in conversation, but eventually he answered. "Bryce."

"Why change it?"

"When the Alpha Pack burned down our house with my parents in it, they thought we were inside, too. We assumed new identities and let them continue to think Bryce and Christopher were dead."

"The Alpha Pack burned down your house with your parents inside?" My stomach twisted. "How do you know it was them?"

Another pause, and then a deep breath. "My parents met in Romania when they were both in training to be part of the Alpha Pack," he began. "My mother's family is one of, if not *the*, most powerful line of Seers in Europe. At least one girl from every generation was invited to become a Potential once their powers manifested. Usually they waited until they were eighteen to actually move them to the Den, but Mom went when she was fifteen. Future Seers are very rare, and they wanted her immediately."

He didn't look anywhere near me as he talked. It was as if he was telling his story to the mountains, but I was okay with that. As long as I got to hear it, I didn't care who he told.

"My dad was nineteen when he joined. His Pack wasn't very large and held very little Territory in Germany, but he was Dominant enough to catch the Alphas' eye. Gerard was the Alpha Male at the time, and he took Dad under his wing, preparing him to become a Stratego.

"They never said why they left. Mom would occasionally allude to things, but never said anything concrete. All I know is that after three years, Dad was granted a special Lone status and moved to Canada, taking Mom with him. Two years later, I was born.

"Our childhood was fairly normal, or at least I thought it was. We learned about being Shifters the same way human kids might learn to be Catholics. It was just part of who we were. They talked about the Alpha Pack in the same terms your parents would have spoken about the President or something. They were part of the social structure, a governing body that made and enforced our rules.

"Things changed when I was nine. That's when my sister was born."

A sister....? "Nicole."

Liam nodded. "You know how your siblings are supposed to annoy the shit out of you just because that's how life works?"

"As you may remember, I tried to kill my brother earlier today."

"We never felt that way with Nicole. She had Alex and I tied around her tiny little finger the moment we walked into the hospital room and first saw her angry red face." He laughed silently at the memory. "Mom said she was furious at having been born. She apparently liked the womb a little too much. Mom finally agreed to induce labor when it was two and a half

76

weeks after her due date and she still hadn't made an appearance.

"At first, everything was fine, but when she was six months old we got a visit from some Alpha Pack Seers. Dad had sent me and Alex to our bedrooms, but we snuck out into the hall to eavesdrop. I didn't understand much of what they were talking about, I was just a kid and they were talking about grown-up stuff, but I got the general idea of it. They wanted to take Nicole back to the Den with them. I didn't know at the time that was the standard procedure when a girl is born to Shifter parents."

"It is?" I hadn't heard that before. All Alex ever told me about female Shifters is they never make it to adulthood because the Change is too much for their body to handle. "All of them?"

"Initially, yes. Actually, parents are supposed to take their female daughters before the Alpha Pack immediately following birth. The ones who don't show any signs of carrying the Shifter gene are sent home, but the others..." Liam rubbed a hand over his hair. "They say they're trying to find a way to save them. Most parents let them go without much of a fight because they want to save their kid, and if they can't, then it's better to not have grown too attached, right?"

"They seriously just leave their babies with those psychos?" Even if I hadn't known Sarvarna was completely unhinged, I don't think I would be able to just walk off and leave my baby with someone else. And I couldn't imagine it would take anyone more than a few seconds with the Alpha Female to realize she shouldn't be trusted with a goldfish, let alone a baby.

"It's the way things have been for as long as anyone remembers. When a Shifter gets married there is this blessing everyone puts in their wedding cards and stuff. It says, 'May your days together be many and blessed, and may your children be born male. And should you have a daughter, may she See with the eyes of God.'"

"You are one seriously messed up group of people."

Liam actually turned his head and looked at me. "You don't even know the half of it."

"So tell me the rest. Did your parents let them take Nicole back to Romania?"

"No. They thanked the Seers for their time and concern, but Mom told them she Saw Nicole's future, and it was as a Seer, not a Shifter."

"She lied." Because I had seen Nicole in her wolf form and knew better.

"She lied, and the Seers didn't know any different, so they left. My parents thought that would be the end of it until Nicole actually Changed, but they underestimated the Alphas."

"They came back?"

Liam shook his head, his normal scowl replaced by something a lot more heartbreaking. "Christine, the Alpha Female, called a few times and expressed her concern, but Mom always brushed her off. Then, just before Nicole's fourth birthday, Mom had a vision.

"Future Seeing isn't always clear-cut. The Seers get a bit of this or that, but never any context or timeline. Mom wasn't sure what was going to happen, but she knew the Alpha Pack would be coming back for Nicole. She got really over-protective, always wanting to know where we all were and what we were doing. I was thirteen, which isn't the most intelligent time in a guy's life, and thought she was being crazy. So, when she told me to stay at home with the doors locked and watch my siblings, I didn't listen."

I did not like where this was going.

"I had a girlfriend at the time. Her name was Elyse, and I thought she was the love of my life. When she called and asked me to meet her at the gas station down the road from our house, I went and took Alex and Nicole with me. I didn't want to seem uncool, so I made them stay on the sidewalk out front while Elyse and I made out around the corner.

"I had only been Changing for about a year and a half, but my senses have always been sharper than a normal human. I heard the car turn onto the street and something inside me just knew what was going to happen. I ran as fast as I could, but I was too late to save them both." Liam's voice shook. I continued to look at the night sky, allowing him to have his moment. "They called it a hit and run, but it was a murder. I saw the driver. I smelled him. A Shifter ran over my baby sister on purpose, and then drove off, leaving her bloody body on the side of the street.

"After we buried her, we moved. We weren't allowed to tell anyone where we were going or say good-bye. To the citizens of Provost, we were there one day and disappeared the next. In reality, we just relocated off the grid. Shifters tend to like places with small populations, but our new place was miles from civilization. We weren't allowed to have Internet or go to school. Mom taught us from books she borrowed from the library while Dad kept taking off on 'business trips'. Sometimes his 'business partners' would come to the house for meetings. They were all Shifters."

"Were they part of the Alpha Pack?" I asked.

Liam snorted at the thought. "Exact opposite, actually."

"What's the opposite of the Alphas?"

"Shifters who want to bring the Alpha Pack to their knees." He seemed to consider what he said for a moment before adding, "And then cut off their heads."

Well, that was pretty opposite. "So, you're talking about a rebellion."

"Exactly. My parents went from being Potentials to becoming the leaders of the group secretly plotting to overthrow the Alphas."

"And the Alphas found out?"

"I don't know… maybe. Or maybe they were just too worried about how powerful our little family Pack was becoming. Mom was the strongest Seer other than the Alpha Female in the world, Dad was beyond Dominant, I was following in his footsteps, and Alex could See and Change. Either way, we were a threat."

Liam shook his head and took a deep breath before continuing. "It was a Tuesday. I knew something was up. Mom had a vision the day before, and they had been acting weird ever since. They kept hugging us and giving us these *you know we love you* talks, but since Nicole's death they did that every once in a while. That night, though, the talk went on for a long time, and before it was over they were talking about things like revenge and tempting destiny.

"In my gut, I knew something was very wrong, but they were my parents. I trusted them, so I didn't ask any questions when they gave us each a backpack and loaded us into the back of a delivery truck. They made me memorize an address in the United States and told us they would meet us there in a week.

"They died that night."

My heart ached for the boy Liam had been. "If they knew what was coming, why didn't they leave too?"

"I don't know." I knew that note in his voice. It was grief, pain, and confusion. They were old, dear friends of mine.

"Maybe they did," I ventured. "Maybe they're out there and just don't know how to find you--"

"No. They're dead." Liam reached into his pocket and pulled out an old, tattered piece of folded up paper. "This is my parents' farewell letter. I found it in my backpack that night, but didn't really believe it until Alex woke up in the middle of the night, covered in sweat, and choking on smoke from hundreds of miles away." He turned the note over and over in his hand. "That night Christopher and Bryce died. In our backpacks we had new IDs with names to remind me of everything I had lost, everyone I let die. William became Liam. Alexandria, Alex. Nicole's name we both carried with us. They made sure I would never forget the people I failed to save."

He wasn't being melodramatic. He actually believed it.

"I don't think that was their intention. No one would blame you, especially not your parents."

He acted like he hadn't even heard me. "You know the last thing my mom said to me? She said, 'Take care of your brother. It's his destiny to follow his heart, but it's your job to protect him.' And I tried. God, I tried." Liam pinched the bridge of his nose between two fingers. "I failed him, too. My whole family is dead because I couldn't protect them."

No wonder he was so grouchy all the time. I would be mad at the world if my whole family was dead, too. "Your family is dead because the Alpha Pack is a bunch of corrupt, power hungry monsters."

Liam cut his eyes towards me. "Yeah. Well, that too."

"So you've been on your own since you were what? Fifteen?"

"Fourteen. Some of the other 'rebels' looked after us for a bit, but we didn't stay any one place too long. I had trouble quelling my Dominant instincts, and no matter what someone's intention might be, adults have trouble submitting to a kid."

"And you couldn't just submit to someone else for a little while?"

"Could you?"

I thought about it. "Not now."

"Once I could drive, it wasn't a big deal. Actually, it worked out really well because we roamed all over the place trying to find other Shifters who might be sympathetic to our cause. That's what we were doing in Kentucky. We heard there was a large Pack of strong Shifters there who kept to themselves more than normal. We thought maybe it was because they were less than sold on the whole Alpha Supremacy thing, so we came to see if we could worm our way into their good graces and find out where their loyalties truly were."

"And they were receptive?"

"No. Not at all."

"So why did you stay so long?"

Liam tilted his head skyward. "You."

Something happened inside my chest. It was as if my heart tried to swell and constrict at the same moment. It was an altogether unpleasant sensation.

"Me? Because of Alex?"

This time, Liam didn't just look at the landscape stretching out in front of us, but turned his head completely away from me. "Partially."

"And the other part?"

"Do you remember the first time we met? It was at that burger stand down by the lake."

Some people you have to meet four or five times before you start to remember them. Liam Cole was not one of those people. I could remember every moment of our first encounter at The Strip, from his insulting stare to his threats against me and my family.

"Seems to ring a bell."

"I knew right then we couldn't just leave." He wasn't looking over his left shoulder anymore, but he wasn't exactly looking at me either. "The way you smelled, I had only smelled it on one other person in my life." He took a deep breath, and this time decided to shift his gaze to the stars. "You smelled like Nicole."

"What do you...?" The pieces slid together slowly in my head. "You mean, you could tell I was a Shifter?"

"I knew you had the potential to be one. I've met two of the other female Shifters, and you didn't smell like them. They had a stronger, more demanding scent. And there is this whole aura of power other Shifters have--"

"I've noticed that."

"You didn't have that then. There was just this faint scent layer underneath your normal smell. It was like a ghost of a smell, barely perceptible."

"So, it wasn't something that happened the night--" I stopped myself before saying, *the night Alex died."* It was getting easier for me to accept, but saying it in front of Liam seemed callous and mean. "I've always been a Shifter."

"Honestly, Scout, I have no idea. I think you've always had the potential to be a Shifter, but something happened that night to trigger it. And before you ask: No, I don't know why the potential was there. Your dad isn't a Shifter. It shouldn't have been possible. And I don't know what caused you to Change either. Maybe it was your connection to Alex, or maybe it was something the Hagans did. I don't know, so don't ask."

I closed an imaginary zipper over my lips, turned an imaginary lock, and threw away an imaginary key.

"It wasn't until you Changed that Toby began to understand the threat of the Alphas," he continued.

"Just Toby? What about the rest of the Hagans?"

"Jase, Charlie, and Talley are obviously pro-rebellion, but the others don't know anything about it. After Alex died, I asked Toby to hide me as payback for the unlawful death of my brother. It's one of those Shifter customs dating back to the dawn of time but nobody ever really remembers or uses. I was a little worried he would refuse, but in the end he agreed.

"To keep my whereabouts secret, we decided to only tell Charlie and Jase. They were both so shattered by what happened they wanted to repay me however they could. At first, we were just going to try to figure out a way to join the rebellion without causing Toby to have to face a dozen different Challenges for Pack Leader, but then you Changed and so did our priorities."

"You knew they would come after me."

"You're a female Shifter. There is no way they would let you live."

Goosebumps broke out over my arms.

"There is something I don't get," I said, mulling over the whole Cole-Hagan relationship. "Why didn't Toby Challenge you when you first moved into their Territory? That's how it normally works, right? Did he just meet you and realize there was no way he could take you down?" That didn't really sound like Toby, whose cocky arrogance might have been more annoying if it hadn't been hard-earned, but since neither he nor Liam was dead, something had to have happened.

"Not exactly." When he didn't elaborate I prodded. "Then what exactly was it?"

"I convinced them I was part of the Alpha Pack."

Here's the thing, if I didn't know any better, I would assume Liam was part of the Alpha Pack myself. He's the sort of person even normal people who have no clue about supernaturals would steer clear because of his animalistic personality. As a Shifter, it was even more pronounced. The amount of power radiating off of him even under the new moon was overpowering. I had been in the same room with the Alpha Male, and I wasn't sure which - Stefan or Liam - was actually more Dominant. So, I could have just left it alone, assumed that was all there was to the story. But the way he said it, as if he was embarrassed and wanted to let it drop, made certain I wouldn't do that.

"How?"

"How what?"

Ha! He was hiding something. "How did you convince Toby you were part of the Alpha Pack?"

I thought he was going to ignore me, but then he did something totally unexpected. He unbuttoned his pants.

"Whoa! Wait a minute! Britches stay on. That's a rule." It was an unstated rule, but one everyone should know.

"Calm down. I'm not going to offend your virgin eyes." My face flamed at the v-word, which was probably the only confirmation anyone needed that his assessment was completely accurate. "It's right here..." He pulled down the edge of his pants to reveal his hip. It was hard to make out due to the lack of light, but I thought I could see a mark on his skin.

"Is that a paw print?"

"Yes."

"Like a wolf's paw prin?"

"Yes," he said with no small amount of annoyance.

"You got a tattoo of a paw print on your hip to make Toby think you're with the Alphas?"

"All members of the Alpha Pack have one there."

Kind of a less-than-masculine place to put a tattoo, in my opinion. "So why doesn't everyone who wants to pass as a member get one?"

Liam quirked a lip at me, which was so reminiscent of his brother my heart clenched. "I'll give you two guesses, but you'll only need one."

Of course. It was the Alpha Pack. What was I thinking?

"Let's see, could it be..." I paused for dramatic flair. "Death to all who fake a paw print tattoo?"

That earned me a full-on smile. "Exactly."

"So, why risk it? Aren't you afraid of being severely punished for your ink?"

The smile disappeared. "I'm a dead man walking as it is. A tattoo isn't going to change that."

We were quiet for a long time. There wasn't really anything to say. As far as the Alpha Pack was concerned, we were both living on borrowed time. I thought of Jase, Talley, Charlie, and the others who were putting their lives on the line as well. Was it worth it? If this had all just been for me, then no. But it wasn't about me. It never was, even though I had been too self-centered to realize it for far too long. Liam was right. I was just a pawn.

"Your grand plan," I said. "I'm the bait, aren't I?"

Liam looked at me, like really looked at me. The kind of *"looked at me"* which makes you feel like a bug under a microscope. "Not bait," he said. "You're the secret weapon."

Chapter 11

Jase was no longer on the couch when I went back into the house. Instead, he was on the air mattress, his front to Talley's back. His arm was draped over her waist, and his fingers were once again entwined with hers.

Good grief, could they not go five whole seconds without holding hands? I mean, for the love of all things shiny, they were *asleep*.

"Everything okay?"

I nearly jumped out of my skin at Jase's voice. The heel of my hand pressed my chest to keep my heart from pounding through my ribcage.

"Fine. I couldn't sleep."

"Yeah, me either." He slowly worked his way into a sitting position. The process involved carefully unlacing his fingers from Talley's and then reclaiming her hand once he was in position.

"Seriously, Jase, I don't think she's going to wander off." His eyebrows knitted together, and I gestured to the hands-which-nothing-can-asunder.

"She's been having nightmares," he said as he brushed a piece of hair off her shoulder. It was really sweet, but I still felt like I wandered into some sort of alternate reality. Maybe in this world Sarvarna was a good guy and asparagus tasted better than ice cream. "She doesn't have as many if she can See me, and this way I can wake her up when they start."

"Isn't this a bit much?" I asked. "I mean, weren't you the guy having a hissy fit over the fear of Talley getting into your head just a month or two ago?"

Jase looked down at a sleeping Talley, a truly goofy smile on his face. "I was a coward."

"You're creeping me out."

When he looked back up, his face was serious. It's not like I'd never seen him serious before. It's not his default frame of mind, but it's happened. It's just that usually his seriousness came with a large helping of righteous indignation. Not so much this time. This time, he looked more exhausted than angry. "You think I'm going to hurt her."

"I know you are." Maybe I shouldn't have said it, but it was the truth. And my new policy was all truth, all the time.

"You used to have more faith in me than this. What happened?"

"You lied to me. You were a Shifter, and you never told me." And really, this was the crux of our problems. Everything that had gone wrong between us over the past year came back to this single point.

"That isn't lying. I never said, 'Hey, Scout, I'm *not* a Shifter.'"

I sank onto his abandoned spot on the couch. "But you didn't tell me you were. You didn't trust me then, so I can't trust you now. Not after everything."

Jase clenched his jaw, preparing for an argument. I lay back on the pillows, suddenly too exhausted to keep my head up.

"It was an act. An act, Scout. I would have never done that to you, and I'm still more than a little pissed you think I would."

He didn't sound pissed. He sounded sad, and I couldn't handle it.

"I don't want to talk about it anymore."

"We haven't talked about it yet!"

I threw an arm over my eyes. God, I really was tired. After a few minutes of silence I felt my muscles relaxing as my mind started to drift...

"You're not fooling me."

I made a conscious effort to keep my breaths slow and deep.

"Scout, we need to talk about this. Now. Talley and I have to go back to Lexington tomorrow, and I don't know when we'll see each other again. I'm not leaving it like this."

"You know," I said, still refusing to open my eyes, "if you would have asked, I would have said yes."

"Asked what?"

"To go along with Liam's plan." I couldn't decide if I was hurt or angry. Probably both. It seems that true anger is rooted in pain. "I would have gone along with it. Heck, if it would have helped, I would have turned myself into the Alphas. The truth of the matter is you didn't trust me, *yet again.*" I finally opened my eyes. "How can you blame me for not trusting you when you obviously have never trusted me."

Jase's jaw tightened again, but before he could say anything, Talley stirred beside him. "Shhhhh..." she muttered, still about ninety percent asleep. "It's okay. Shhh..." Jase once again brushed her hair back from her face and then leaned down to kiss her temple. Something passed between them, I could see it on his face, and I was forced to re-evaluate my entire stance on this new relationship. Because what I saw in that moment wasn't the popular jock who changed girlfriends with the same frequency as a Hollywood heartthrob. Actually, I wasn't completely sure who he was anymore, and maybe that was the problem. Maybe I never actually knew him.

"I've made some bad decisions," he said when he looked back up. "I'm the first to admit it. But I've always done it to protect you."

"Did it ever occur to you I don't need protecting?"

He smiled, but it didn't reach his eyes. "It did. Around the same time you took down the Alpha Pack's elite while in handcuffs."

Travis's face flashed in my head, abruptly killing any pride I might have felt.

I rolled onto my side to face him. "Are you really fully on board with these... rebels or whatever?"

"Yes," he answered without hesitation. "And it's 'Jedi'."

"Seriously?"

This time his smile was genuine, lighting up his entire face. "No, but it should be."

"I suppose you're the Luke Skywalker of this Jedi rebellion?"

"Don't be ridiculous. I'm the Han; she's the Leia," he said, indicating Talley with a nod of the head, "and you're the Luke."

"Liam and Charlie?"

"Yoda and Chewy, obviously."

"Sorry, but no. If I'm the Luke, then you have to be the Leia and Talley the Han. Charlie can still be Chewy, but no way is Liam Yoda. Maybe a pre-Dark Side Anakin?"

Jase cringed. "Really? You're going to bring those horrible prequels into this? Are you sure we're related?"

"You know, I'm not sure we've really got a Star Wars feel going on here anyway. I'm really feeling more like a Harry Potter to your Ron Weasley and Hermione Granger."

"Harry Potter? Someone is awful full of themselves."

"And this way Charlie can be always-loyal and cooler than cool Neville Longbottom, and Liam gets to be Sirius."

Jase shook his head. "Sirius dies."

"Lupin?"

"Also dies."

"A Weasley twin?"

"Liam isn't that funny, and Fred dies."

I searched over the entire cast of *Harry Potter*. "All the cool people die."

"Which is why we should stick to Star Wars and Jedi. What kind of cool team name would we get if we went with the wizards? Team Gryffindor?"

"Or, you know, Order of the Phoenix."

"I think we're more like Dumbledore's Army," was Talley's sleepy reply. "Although, we're more like Liam's Army."

"You're awake?"

"She has been the whole time. She was just trying to give us some alone time," Jase said to me before leaning down to plant another kiss on her cheek. "Yes, it was a very good try, but you're not getting anything past me, Tal. I'm way too clever for you."

"It's a good thing I've gotten used to your arrogance over the years," she said.

"You love my arrogance."

"I *tolerate* your arrogance," she corrected.

"Same thing," he said before moving his kiss to her lips. It was just a little peck in the beginning, but then she tilted her head, and the kiss deepened. It took all of two seconds for me to get very, very uncomfortable.

"I'm still sitting here," I reminded them, but they kept going. "Like, two feet away from you." Still no response. "Seriously, I can hear all your yucky smacking noises and stuff. I would really appreciate it if you would stop." I was going to have to gouge out my eyeballs if they didn't.

"Sorry," Talley said, *finally* pulling back. She pressed the back of her hand to her lips, and even in the darkness of the room I could see both the blush on her lips and stars in her eyes. "This whole newly-promised-to-be-mated things is kind of intense. Charlie has started keeping a water gun by his hospital bed to use on us."

Since everyone was fully awake I went ahead and sat back up. Exhaustion made my body heavy, but if this was the last time I was going to see my brother and best friend, I wanted to be awake for it. My foot rested on Talley's calf, and before she could wrestle with the ethics of Seeing what was going on with me, I opened myself up to her.

"You talked to Liam," she said. "Good."

"Yeah, he's considerably less annoying when he isn't being all broody and silent. And it's kind of nice being caught up on everything for once." I shot Jase a look to let him know he still wasn't completely forgiven.

"Give him some slack," Talley said, and I wasn't quite sure if she was talking about Liam or Jase. Maybe both. Knowing Talley, she meant humans in general.

I was willing to give Liam some slack, especially now that I knew what he had been through, but I wasn't trusting him to become a regular Chatty Kathy and start sharing on a regular basis. Knowing this might be my last chance to gather information from people who really did care about my place in all of this, I ventured into an area of conversation I was mostly sure Liam wouldn't approve.

"I don't suppose you guys are in on The Plan? Like what happens tomorrow, or the day after, or the month after?"

Talley and Jase shared a look, and then Jase answered. "Liam is supposed to be training you. I'm not sure of any particulars as to where you are going or anything, but Toby and the others are busting their asses off to recruit as many Shifters to our side as possible before he declares you ready."

"Ready for what?"

Talley's eyes flicked towards the back porch where Liam was supposed to be sleeping.

"He's out by the barn," I said, able to hear him walking around. He had to be as tired as I was, but I understood. He wasn't really in a good place emotionally when I headed in, but it was the kind of thing you had to be in your own head for a while to get through. I knew. I had been there myself. "I don't think he's actively listening to our conversation." Although I went ahead and dropped my voice a few notches.

She nodded. It seemed more like a *"Yes, I'm going to go ahead and do this,"* than *"Good to know."* "You're supposed to Challenge the Alpha Female."

"I can do that?" It seemed logical, I guess. Although, there was no way in Hades I was going to become the new Alpha Female. Running an entire race of people wasn't really something I am super-qualified for. "Why would I have to train for that? Not to be too horribly boastful here or anything, but I'm pretty sure I could take that skank down with one arm tied behind my back. I'm a Shifter. She's evil, but a pampered princess all the same. It'll take me less than two minutes to have her bleeding and broken."

"But can you kill her?"

My heart paused dramatically in my chest. "I've killed before." I could still feel the gun in my hand; see the shock and then nothingness in Travis's eyes.

Being more perceptive than normal, Jase said, "And you can't think about it without turning green. That was in self-defense, kill or be killed. Right now could you honestly issue a Challenge to Sarvarna knowing you're going to end her life?"

"If I had to--"

"And to claim the Alpha spot, you would also have to kill Stefan."

"He's in a coma."

"Yes, he is," Jase said. "Could you do that? Kill a defenseless man?"

I wasn't a fan of Stefan by a long shot - he did lock me in a cage and agree to have me killed - but I didn't hate him with quite the same passion as I did Sarvarna. When it came down to it, he didn't really want me dead. He regretted having to do it, but felt it was necessary for the greater good. Even though I disagreed, *strongly*, I understood. He was sort of noble in this really screwed up way. It was the kind of screwed up nobility which would have kept him from attacking someone in a hospital bed.

No, I couldn't do that. Not at all.

"I don't want to be Alpha. Can't we just stage a coup and then have an Alpha election?"

"That's not the way it works," Jase said.

"It can't work that way," Talley added. "Wolves and coyotes need a hierarchy based on strength. Once you beat the Alphas, you'll have to face Challenges, both from within the Alpha Pack and outside. Every Dominant in the world will see it as a time to make a bid for power. You will have to fight every day, kill every day, for as long as it takes to prove you're the strongest, most capable Shifter."

"But I'm not." And I would never be prepared for what Talley was talking about. A life of fighting? Of killing? There was no amount of training Liam could do to prepare me for that. "Why not Liam? Why doesn't he Challenge the Alphas?" I knew he was capable of taking them on, and might even have the fortitude to keep fighting once the initial battle was done.

Jase's mouth set as he slowly gave his a head a wish-I-knew shake. "I guess he figures there is no need to fight a war when you can program someone else to do it for you."

"That's not it," Talley said. I could see her wrestling with those morals of hers, but finally she came down on the side of sharing what she knew despite the invasion of Liam's privacy. "He doesn't feel worthy. He thinks he'll fail."

"And I'm going to do a better job?" I snorted out a laugh. "Seriously, Tal? He has to know this is a suicide mission for me."

"No, it's not!" Jase practically yelled at the same time Talley said, "You can't think that."

I held up a hand to quiet them. "Listen, I don't want to die, and I'm certainly going to do everything in my power to keep from biting the big one, but you both know I'm not going to be able to go all River Tam on the Shifters of the world." I looked at Talley. "And we both know what you've Seen. It doesn't look like I'm going to make it past Round One."

"I don't See--"

"Talley."

She took a deep breath. "The vision changes all the time. It's not a definite thing."

"How many times does it not include me getting stabbed?"

Her silence was answer enough.

"I'm not lying. I'm scared, and I don't want to die." While part of me yearned to be at peace with Alex, I knew it was the coward's way out. Not to mention, there were still things I wanted to do in this world. "But they can't win. I'm not saying I'm going to go along with this whole Scout-Challenges-the-Alphas plan, but I'm willing to fight for the cause. If there's going to be a war, then count me in as a soldier."

"That's why we're trying to gather up as many Jedi as possible," Jase said. "You'll need backup, an army at your command. Plus, the more people we already have on our side, the fewer Challenges you'll have to take on. Those who sign on with us will already be willing to follow your lead."

Jase believed it. I could tell he actually thought I was going to go out there, take on the world, and win. He believed that Liam's Army would put their faith in the leadership of an eighteen year old girl. I could have corrected him, pointed out how I was, as Liam had said, just a pawn. I could have told him that if destiny existed, mine wasn't to lead a rebellion but be the catalyst for a revolution. I understood where I fit in to all of this. It didn't take a genius to figure it out, just a realist. But Jase couldn't see it, because he didn't want to believe it, and I wasn't about to be the one to open his eyes.

"What's your role in all of this?" I asked.

My brother tried to look all haughty. "We're spies, of course."

"Of course."

"We've earned Sarvarna's trust," Talley said. "We're able to move about freely with no one tailing us or tapping our phones. We can pass information to Toby, who in turn passes it to other members of the rebellion, without any problems."

"Are you crazy? What if they catch you?" The idea of what could happen to them was enough to make my stomach hurt. "It's too dangerous. You have to stop. Like, now."

Talley leaned against Jase's arm. "It's a dangerous world we live in, Scout. We all have to play our parts, do what we can."

"This is too much," I said. "We're kids. Why should we be the ones to save the world? Aren't there adults much more qualified for this task?"

"The adults have sat around and let the Alphas do whatever in the world they want for way too long. It's our turn now. Our generation has to be the change we want to see in the world."

I was a little slack-jawed. "That's very profound."

"It's Ghandi," Jase admitted. "But it's true. If we want things to be different, we have to make them different, even if it means sacrificing our own safety for the future."

"It's still not fair," I said. We were supposed to be worrying about what classes to take and our roommate's lack of hygiene or constant stream of sex partners. Normal college freshmen stuff. Instead we were planning to take down the Alpha Pack and putting our lives on the line. "I want to grow old with you guys. I want to be an aunt to your kids and teach them all the ways to annoy you."

"You will," Talley said. "We'll make it through this."

"How?"

Jase met my eyes. "You're the smart one. You figure it out."

Chapter 12

Heaven smells like bacon. Well, not Alex's part of heaven - if that is heaven - but the part with the pearly gates and harps and all that jazz? Fried porky goodness wafts through the air. It's a truth I hold in my heart.

I woke to the most wonderful of all wonderful smells to find Liam standing over the stove, spatula in hand, while Talley sliced a tomato at the counter. Jase was seated at the table, still in his pajama bottoms and UK Wildcats t-shirt. His face was a living testament to my rage the day before, swollen and bruised all over.

"You trust the Alpha's doctor?" Liam asked.

"We don't really have much choice," Jase said, "but I can't imagine why he would lie. If he wanted to hurt him he would've just let him die. He worked too hard to keep him alive to be screwing with us now."

"Damn. That's just..." Liam stabbed at the skillet with undue force. "He deserves better."

"What's wrong?" Jase and Talley both jumped at the sound of my voice, but Liam just scooped up the bacon and placed it on a plate. "What's wrong with Charlie?"

"Nothing," the three of them said in unison.

I sat up on the couch, eyes narrowed. "Yeah. Right."

"We weren't talking about Charlie." Talley's finger snagged a lock of hair. "It's Stefan. He's not doing well."

Liar-Liar, pants on fire.

"So Charlie is fine and dandy?"

"Since I'm a guy and his cousin," Jase said, "I can't really comment on the 'fine' assessment, but the guy's kind of a slouch when it comes to grooming. I don't think 'dandy' really applies."

I wasn't completely awake, and therefore couldn't come up with a witty reply, so I extended my middle finger in his direction. Talley scowled at the profanity, but soothed me with, "He's fine. Really. You heard him for yourself."

True, he sounded like Charlie on the phone yesterday, which was way more than I was expecting. My overactive imagination had him lying in a hospital bed with tubes sticking out everywhere, his face gaunt, the light gone from his eyes. But I still felt like something was off, that there was something they were keeping from me. *Again.*

"Do you swear it, Talley? In front of me, God, and everybody, that Charlie is okay?"

Talley looked to Jase, who held out a hand to her.

"No! No hand holding." I looked Talley in the eyes. Yes, I was being a bully, but this was the only way I would get any real information. Jase and Liam could both lie with aplomb, but as long as Talley wasn't plugged into Jase's brain, I knew she wouldn't be able to fib, especially since I'd invoked the name of God. She was really paranoid about that sort of thing, thanks to her mother.

I inwardly flinched at the thought of Mrs. Matthews.

Talley took a deep breath and raised her left hand while the right one rested over her heart. "I swear that Charlie is getting better every day, and we fully expect him to almost completely heal."

"Almost completely?"

"We didn't want to you to worry," Jase said, "but there have been some complications. He's never going to be back to where he was before."

99

"But when he Changes..." A realization struck me. "He should already be completely healed. We've had two full moons since he was injured."

Liam, who was scrambling up at least a dozen eggs, answered. "Changing can't fix everything, and sometimes injuries prevent you from Changing at all while you heal."

"Since when?" It didn't make sense. Alex was able to Change from wolf to human after his fall, even with a stick protruding from his chest. Liam seemed disinclined to enlighten me, but I wasn't having it. I stormed over to him, stopping just far enough away that I could look him in the eye without craning my neck. "What kind of injury could prevent a Shifter from Changing?" Liam just stood there. "Tell me, damn it!"

He stepped closer, which pissed me off. Now I either had to look up to him or take a step backwards. I decided holding my ground was more important.

"I don't follow your orders." His words were quiet, yet dripped with hostility. Out of the corner of my eye I could see Jase and Talley watching with rapt interest.

"*Liam.*" It came out as a growl, a warning.

His eyes narrowed. "You have dad's book. You tell me."

I was about to snap that there wasn't anything in the book about injuries preventing a Change, but then it hit me. "Your brain and spinal cord don't Change. They're the same in either form." Dr. Smith hypothesized the catalyst for the Change resided in the Central Nervous System. "Is that it? Does he have a brain injury?"

"His spinal cord is messed up," Jase answered. "The bullet wound was bad, but it was never the real danger. One of those assholes broke his back."

"Is he paralyzed?" On the phone he said something about walking again. In the information bombardment that occurred afterwards I hadn't thought to ask about it.

Liam, obviously bored with this conversation, went back to preparing breakfast.

I plopped down in the chair beside Jase. I felt a teensy bit embarrassed over my outburst with Liam, especially after our heart-to-heart the night before, but there was only so much space in my body for emotions to go, and most of that space was reserved for Charlie-related concerns at the moment.

"He shouldn't have been there. He shouldn't have risked himself like that."

Liam sat a plate in front of me. "He made a choice, knowing the risks. All of us have. We think it's worth it. The question is, do you?"

Was it? Was overthrowing the Alphas worth putting our lives on the line?

If it was a faceless horde we would be liberating, I would have said no. But it wasn't an anonymous population on the line. This revolution or coup or whatever had Talley's fearful tear-stained face from when she thought she would have to go back to the Matthews Pack because of the way the Alphas encourage Shifters to treat Seers like property. It had the face of Nicole, who died just because she would one day Change. It had the faces of Alex and Liam's parents, and Alex and Liam, who had to suffer so much loss simply so a select few could hold on to their positions of power.

"I do," I said. "I'm in. All the way."

***

I tried to be good throughout breakfast. Really, truly I did, but Liam seemed intent on pushing my buttons.

"You weren't kidding," Jase said, squirting ketchup on his eggs because he's weird like that. "Scout really doesn't submit to you."

Liam reached across the table and stabbed a stack of pancakes with his fork. "Took you this long to figure that out?"

"Isn't this whole idea of submission really archaic?"

"No," three voices answered me in unison. "Every Pack needs a Pack Leader," Talley added on to the end of hers.

A little light bulb, like maybe the size of a Christmas light, went off over my head. "That's because we're not a Pack." Oh yes. This was making sense. "We're like two lone wolves peacefully coexisting with one another."

Liam nodded in agreement. "We're both perfectly accepting of the fact that we're equally Dominant, so there's no reason to force the issue."

"Except, you know, we're not really equally Dominant." I snagged my glass of milk, frowning at its pale blue tint. "What we both equally accept is that he's Super-Shifter, and I can't be bothered to care."

"I was wrong," Liam said for perhaps the first time in his life. "We apparently don't agree on anything."

I looked at him over the top of my glass. "Seriously? You do realize you can Shift any time you darn well please and I can barely push myself through it under a full moon, right?"

"Only because you're not trying hard enough."

"Good grief, not this again."

"Well, if you would just put some effort--"

"I am putting effort--"

"*I'm new. It hurts. I can't do it. Don't make me try.*" Liam's voice went beyond mocking and into antagonistic. I didn't realize just how much he pissed me off until the glass in my hand shattered. I jumped back, but my jeans, the only pair I had, were covered in milk.

"I'm blaming you for this," I said between my teeth.

Jase looked at Talley. "They need to spar."

"They definitely need to spar," she agreed.

***

102

Someone may put our first fight down in the annals of Shifter history someday, but hopefully they'll leave out the part where I slipped on a patch of grass covered in chicken poop and Talley almost went into an asthma attack because of a stray long-haired cat who didn't have brains enough to be scared of a bunch of Shifters.

"Liam hasn't had much training, so he fights street." Jase stood behind me, rubbing my shoulders as if I was Rocky Balboa. I was only half listening to him. My body was buzzing with anticipation. I started taking martial arts when I was a kid, and it's one of the few activities I've kept up with over the years. There is something both relaxing and empowering about having the control over your body it takes to execute a perfect move. I hadn't realized it before, but now that it was happening, I needed this. Not to prove which of us was stronger, but just the simple act of fighting. It could have been Jase or anyone else standing in front of me and I would have still felt the same.

Maybe.

"Don't expect him to follow the same rules we're used to," Jase continued. "And remember, this isn't a real Challenge, so if your wolf instincts start to take over, back off."

"Yep. Got it." Whatever it was he said. I just needed him to get out of the way so I could go.

"I'll try not to hurt you," Liam called to me from across the patch of grass we had chosen as our arena.

I flexed my fingers. "Same here."

Jase stepped back.

"You ready?" I asked.

Liam stuck out his hand, palm up, and then flicked his fingers a la Neo from *The Matrix*.

"Oh, please," I said. "That is so cliché. Do you really--" And then he was right in front of me, his way-too-freaking-huge fist barreling towards my face so fast I really didn't have time to dwell on how he got there.

In a move that was both an attempt to show off and an effort to get some space between the two of us, I dove forward, tucking my body in for a summersault once I hit the ground. When I bounced back onto my feet I was at the other side of the grassy area, and he was already coming back at me.

He punched. I blocked. He kicked. I blocked. Punch, punch, punch. Block, block, block. Then, just when I was expecting a kick, his arms clasped around me, pinning my elbows to my side, and he tossed me. I'm pretty sure his plan involved me being on the ground with him towering above, but it didn't work out quite that way. I hooked my foot behind his ankle as I went, which caused us both to tumble.

I could feel the shift as I rolled; my senses got sharper as my mind was overtaken. The human part of me remembered Jase's advice to pull back, but I couldn't. Wolf Scout was already in control, and, if the snarls were anything to go by, Liam wasn't thinking with his human half either.

We rolled on the ground like animals. After over a decade of martial arts training, I knew at least a dozen different moves I could execute from the ground, but I didn't use any of them. Instead, teeth and fingernails came into play. I could smell Liam's blood on the air as well as my own.

I wasn't aware of the screaming until someone ripped me off Liam. I tried to lash out at the arms around me, but that's when Talley's shouts of "Stop!" and Jase's assurances of "I've got you" started clicking in my brain.

"It's okay, Scout. I've got you," Jase cooed into my ear. "I've got you."

"What's wrong with you?" I asked, pushing myself back and only accomplishing landing on my butt.

Jase looked at me as if he didn't know who I was. "You were crying."

Crying...?

"I was laughing, you idiot." I caught sight of Liam behind Jase. He was grinning like he just found out he was getting an extra Christmas this year. "We were having fun."

"Fun? You've got blood gushing from your lip!"

"And you broke something when you hit the tree," Talley said. "I heard it."

"The only thing broken is the tree, and it shouldn't have gotten in my way." I used the bottom of my shirt to wipe off my mouth. "New demand," I called over Jase's shoulder. "We're going to start doing this on a regular basis, or I walk, deal?"

Liam's smile was blood-tinted. "Deal."

Chapter 13

Less than twenty-four hours after trying to kill my brother, I found myself fighting back tears as I told him goodbye.

"Do you still consider me your Pack Leader?" We were alone in the bedroom, the television blaring to cover our voices.

"As long as I live," he said without a hint of irony.

"Good. Then consider this an order. Do what you can to aide Liam's rebellion, but when it comes down to it, your loyalty is to our family. Protect them and yourself, even if it means turning your back on everything else." I didn't have to explain how I was including Charlie and Talley in my definition of "family". Jase knew.

He ducked his head and offered his throat in the Shifter's sign of submission. "Understood."

I wasn't sure how Shifter custom dictated I respond - amazingly, Liam hadn't covered that aspect of our world yet - but after a few seconds of Jase standing in such an awkward pose I had to do something, so I grabbed him and pulled him into a hug.

"I'm lost without you," I muttered into his shoulder.

"I don't care what our blood says," he responded. "You're my sister. My twin. My other half." My rib cage threatened to collapse from the pressure his arms. "I would die without you, so please stay the hell alive."

"I'll try."

He released his hold enough that he could pull back and see my face. "Pinkie promise?"

My eyes pricked, but I blinked the tears back. "Pinkie promise," I said, as my little finger slipped around his.

***

Like most families, our vacations always included cars and planes, although we once rode a train to New Orleans. Traveling via Greyhound was new to me, but I've traveled on charter buses for long school trips, and the bus Liam and I boarded in Lexington three hours later was much the same. The floor was a little stickier, the seats a bit more worn and stained, and the smell just a hair on the wrong side of pleasant, but if you've seen one big bus, you've seen them all: High-back seats covered with loud, patterned fabric were arranged in two rows of two. Long, tinted windows stretched the entire length. A small closet-type thing occupied the back corner and was the source of the odor.

Liam led me straight to the back and motioned for me to take the window seat. There were plenty of empty seats available, but he parked himself in the one beside me. I wanted to ask him what he was thinking picking the seats closest to the bathroom when we both had super-smelling abilities, but then I noticed how the other passengers would get near the back, notice the smell, and then head closer to the front.

As we pulled out of the city and onto the Interstate, neither of us spoke. We were both perfectly happy being lost in our own head space. I would have also enjoyed being lost in my own physical space, but even though Liam in no way spilled over onto my seat, his size and power made me feel dwarfed as I pressed as tightly to the window as possible.

We were already leaving Cincinnati, the first of a million stops, when Liam asked, "What are you thinking about?"

My eyebrows shot up. Liam was starting a conversation? One that wasn't a lecture? And he was doing so by expressing interest in what I was thinking?

Since I was sitting down with a seat back behind me, knocking me over with a feather would have been impossible, but you could've stabbed me with the pointy end without me noticing.

"I was actually thinking about you," I answered honestly. When Liam pulled back a smidgen, his eyes full of unease, I rushed to clarify. "I was thinking about your ultimate betrayal."

"My ultimate betrayal?" His shoulders slumped. "Listen, Scout, I--"

"I mean, Canadian, Liam? You're a freaking Canadian? How am I supposed to deal with that?" I had to work at not breaking into a grin at his startled response. "Do you secretly listen to Celine Dion and Avril Lavigne? Do you douse all your food with maple syrup when I'm not looking? Do you have a poster of Alex Trebeck stowed away in your overnight bag?"

Liam smiled, one of his real folded-cheeks smiles, and I fastidiously ignored what the sight did to me. "You are impossible."

"Although, this could work to my advantage," I mused. "Do you happen to know Ryan Reynolds? Because it would be kind of cool to meet him. And talk to him. And maybe touch him..."

"Yes. Of course I do. You know, all Canadians know each other. I've got Estella Warren on speed dial."

"Who is that?"

"Americans," Liam sighed dramatically.

"And *Bryce*? Really?"

That wasn't met with even a hint of humor. "Bryce is dead."

"I'm just trying to imagine the person he was," I railroaded on. "Bryce. *Bryyyyyyce.* That's the name of a Mustang-driving, cheerleader-dating, popular quarterback if I've ever heard one."

At first I thought he wasn't going to relent, that I had gone too far with bringing up his past, but then he said, "Americans are quarterbacks. Bryce played center."

"Basketball?" That I could understand. We Kentuckians are all about some hoops, and my family is particularly enamored since Jase is pretty much a basketball rock star.

"Ice hockey. It's Canada, remember? Try to keep up."

I leaned into his personal space, putting my face mere inches from his.

"What are you doing?"

"Looking at your teeth," I said. "You have all of them. I don't buy this hockey story."

He flashed his teeth, something between smiling and baring them, and I saw my assessment was right. They were all there.

"This one, this one, and this one," he said, pointing at three different teeth, "have all been broken."

"Ah-ha. The old Shifter thing worked to your dental advantage."

"Yeah. Thank God I didn't knock any out, or they would still be gone."

I thought about that. "Because the Change repairs damage but can't regrow something that's gone?"

"Exactly. Matter can't be created or destroyed, only changed. Or Changed. Or something like that."

We sat there for a bit, me watching the world whip by while Liam tried to derive meaning from the stains on the upholstery.

"So," I said, once my curiosity could no longer be contained, "I need you to say it."

"Say what?"

"*It.*" I nodded my head slowly, giving him a come-on-you-know-what-I'm-talking-about look. "You might as well get it over with."

"I honestly have no idea what you're talking about."

"Say it, Liam. Say 'out and about'."

His laughter was so abrupt and loud many people turned their heads in our direction.

He never did say it, but it was okay. I made him laugh, and not by ineptitude. It was a small victory, but it felt more like winning the war.

***

We had to change buses in Columbus. There was enough time to grab something to eat before we hit the road again, so we found a little run-down place selling barbecue and filled our bellies. Liam is a pie man, and since I honestly can't think of anything to say against them, we ended up splitting a homemade coconut cream pie that tasted like it was made by a blue-haired granny who loved butter like a grandchild. We didn't chat the entire way through the meal the way I would have if it had been Talley, Jase, or Charlie keeping me company, but it wasn't the absolute silence of meals past either. We remarked on our food and fellow diners. Liam asked why Western Kentucky barbecue was so superior, and I explained something about dry rubs, smoking processes, and sauces that may or may not have been one hundred percent true. It was, for lack of a better word, nice.

There was a three hour ride until our next stop, and during that time I drifted off to sleep. I was somewhat surprised to find myself back on a familiar stretch of beach.

"Alex Cole," I said, making my way to where he lounged on his favorite rock. "It's been a while."

"Yes, well, it seems I'm not quite as trusted as I once was." Nicole scampered up behind him. "My comings and goings are more guarded these days, and all extraneous visits are nipped in the bud."

I sat down beside him and greeted Nicole with a scratch behind her ears. "So what you're saying is you need something and that's the only reason you're here?"

Alex lifted a shoulder. "Apparently, not that anyone will tell me what that might be." He directed his last words to the clouds.

"Are you talking to God or the angels?"

He turned, dropping one leg to the ground to brace his weight. I readjusted ever so slightly so we would be face-to-face. "You know I can't answer that, right?"

"I know," I said. "But you know I can't keep myself from asking."

His dimples showed. "I know."

Nicole, not liking her place in our new seating arrangement, got up and moved around until she could drape herself over both our legs. I stroked a hand through her multi-toned fur, marveling at the softness. She was even fluffier than I remembered Alex being, probably because she was still a puppy.

"Her coloring is almost exactly like yours," I said to Alex. "I really should have figured out she was your sister sooner."

Alex's eyes flew wide. I didn't realize he was holding a breath until it came rushing out in something between a sigh and laugh. "And that, I assume, is why I'm here."

I continued stroking Nicole's fur. "Liam and I talked."

"About...?"

"Everything." I was still coming to terms with it all. I thought my story was a sad one, but Liam and Alex experienced more tragedy in a few short years than most people are forced to endure over their entire lives. Then there was the whole anti-Alpha movement, and the fact they wanted me to be their champion or sacrifice, depending on how you looked at it. "It was a long talk," I said.

"So, to clarify, you know about...?"

"Nicole. Your parents. The role the Alpha Pack played in their deaths." Nicole whimpered. "I know about Liam's Army and what they expect of me."

Alex soothed his sister with a kiss on the forehead. "Liam's Army?" he asked as he continued to nuzzle her. The sight reminded me of the way Wolf Scout and Wolf Liam comforted one another.

"Yeah, it's like Dumbledore's Army, but instead of going against an evil witch cum temporary headmaster, we oppose an evil Seer cum temporary Alpha."

"Temporary Alpha?"

"No matter what, she's not going to hold that spot for long." I knew the position itself was corrupt, but I couldn't image a more vile person than Sarvarna in the spot. She had to be removed from power, even if it meant I was going to have to kill her. I might not be ready to do it now, but Liam would get me there. Of that I had no doubt.

"You know, I'm not really sold on 'Liam's Army'. How about 'The Jedi' since it's this whole rebellion against an evil Empire thing?"

I snorted. "That's what Jase wanted to call it."

"The guy has good taste."

"Well, he certainly chose a good mate," I said. "Couldn't have chosen a better one for him if I had accidentally made him declare himself to her myself. Oh wait. I did do that, didn't I?"

I got to see Alex's completely shocked expression yet again. "Jase and Talley? Seriously?"

"They seemed pretty serious to me."

Alex leaned down to talk to Nicole. "You're right. All the really interesting stuff happens after you die."

His words were light, but they sat heavy in my heart all the same. True, these dream meetings were better than nothing, but I missed him. I wanted him with me in the real world. What would this have been like if he had been by my side? Would he have been the one to save me from the Alphas? Would he be the one absconding with me? Would it be his job to teach and train

112

me? Or would all those responsibilities still have fallen to Liam? And if so, would Alex have come along for the ride?

Of course, if Alex hadn't died, there was a good chance none of this would have happened. The exact cause of my ability to Change was still very much up in the air, much to my chagrin, but most every theory centered around the night Alex died. If he was still alive, I would probably still be a normal, boring human, and the Alphas would have never known I existed.

And they would have gone on terrorizing the Shifters of the world for God knows how long.

That's when I had a revelation. I was already beginning to accept my life as a Shifter, but at that moment, I was happy I Changed. I might not be looking forward to the battle ahead, but it was one that needed to happen. Some things are worth fighting for. For me, this was it.

"I'm going to do it, Alex," I said. "I'm going to Challenge Sarvarna."

His hand froze on Nicole's neck. "Now?"

"No, your brother has made it abundantly clear I'm not ready yet, but once I am..." In my head I saw myself on a field with tall evergreen trees and a winding stream. The ground was littered with the wounded and the dead, and in the middle I stood in front of Sarvarna, her knife lodged in my stomach.

No, I told myself. *It's not happening. Talley said it was a future not set in stone.* Or maybe that was The Terminator. Either way, I had to believe that. I had to believe there was a way I could come out of this in one piece. And if there wasn't... well, I had to ensure there was a back-up plan, someone else to swoop in and save the day.

"You don't have to do this," Alex said, snapping me out of my thoughts.

I looked into the grey eyes I would never forget no matter how long I lived. "Don't I? Isn't this the destiny you've been pushing me towards?"

***

I was jerked out of my dream. You know those times when you wake up from an accidental Sunday afternoon nap by a ringing phone, and because you're so confused and discombobulated, your heart beats so hard it literally makes your chest hurt? Imagine how much worse it would be if instead of the familiar ring of your cell phone it's the sound of a horn and some random stranger's scream that wakes you.

"What the Hades?" I asked, my fingers digging into the first thing they could reach.

"Some idiot on a motorcycle cut in front of us," Liam said. He motioned towards his thigh. "You know, that kind of hurts."

I looked down to see my fingernails embedded in the denim of his jeans. "Oh, sorry!" I jerked my hand away as if his leg was scalding hot. "So sorry. I was...ummm..."

"Asleep and awoken suddenly by a potentially deadly near-accident? Yeah, I get it. It's not a problem."

Of course it wasn't. There was no need for me to be embarrassed, which is exactly what I tried to explain to all the blood rushing up to the surface of my face and neck.

I leaned back and waited for the color in my cheeks to return to normal. According to the road signs, we were getting close to Indianapolis, our next stop. That meant I had been asleep for at least two hours. I took a moment to marvel at how time turned into a wibbly-wobbly ball when you were asleep. I could've sworn I was only on that beach with Alex for a brief period of time, twenty minutes max, but in the waking world hours had passed. Timey-wimey stuff, indeed.

"I sometimes dream about him, too." It wasn't even a whisper, just a breath of words I wasn't sure I'd actually heard.

Nothing about Liam's body or face said he'd spoken, they were still in the relaxed-and-bored-bus-passenger mode, but still I waited for more. It wasn't until I turned away he continued. "Most of the time it's nothing. We'll be doing something really normal and lame, like sitting around watching television and then I'll start noticing that something is wrong. Off. And then I'll remember."

Still no change in position or expression, but the knuckles on the hand resting on the thigh I had just molested were turning a startling color of white. "Once I remember he's dead, the dream is over. I never get to talk to him." Finally he turned, and I really wish he hadn't. I wasn't prepared to deal with the pain in his eyes. "Not like you."

"I have dreams like that, too." Of course, my dreams like that weren't about Alex but the man I killed, but Liam didn't need to know that part. "I think Freud would tell us they represent unfinished business, a need to communicate that one last thing we never will be able." Not that I gave it much thought, unless you count hundreds of hours of obsession as "much".

"But you were talking to him," Liam countered.

"How do you know?" Could he reach into my head like Talley?

Liam looked so uncomfortable I really thought he might be about to admit to keeping the fact he was a Soul Seer from me. "You said his name," he told his knee. "And then... ummm... you smiled. And then frowned. And then... I don't know. I could just tell you were having a conversation. You had conversation face."

"Conversation face? That's a thing?"

Without an ounce of humor Liam said, "It is when it's you."

I wasn't one hundred percent certain what he meant, but I felt confident it wasn't a compliment.

I considered what I was willing to share. My meetings on the beach with Alex were private. I didn't want to share them with anyone, let alone someone who would have no problem telling me just how stupid I was for letting myself believe they were really Alex reaching out from beyond the grave. But my conversation with Jase was still swirling around in my brain. All of this came back to trust, and last night Liam had trusted me with his past. I knew without having to ask, it wasn't one he easily shared.

It was time for trust to become a two way street.

"Sometimes I have these really vivid dreams about Alex. They're like the ones before--"

"The ones before?"

"Before the accident." That word still felt so wrong in my mouth, even though I now knew it to be the truth. "I had these crazy vivid dreams where I was standing on one side of the lake, and Alex the other. And when I say 'crazy vivid', I mean 'could feel the wind and taste the rain' kind of vivid."

Liam nodded like he understood.

"In the dreams, that part of the lake was completely foreign to me, but it was where Alex took me the night he died." It had been a date, our one and only. "I told him about how I had seen it in a dream, and he seemed upset about it, but he couldn't exactly tell me why." Because he was in wolf form at the time. We managed to communicate surprisingly well for one of us to be without the ability to speak, but not well enough to discuss the finer points of dreams.

"Now, when I dream about that same place, he's there. It's the same as before. Everything is so *real* it's hard to remember it's a dream." In the beginning, those dreams had been my escape. In them, Alex held me in his strong arms and kissed me with his warm mouth. I was able to feel every brush of lips, taste the salt of every tear. "It's not like the accident never happened, but it's as if he's come back to me. It seems like he's trying to help the only way he can now, giving comfort and guidance through dreams." I couldn't look at Liam. "I think..." A deep breath. "I think they may be real."

He didn't answer immediately, which made me think he was ignoring me. I should have realized, though, that Liam does that when conversations start getting intense. And while it may make the person having a conversation with him go a little bonkers from time to time, it was probably a good practice. I could use a bit more time to think before I speak quite often.

"My great-grandmother was a Dream Walker," he finally said. "She died before I was born, but my mom talked about her a lot. Sometimes, when she would have a particularly confusing vision, she would worry about it for days until the answer would come to her in a dream. She said it was her grandmother who helped her figure it out, that she came to her in her dreams. When I was a kid, I believed it absolutely. Of course her grandmother was able to talk to her in her dreams. It made sense, especially since I watched my dad Change into a wolf once a month and knew my mom could predict snow days."

I was disturbed at the idea of a child watching the painful and, let's face it, grotesque, act of Changing, but instead I said, "You were in Canada. It couldn't have been that hard. Don't you guys have snow on any day of the week ending in 'y'?"

"As I grew older, I started having my doubts," Liam continued on as if I hadn't spoken. "I thought it was just her way of working through stuff, but now..." He blew out a breath and rubbed the back of his head. "What does he talk to you about?"

"I don't know... everything?" I tasted blood and realized I had just bit through the inside of my lip. "In the beginning, he was there every time I went to sleep, so we literally just talked about anything we could think of." In those first weeks, they were the only normal conversations I would have. "Once I Changed, he came less often, and the conversations got more focused. We theorized on how I became a Shifter. He listened to what was going on and offered advice." Not that it was easy to understand advice, but he did try. "He got grounded after The Great Escape and wasn't able to visit me for a month, and the visits have been really sparse since then, but it's still basically the same thing. I tell him stuff, he responds with less-than-helpful answers, and then I beg him to elaborate. He swears they won't let him." I tried for a smile, but fell short. "Today we talked about how I now know about the rebellion and my role in it."

Liam's scowl wasn't unexpected. "Who are 'they'?"

"Angels? Gods? The Fates?" Not that I necessarily believed in all of those. "I don't know. He's pretty cagey when it comes to that stuff. He said if he reveals too much his visitation rights will be revoked."

The traffic had picked up as the Indianapolis skyline became visible. Liam took a keen interest in the vehicles passing by the window over my shoulder. I couldn't read his face. The ever-present scowl was gone and replaced by something less self-assured. Sadness? Confusion? Heartache? Disbelief? We weren't close enough for me to know for sure, but they were all valid emotions. I had a healthy mix of each going on.

"I'm glad he has you," he told minivan full of middle school aged soccer players. "It's good he's not alone." There was a tremor in his voice I would have attributed to unshed tears on anyone other than Liam.

"I don't think he's ever alone," I told him with complete honesty. "I get the feeling he's usually with others and our time at the beach is supposed to be private, but Nicole always follows him there."

When Liam's eyes met mine they were definitely wet. "Nicole?"

I nodded. "That's how I knew your sister's name. She stays in wolf form, but she's almost always there." I smiled at the thought of the little wolf pup who wiggled when you scratched just the right spot behind her ears. "She's happy. Alex is... Alex. He worries about me and you and everything that's going on out here in the living world, but he still smiles like an idiot at the drop of a hat. I think if it wasn't for us, for all this crazy mess with the Alphas, he would be very happy and at peace there, too."

Liam closed his eyes. "Thank you." His voice was husky. My heart cracked straight down the middle at the sight of him. I wanted to wrap my arms around him to offer comfort, but thought he wouldn't want it. Although, if I knew he would be kissing me less than twenty-four hours later, I would have chanced it.

Chapter 14

The whole sitting-by-the-bathroom-so-no-one-will-sit-near-us thing worked out pretty well most of the trip. The problem occurred when we changed busses in Minneapolis, and to be perfectly honest, it was mostly my fault.

Okay, okay... It was *all* my fault.

The thing about taking a bus across the great nation of the United States of America is it takes *forever*. Like an infinite amount of time, plus one more day. Sure, you think it's going to be no time at all since there are only 3,000 miles from one coast to the other and you're not doing any overnight stops, but what you are doing is a million and a half little stops. Thirty minutes in this small city, an hour or two in this big city, and ten minutes in every little town in between. So, by the time we got to Minneapolis we had been on the road for over twenty hours. I was tired. Cranky. And my stupid wig was so hot and itchy I considered asking the spaced out chick with evident track marks on her too skinny arms if she had any Xanax to share.

As far as mistakes go, what we came to call The Minneapolis Incident was one of my more idiotic screw-ups, but I still contend that an insanity plea should be accepted considering the circumstances.

I was in the bathroom at the terminal. I thought I was alone, but honestly I wasn't really paying attention. All I knew was my head was going to explode if I didn't take off the wig and the plain black knitted hat I had replaced my UK hat with back in

Indiana. So, I did. I sat them both carefully on the ledge of the mirror, leaned my head over the sink, and ran some gloriously cold water over my head.

When I straightened back up an older woman was staring at me.

"Hi," I stammered out. She didn't say anything. She just kept staring at me, and I could almost see her matching my face and hair with the picture they flashed on TV for weeks. "Looks awful doesn't it?" I grabbed a handful of paper towels and started rubbing them over my wet head so I could put the wig back on. "They said it would look different after it started growing back in, something about the chemo and chemicals and hair follicles and stuff, but no one said it would look like this." Her expression didn't change, so I just kept on rambling. "My mom won't let me dye it yet because she thinks it'll make the cancer come back or something crazy like that, so I'm still stuck with the wigs." I lifted mine up to demonstrate. "I really thought I would be able to throw these away by now, but there is no way I'm going around with my hair looking like *this*."

The old lady turned around and left the bathroom without saying a word. Once I got everything back in place, I went in search of Liam.

It didn't take long since he was waiting for me on the bench just outside the restrooms. It wasn't nearly enough time for me to finish my internal debate over whether or not I was going to tell him what happened. On one hand, we were trying this whole new honesty thing on for size. On the other hand, Liam was scary when he was mad, and this was really going to piss him off good.

On a third hand, or perhaps a foot, he still hadn't told me why we were going to Fargo, so we weren't really doing very well with that open communication thing yet, anyway.

Yeah, there was really no need to tell him.

The bus was crowded, more so than any of the others had been. Liam and I got on first and took our customary stinky seat. It wasn't until almost everyone boarded that she climbed on and sat directly across from us. She settled herself into the seat, placed her bag of knitting supplies in the empty seat, and then turned to stare at me again.

"Liam?" I said as quietly as I could without moving my lips. His lifted eyebrow told me to continue. "See that lady across from us?" A slight nod. "She may have seen me without my wig on."

Liam rolled his eyes to the heavens and took in a deep breath through his nose and then let it out slowly through pursed lips. "Follow my lead," was the only warning he gave before grabbing onto my face and placing both thumbs over my lips. Then he leaned in and placed his own lips on the other side of his thumbs.

What the Hades...?

It took me a second, but I realized the wet smacking noise was coming from Liam's mouth, which was separated from mine by less than half an inch. When he moaned out my name I knew he meant it as an admonishment for not joining in quickly enough, so I grabbed onto his shoulders, tilted my head, and attempted to make my own make-out noises.

At first it was awkward and weird because, come on, I was fake making out with Liam freaking Cole. But then something changed. I don't know what it was, but one minute I was feeling more than a little ridiculous and the next my heart was going all pitter-patter. Occasionally the corner of Liam's lip would brush against my flesh and it would cause little electrical storms of sensation to travel from that spot all over my body. Being that close, his smell, which Wolf Scout has always appreciated, completely encompassed me. I found myself flicking out my tongue to see if his skin tasted as good. And then I might have sort of tried to suck his thumb into my mouth. Fortunately, somewhere between opening my mouth and actually doing something stupid, I realized what I was doing and jerked back.

"She's gone," I croaked out through my now too small windpipe.

For the record, Liam looked like he just finished changing the batteries in a remote control. "Good."

I pressed tightly up against the window. It was too bad I couldn't pull a Kitty Pryde and phase through the side of the bus. Sure, we were running seventy miles an hour down the Interstate, so there were some risks involved there, but I was willing to take them if it meant getting the Hades away from Liam.

"What was that?" I finally asked since my attempts at becoming intangible weren't panning out.

"What was what?" If I hadn't been focusing so hard I might have missed the way he said the words a little too fast or the way his pulse sprinted erratically in throat.

"You kissed me."

"I created a diversion." Definitely not my imagination... he was talking *fast*.

The corner of my mouth lifted slowly and little bubbles of glee bounced under my skin as redness started creeping up the back of his neck. *He's blushing*, I thought. *Just like--*

And with that thought my mouth flattened and all my bubbles popped.

What was I doing? This wasn't some random cute guy. It was Liam. Alex's *brother*. How could I even think of thinking the sort of thoughts my brain was starting to think?

"I'm sorry," I said, my voice back to normal, if you call really quiet and slightly freaked out normal. "I wasn't being careful. I won't let it happen again."

Liam's head jerked in a quick nod.

"Do you think she knows who I am, or that she'll tell the police?" It was an honest concern, and really should have been the more important issue at hand. Being more worried about who I was kissing or almost kissing than whether or not we got caught said something about my priorities, and it wasn't a very nice something.

Liam didn't look at me when he answered. "I think she's just a nosey old lady." I followed his gaze up the aisle where she was now blatantly reading over the shoulder of the middle aged woman she was sitting beside. "But we'll have to be extra cautious once we get to Fargo."

"I can do that."

The look I got in response said he highly doubted it.

***

Fargo looked nothing like I imagined. In my head, it was a quaint little place with a general store ran by a man named Fred who wore flannel and flirted with Sally the waitress at the diner down the snow-filled street. In reality, it was just like any other mid-sized American city. The buildings were industrial looking and dirty, the stores boasted names so familiar they felt like old friends, and there wasn't a flake of snow to be seen. Sure, it was cold, but not so much that it made me happy to have on the wig and hat.

Liam was back to the silently aloof person I met over a year ago, which was fine by me. I needed some distance. What happened on the bus, the way I reacted, wasn't okay. At all.

At the bus station Liam pulled out an until-now-unseen phone. "I'm at the Greyhound station," he said by way of greeting. "How soon can you be here?"

Almost no time at all later, a silver BMW pulled up to the curb. Liam was opening the back door before I understood this was supposed to be our ride. I rushed to catch up, and jumped into the seat beside him. I felt kind of silly with both of us getting into the back, but since Liam had left the door open and slid over behind the driver's seat, I figured it was what was expected of me. The seats were upholstered in a soft brown leather that smelled new and the windows were tinted so dark I wondered if they were actually legal. The driver was a black man in his mid-fifties who sported what appeared to my untrained eyes to be a rather expensive business suit. With the two of us in the back seat and the driver looking all posh while silently driving us through the city, I felt a bit like I was being chauffeured around, which would have been ridiculous enough for a girl like me even if I hadn't just finished a twenty-seven hour bus ride and was in dire need of a shower and change of clothes.

We ended up in one of those rich people subdivisions, which apparently looks the exact same no matter where you are. The BMW didn't stop until we made it to the very back corner of the little community. The house wasn't one of the biggest we had passed, but it wasn't exactly small. The arched doorway and professionally manicured lawn made it look more impressive than it actually was, as did the detached three car garage where we parked.

"That's a Rolls Royce," I said, staring at the car next to us. I had no idea as to what model it was, but I did know it was old and in pristine condition. I decided there was no way I was getting out on my side. I would crawl across Liam's lap if I had to, but I didn't want to accidentally ding a car worth more than my parents' house.

"You know cars?" the driver asked, speaking for the first time.

"Just enough to know a Rolls when I see one," I answered honestly.

He smiled and it was one of those great big smiles that show all your teeth. I felt myself relaxing at the sight of it, despite knowing beyond a shadow of a doubt this man was a Shifter, and if my aura-reading was anywhere near accurate, a fairly Dominant one. "I'm not exactly an aficionado myself. My wife picked this one out for me, and that one was an inheritance from my father."

"That's an awful nice inheritance."

"It is," he agreed, "but I'd rather have my dad."

"I'm sorry," I muttered. I could feel my face flaming red. Seriously, how stupid could I be? I really shouldn't be allowed to speak. "I didn't mean--"

His smile was more subdued, but the kindness in his eyes was evident. "Of course you didn't, sweetheart. I wasn't chastising you, just voicing my grief." He opened the door and got out of the car. I was waiting for Liam to move so I could scoot across the seat when my door opened. Our driver stood outside and offered me a hand. "You know, my dad died more than ten years ago, but I still miss him every single day."

"I know what that's like," I said, letting him help me out of the car. His hand was roughly the size of my mom's favorite frying pan, but having it wrapped around my elbow made me feel protected, not shackled.

"I thought you might," he said. His hand squeezed my elbow ever so gently. "It's in your eyes."

"Funny, it's my heart that hurts."

With a small, sad smile that said he understood, he let go of me and gestured for me to walk ahead of him toward the door. I wasn't completely comfortable at having another Shifter at my back, but I allowed it since he seemed to be one of the good guys.

"You went and found yourself a poet," he said to Liam, who waited for us by the door.

Liam didn't even acknowledge the statement or anything it implied. "Thanks for coming so quickly."

The older man clasped him on the shoulder. "You know I'll always come for you, son. Always. No matter what."

126

And with that I knew this man, no matter who he was, had my trust, one hundred percent.

We entered the house through the backdoor, which opened up into the kitchen. More specifically, the kitchen where a curvy Latino woman with greying hair was making cookies that smelled like warm-baked heaven. "Liam!" she squealed in a way more suited for a fourteen year old girl than someone old enough to be the mother of a fourteen year old girl.

Liam wrapped his arms around the lady, his face filled with pure joy. She squeezed him back with as much zeal as you would expect from an adult who squeals.

"And who is this you have with you, *Bombon?*" She asked once she pulled back.

"This is Scout. She's a Shifter."

I'm pretty sure neither of the adults would have looked more shocked if he told them I was an alien.

"Hi," I said, bouncing awkwardly from one foot to the other. I lifted a hand, thinking I would shake theirs in that whole nice-to-meet-you thing done in polite society, but then decided that would just make things more weird, so I stopped with it kinda stuck out, but not really out far enough to be seen as an invitation. As an attempt to make things, me in particular, seem less awkward, it failed miserably.

"Forgive Liam's manners," the lady said, recovering much more quickly than I did. "I tried to teach the boys, really I did, but this one was a lost cause." There was no real venom in her admonishment, just the same exasperation my mother had in her voice when she spoke about Jase. "I am Miriam, dear. And this is my husband, Hank." As she came forward I offered out my hand nice and proper, but she ignored it to wrap me in a hug almost as bone-crushing as the one she gave Liam. "We are so, so very happy to have you here, *Princesita.*"

Over Miriam's shoulder I could see Liam. I had already figured it out, but if I hadn't, his complete embarrassment over her enthusiasm would have clued me in on their relationship. If I had to venture a guess, I would say these were the people who took in Liam after his parents died.

"Oh, you're a beautiful one," Miriam said pulling back. I decided she was either really blind or really kind, because not only did I look wrinkled, rumpled, and generally icky, I smelled it, too. "I don't think I've ever seen another arctic wolf, and certainly not one such a pure, silvery white. And your eyes, it's like God carved out two perfect pieces of a glacier and put them in your head." She patted my cheek. "Honestly, I don't know if beautiful is a strong enough word. You, my dear, precious child, are magnificent."

"Ummm.... Thank you?" I blinked my eyes a couple of times to make sure that my contacts were still in place. "So, you... what? See a Shifter's animal form?"

"No, dear. I see a person's true form."

My true form? I was in my true form. Okay, minus the contacts and wig I was in my true form.

"Speaking of true forms," Miriam continued, "where is my little imp? Did you leave him to carry in all the luggage again, Liam?"

There are a whole host of things I firmly believe I will never see in my life, like the University of Kentucky winning the Rose Bowl, Paris Hilton taking home an Oscar, or world peace. Up until that moment, seeing Liam Cole, who spoke of the murder of his parents and sister with complete stoicism, cry was at the very top of that list.

"How long ago?" Hank asked when Liam just stared at the floor instead of answering the question. Miriam moaned, a truly heartbreaking sound. When Liam looked up, a single tear traveled from the inside corner of his eye, down his nose, and gave up just shy of his mouth. One tear, and it ripped me apart more than any of Talley's sob sessions had ever done.

"April." I didn't even realize I was crying too until I spoke. "Alex died in April."

"How?" It was Miriam who asked. "Did they find--?"

"It was an accident. He fell." Liam cleared his throat. "The Change couldn't fix it because there was a lot of debris, and--"

He didn't get to finish his sentence because Hank had grabbed him up in a fierce kind of hug. A second later, Miriam joined in. As I stood there and watched the people who had loved Alex mourn his death, I couldn't help but think he was finally getting the memorial he deserved.

Chapter 15

Miriam called it the guest room, but I knew better. A tattered copy of *Ender's Game* and an old PSP resided in the top drawer of the bedside cabinet. Framed pictures of famous Parisian landmarks hung on the walls, but a Halle Berry poster hid on the inside of the closet. And, most telling of all, the pillows inside the shams sported Spider-Man pillowcases.

I expected to dream of Alex that night since I was surrounded by his things, but I woke up disappointed. I considered hiding out in the room until someone came and forcefully removed me, but the smell of pancakes proved too great a temptation. I found Miriam alone in the kitchen, her hips swinging in time to Cee Lo as she spooned more batter onto the grill.

"Butter and syrup, fruit, or chocolate chips?" she asked without turning around.

I pulled myself up onto a barstool. "Chocolate chips, please ma'am."

Miriam's laugh was just as warm as the rest of her. "A southern arctic wolf. Doesn't that just beat all?"

It didn't seem like the sort of question that required a response, so I didn't give one. I liked Miriam and all, but I've never enjoyed interacting with strangers. I never know what to say or how to act. If it wasn't for the promise of a carb and sugar ladened breakfast, I would be taking my introverted self elsewhere. Miriam seemed to understand, focusing on her chef duties instead of interrogating me or trying to make idle chit-chat the way some people might. I snagged a left-over cookie from the Snoopy cookie jar and watched her work while my mind floated off to unhealthy places, like trying to imagine Alex and Liam sitting in this kitchen waiting for their breakfast before school. What were they like then? She had called Alex an imp. Did he pull pranks? Use his charm to get out of trouble? And what about Liam? What kind of teenager would he have been when there were adults around to take some of the responsibility off his shoulders? Did he smile? Laugh?

"You're thinking awfully hard for someone who just woke up," Miriam said, sitting a large plate of pancakes and sausage in front of me. "Just a warning, dear, the sausage is turkey. Hank has some heart issues, and I'm trying to make him eat a bit healthier."

"We have turkey sausage for the same reason at my house." I took a bite, smiling as I chewed so she would know I liked it. Or, at least, that was the emotion I meant to convey. Instead, I looked like a mentally challenged homicidal maniac. I know because I caught my reflection in the super-shiny refrigerator.

Miriam didn't seem to notice. Or if she did, she was too polite to cringe and run the other direction. She wasn't, however, too polite to stare at me. Intently. For a really long time.

"I'll put the contacts and wig back on if it'll make you more comfortable." I tried to sound nice about it, really I did, but my annoyance was more than evident.

"What?" Miriam looked perplexed, but then the pieces slid together. "Oh no, dear. There is nothing at all wrong with the way you look."

Of course there wasn't.

"Listen, I like you. You've given me food and a bed, even knowing what I am and how dangerous it is for you to do so. I appreciate it more than I can say. So, please, don't screw it all up by giving me that crap. We both have eyes, and I'm way past the point of being sensitive about it. Pretending I look like a normal girl is just going to piss me off."

I usually wasn't so blunt about it with adults, and the few times I had said something similar to teenagers it was met with lots of stuttering and red cheeks. A few even got a little angry themselves. Miriam surprised me by laughing a big, natural belly laugh.

"Oh, this is good," she said once she regained her breath. "Liam has finally met his match."

I decided she deserved my ire. "Speaking of His Royal Crankiness, where is he?" I couldn't scent him in the house anywhere, nor could I hear him outside.

"That nice but entirely too serious young gentleman you came with is out taking care of some business today. It's just us girls."

Uh-oh. I did not like the sound of that one little bit. I am so not a Girl's Day kind of girl. I'm more of a Nose in Book Day or *The Walking Dead* Marathon Day kind of girl. If she expected me to get a pedicure and talk about my feelings we were in for a long and painful experience.

"When you get done with breakfast we're going to head into town to do some shopping."

Oh God. It was worse than I thought.

"I'm actually supposed to be keeping a low profile..."

"No worries," she said with a wave of her hand. "The shop we're going to belongs to a friend of mine. They're closed today, but he's going to let us grab what we need."

Knowing we wouldn't be surrounded by a bunch of people or get harassed by saleswomen who seem way too eager to give me a bra fitting helped. I wouldn't say I was excited to change into my one and only clean outfit and head out into the not-so-thriving metropolis of Fargo, North Dakota, but I wasn't dreading it with every fiber of my being either.

***

"Miriam!" The owner of the quaint little store stood waiting for us on the sidewalk. "It's simply marvelous to see you." Krummholz was a sporting goods place, so I was expecting a gruff old hunter or maybe a has-been athlete. Instead, I got a gay man with skin a bit too dark for the frigid North and rock hard abs evident beneath his thin grey sweater.

"Spence, you are so sweet to agree to see us today," Miriam said, kissing him on the cheek as if we were French or something. "I owe you one."

Spence's face lit up and I couldn't help but notice how handsome he was. The handsomeness, however, was lost in the tiny surge of power I saw come off of him at the same moment.

"What are you?" The words slipped out before I realized it was probably a bad idea.

"I'm a small business owner. What are you? A pseudo-goth? Misguided hipster?" He reached out to flick the ends of my wig, and I growled at the invasion of my personal space. Spence snapped his hand back as if it was on fire.

"Sweet baby Jesus and his mama Mary! You're a... You're..." His eyes darted up and down the street. "In the store. Now. Both of you."

I scurried right in, but Miriam sauntered her way through the door, rolling her eyes when they met mine. "Spence, I would like you to meet Elizabeth."

Spence threw the deadbolt on the door. "Please, tell me that's not your real name." He threw up a hand. "No. Don't. Don't tell me anything. I don't want to know anything." He turned to Miriam. "I mean it. I don't want to know anything at all. This isn't my world. Not my problem. Not my neck to be stuck on the line."

"Don't be silly, Spence." Miriam breezed towards the back of the store. Not knowing what else to do, I followed. "Of course this is your problem. A Seer cannot simply hide his head in the sand just because he doesn't like politics."

"A Seer?"I stopped next to a display of bug repellent. "But you're a boy."

Spence lifted an eyebrow a full inch up his forehead. "And you're a girl, Little Miss Shifter. These things do happen, you know." He studied the display with a critical eye, moved around a few canisters to make the shelf look fuller, and then continued. "And, for the record, I'm a man. I passed 'boy' without so much as a glance many years ago."

Of course I knew guys could sometimes See things, but it was still strange to me. I was certain Spence wasn't a Shifter, and somehow I had, without conscious thought, decided all male Seers were like Alex.

"What do you See?" I asked, once again trailing behind Miriam.

"Jesus, have you no manners at all? I thought Southerners were supposed to be all genteel and shit."

"And I thought gay men were supposed to be fashion-conscious," I said looking at the ugly white tennis shoes peeking out from underneath his slightly wrinkled and overly long khaki pants.

"Are you stereotyping me?"

I finally caught up with Miriam, who was looking at a wall of shoes. "You did it first," I retorted.

"Children, please," Miriam said, picking up a hiking boot. "*Dulzura*, Spence doesn't like to speak of his gift and prefers to ignore it. Please be considerate of his wishes on the matter." She turned to Spence. "As for you, she is a Shifter in need of your assistance, not to mention still a child. Quit antagonizing her, and help her find a pair of boots. Liam said she needs something good for climbing, and they have to be weather-resistant."

Spence's eyebrow traveled way up north again. "Liam? She's Liam's?"

"I came here with Liam. I don't belong to him like a piece of property." Of course, that wasn't exactly what he was implying. My blood threatened to rush to my face at what he was implying, especially since it brought the memory of our not-really kiss up to the forefront of my mind. "Why do I need boots?" I asked Miriam to distract from the whole issue of Liam and me.

"Dear, I don't question Liam. I just do as he asks, and he asked me to get you some boots and thermals." She held up the hiking boot. "What do you think?"

"It's ugly?" I'm not really into clothes and shoes and stuff, but I wasn't sure the leather and mesh lace-up atrocity she displayed was even intended for females. "Do you really take orders from Liam?"

"It's not supposed to be pretty, it's supposed to help you navigate the wilderness and protect your feet." She looked at the shoe and wrinkled her nose. "And of course I take orders from Liam. He's a Dominant, and I'm a Seer."

"But you're like his step-mom. Moms don't take orders from kids." It was something my mother reminded me of often during my middle school years.

"If they're going out during the winter she's going to need a mountaineering boot instead of a backpacking one," Spence interjected. He grabbed one of those silver foot measuring things I've never actually seen anyone use from a bench. "Sit down and take off your shoes," he said to me.

I thought about resisting, but realized it would be a bratty, spoiled child-like thing to do.

Miriam put her selection back in its spot. "Even those of us who don't fully support our Alpha Pack have certain rules to

135

follow. It's part instinct, but mostly it's to ensure that chaos doesn't reign. Liam is a strong, trustworthy Dominant. He loves and respects me, so if he asks me to do something, I do it."

"And if one of the Alphas asked you to do something?" I asked as Spence grabbed my foot and put it in his contraption. The metal was cool and his fingers soft as he arranged it just so. I bit my lip to suppress a completely inappropriate giggle.

"Outright defiance is harder for us," Spence answered. "Since she can get into our heads anytime she pleases, we have to at least have the appearance of being her loyal servants." He finally stopped tickling my foot and released it. "Wait here. I'm going to grab a few different styles for you to try on."

There was something about what he said that was bothering me. "She can reach you guys anywhere, any time, right?"

"Yes," Miriam answered, "the Alpha Female is able to contact her Seers no matter the distance or time of the month."

"So, she can only do the brain-talk thing with Shifters when she's in a certain range?"

"Yes. Like the rest of us, she has to be within a few miles during the full moon to communicate with a Shifter."

"But not just during a full moon."

Miriam's attention had returned to the shoes on the wall. "No, it's just during the full moon. Her connection to Shifters is no different than mine or Spence's."

"That's not true," I said as Spence came from the back room with a stack of shoe boxes there was no way he could see over. "When they had me captive she mind-melded with me in the middle of the day, and it was a few nights after the full moon."

Spence dropped his haul without an ounce of grace. "She knows you exist? You've talked to her?"

"It wasn't voluntary on my part," I said. "Although, it's hard to refuse when she's got you locked in an electricity-fortified steel cage."

"The Alphas had you captive? And you got away?" Spence's eyes nearly popped out his head. "How?"

I shrugged, hoping I made it look like it was no big deal. "Charlie, Liam, and I killed some Stratego, and then Liam and I made a run for it."

His wide-eyed gaze swung to Miriam. "You're going to get me killed!"

She ignored him to focus on me. "Are you sure? Sarvarna spoke to your mind in daylight?"

"Well, I can't be sure about the daylight part since I was in a basement, but I do know it wasn't a full moon."

Miriam's face, which always held a kind of softness before, hardened into a mask of complete seriousness. "What did she say?"

"I don't remember exactly." A lot had happened between then and now. "She was talking crazy. Something about how I didn't think she would find me and how I was breaking some sort of rules. It didn't really make any sense to me, although she really thought I should know what she was talking about. I think she thought I was someone else. She even called me the wrong name."

"What did she call you?" Her voice was high and reedy.

"Ummm... Lydia? Lilly? Lilith?" That was it. I remembered thinking I had heard that name used in some sort of mythology before. "Yeah, Lilith."

Miriam visibly paled.

"What is it?" Spence asked. "What are you thinking? How much danger are we in?"

She swallowed deeply and smoothed her hair down. "Spence, dear, let's see what treasures you've brought us."

"You promised me when I moved here I would be kept safe," Spence said, jaw clenched. "You said I could stay out of all of it, live my life like a normal person under your protection. Now you're bringing a girl who throws off enough Dominance to make the hair on my arms stand on end, and has murdered part of Her Majesty's Elite Guard into my store and asking me to aide her. That isn't staying out of if, Miriam. That's standing right in the middle of it with a bull's eye painted on my chest."

Her eyes didn't even flicker. "The boots, Spence."

"Tell me why, Miriam. Who is she? What's going on?"

Miriam walked over to the pile of shoe boxes, picked up the one on top, flipped open the lid, and dug out a boot. "There's nothing to tell," she said, handing me a monstrous shoe. "You now know what I do. The girl is a Shifter, she was being held by the Alphas, but she escaped."

"There's more."

Miriam sighed. "There is always more, but I don't know what that is any more than you do."

Spence wasn't buying it. For the record, neither was I. "That name, what does it mean?"

Miriam bent down to help me with the laces.

"Who is Lilith?" Spence asked, growing more agitated.

Still no response.

"I'm curious as to the answer to that one myself," I said as she shoved the boot onto my foot with way more force than necessary. "Is she another Seer or a Thaumaturgic?"

"Thaumaturgics aren't real," Spence said condescendingly.

I glared up at him. "Glad you think so. I'd hate to see your reaction to finding out I was convicted of being one if you were a believer."

He threw a hand over his eyes, using the one hand to massage both temples. "God, this keeps getting better and better."

"Really, Spence, your theatrics aren't entertaining anyone. Get a grip." Miriam twisted my laces together so tightly I feared I would end up losing a foot from lack of blood flow. "Get up and walk around a bit. Make sure your toes have some wiggle room and the width doesn't pinch or slide."

This time there wasn't even the thought of not doing as she asked. Her tone and face were still completely schooled, but she was one second away from snapping. I didn't fear her physically, but Miriam was a tough lady, one whose path I didn't want to be in when she went on a rampage. I had a feeling anyone equipped to keep a young and angry Liam Cole in line could handle me with little thought or effort.

"Like Thaumaturgics, Lilith is just a myth and legend," she said as I walked up and down the aisles trying to decide if the boots were supposed to be this uncomfortable. "We can't know what Sarvarna was thinking by calling you that. Maybe she really believes you are her reincarnation, or maybe it's another one of her ploys."

I wiggled my toes. "Am I supposed to be able to feel the stitching?"

"No, try these," Spence said, grabbing a box from the middle of the stack without making the whole thing topple.

"So this mythological Lilith, who is she?" I asked as I sat down and began wrestling my way out of the boots.

"According to legend, she's the first Seer."

"You mean the chick who fell in love with a wolf?" It was the Shifter and Seer origin story Talley told me. "She has a name?" I tried to remember more details from my best friend's disturbing supernatural bedtime story. "Wait. Does your version say what this Lilith person looked like?"

It was Spence who answered as he helped me into the second pair of boots, which were slightly less hideous than the previous pair. "She was the moon incarnate."

"So, all monochromatic and silvery?"

"I think the word my mother used was 'luminescent'."

"This doesn't make sense. Sarvarna definitely thought of Lilith as a bad guy. If she was the first Seer, shouldn't she and the Alpha Female be BFFs?"

Spence snorted. "Sarvarna? BFFs with a more powerful Seer? What kind of fairy land are you living in?"

"There is another version of the story," Miriam said. "In it, Lilith was a manipulative demon, so evil all the color had leeched from her. Of course, that is just a warped version of the true legend used to frighten children."

Of course it was. Although, now I could kind of see where Sarvarna was coming from. A female with pale skin, silvery hair, and icy blue eyes? Not a ton of us running around out there. And if she actually believed that version...

On second thought, I didn't really see where she was coming from at all.

While I was dismissing all theories which turned me into a demon, Miriam came over, hunkered down in front of me, and fixed her eyes on mine. I thought she meant to grab my attention before saying something profound, but she just kept staring deep into my eyes.

"Ummm..." I couldn't think of anything to say other than, *"Get out of my face."*

"It's not working," she finally said with a sigh as she stood back up. "You're going to have to try."

I expected outrage or dramatics, but Spence simply said, "No."

"I'm not strong enough. Hank is my mate and I can't connect with him if he gets more than a quarter mile away during the full moon."

"I won't." His voice was calm and quiet. "I don't even know if I can."

Miriam placed her hand over his. "Of course you can. Just let it go." He shook his head in silent refusal, but at the same time turned his hand over and laced his fingers with hers. Then he closed his eyes and did as she asked. I knew because I felt it. His power rushed over me like flood waters breaking through the dam. When he opened his eyes, they were locked onto mine.

"Can you hear me?" The voice in my head was identical to his speaking voice, which probably said something profound about what kind of person Spence is, but I don't really know what that something is.

"No." I didn't want to be able to hear him. I wasn't buying into this reincarnated first Seer crap, especially since I don't See anything, nor did I want to.

The corner of Spence's mouth tilted up. *"Are you saying you want me to pretend that I can't hear you? That you're not what Miriam suspects?"*

"I'm not."

"You could change the world."

"I could get a bunch of people killed because they believe a lie."

Spence nodded ever so slightly. "Sorry," he said aloud to Miriam. "Nothing."

Her eyes narrowed. "Then what was that nod about?"

Damn, she was sharp.

"I was simply acknowledging that I was right." He pointed at me and then mimicked walking around with his fingers. "I can't do it. After more than fifteen years of repressing it, I don't know how to See anymore."

"Malarky. You can't lose your ability to See any more than that girl can stop the Change under the full moon."

I saw jock straps and cups at the end of the aisle and quickly turned back around. "Actually, Liam thinks I should be able to start and stop the Change at will. He's really sold on the whole idea despite the fact I can't even get my body to even consider the possibility."

141

Miriam leveled me with a classic mom-look, which must be taught to all females at some point.

Spence ignored my interruption and Miriam's annoyance. "Yes, well, a male Seer never lives past the age of twenty either. It seems I can be quite exceptional when my life depends on it." He clapped his hands together and turned on the ball of his foot. "Enough of this dreadful *True Blood* wannabe stuff. Elizabeth, how do those boots feel?"

It took me a second to realize he was talking to me. I lifted one knee chest-high and then the other.

"Heavy."

"Are they too tight?"

"No."

"Too loose?"

"No."

"Can you move your toes?"

"Yes."

"Then quit being a whiner. If a ninety pound backpacker can walk in those, so can you."

I ended up getting that pair of boots, although Miriam and Spence made me try on five more pairs. I also got three sets of what Miriam called thermals but my family always referred to as long johns, and a package of really expensive socks. Spence refused to let the conversation return to anything Sifter or Seer related. I think Miriam felt sorry for him, but she gave up with less of a fight then I expected. Then, as we were leaving, he reached out to me telepathically again.

"Don't let them give you any of that 'greater good' shit," he said. *"You're too young to be a sacrifice in an unwinnable war."*

"But what if we can win? What if you're wrong?"

His eyes dropped to my stomach. *"I'm not."*

***

"How does he do it?" I asked once we were back in Miriam's Saab. The day had turned overcast and a cool dampness clung to my clothes. I found it a bit annoying, but not overly so. Miriam, on the other hand, cranked the heater all the way up and was holding her hands over the vents, waiting for them to de-thaw. "How does Spence suppress his Sight?"

Miriam flexed her fingers. "With a great deal of effort." When I continued to wait for an answer she went on. "Seeing is a gift, but sometimes it is also a burden. For Spence, it was more than he could handle. Couple that with being a male Seer and..." She shrugged. "Seeing requires a certain amount of openness to work. We have to connect ourselves to other people, especially Shifters, and be willing to let in whatever it is the universe wishes us to See. However, if you cut yourself off from the world, stay away from others like us, with enough will power you can choke your Sight and hinder your ability to See."

"But Spence runs a store and hangs out with you guys. That doesn't seem very reclusive to me."

Miriam turned down the heat one notch, an action which was met with a silent *"Hallelujah"* from me. "Spence owns the store, but he runs the business from his home. All the day-to-day operations are handled by his managers. And this was the first time I've seen him in... five? Six years?" She shook her head as if she couldn't believe it had really been that long. "He only came today because I called in a favor."

I had been more than a little annoyed with him back at the store, but now I felt my agitation giving way to sympathy. Spence didn't seem like a natural hermit. Hiding himself away, cutting himself off from everyone and everything just to keep himself from Seeing had to be torture.

"What does he See? What could be that bad?"

After a moment's hesitation, Miriam replied. "Death."

"Like that kid on that movie? The one who sees dead people?"

"No, not like that. It's a variation of a Future Seer. When he looks at a person, he can See their moment of death."

My hand automatically covered my stomach, the scars tangible even through my shirt.

"All people?" I asked. "All the time?"

She nodded. "Every person he comes in contact with. Everywhere he looks, all he Sees is death. He knows if you will be young or old. He knows the pain and the peace." She pulled the car into the garage. "Can you imagine what it must be like for him to have that burden on his heart all the time?"

No, I couldn't, nor did I want to. I was with Spence; it was too much for a person to bear. It angered me that Miriam had forced him to open himself up to all that horror just to run a practice test on my weird abilities.

"Spence said most male Seers don't live past twenty. Is that because they all have macabre powers?"

Instead of getting out of the car, Miriam turned to me. "Why are you one of only a handful of female Shifters in the world?"

"Because the Alpha Pack kills all the little girl Shifters so there isn't a threat to the Alpha Female's position."

"So, why do you think male Seers don't have a long life span?"

Good grief. No one told me there would be an oral exam. "Can male Seers challenge the Alpha Female?"

"No, think about it. What does the Alpha Pack claim to value above all else?"

Crap. I really hate not knowing all the answers. "Shifter unity?"

"Tradition." Miriam leaned in. "They rule the Shifter and Seer world with the oppression of tradition."

"Like the whole turning people who don't go through with a mating ceremony into exiles."

"Exactly."

"So... What does that have to do with male Seers?"

"Our entire political structure is based on male Shifters and female Seers. When evolution introduces female Shifters and male Seers in the mix, things start getting confused. The traditional way of picking our Alphas becomes invalid, and when it does, a new way will have to be adopted."

I started to understand. "A way that will take power away from those who currently hold it."

"I knew you were bright."

"But I still don't get it. How do they kill off the male Seers?"

"Most of them they don't kill. Instead, they convince them they're crazy. Those whose Sight can't be refuted usually find themselves involved in some horrible accident before they can get old enough to start causing too much of a ruckus."

In my head I saw Nicole as a human child standing on a street corner, watching a car heading straight towards her.

"This can't go on," I said despite the nausea I was fighting. "This can't keep happening."

Miriam cupped my cheek in one hand. "Then make it stop."

Chapter 16

Miriam is a talker. The woman used more words in a single day than Liam does in a year. During the week we stayed in Fargo I learned about different Shifters and Seers involved in the whole rebellion, including various tidbits about their personal lives, especially the parts they probably didn't want anyone else knowing. She talked about what Liam and Alex were like when they came to live with her after their parents died. She laughed at Alex's non-stop antics and worried at Liam's unbreakable seriousness. I even endured countless stories about her family, including her favorite nephew, Diaz, which explains how Liam knew a gang leader in Texas. However, despite Miriam's love of gossip, I got the impression she thought her nephew was a nice, law-abiding boy.

Hank turned out to be Fargo's most well-respected lawyer, which meant he was either in his downtown office or court most days, but he always made it a point to be home for dinner. He would then spend the evening watching Liam and me spar, offering up some pointers for the both of us, or he would huddle in his home office, talking with Liam about Shifter politics and making conference calls to other Shifters and Seers around the world.

Hank and Miriam's house felt like a home. We didn't know each other well enough for it to be a home filled with love, but feelings of respect, concern, and safety abounded. Even Liam seemed to relax during our stay.

But for me, and I would wager Liam too, there was a sadness clinging to every corner of the house like a cobweb of grief and loss. Every time Miriam shared an Alex story, I could see the ghost of him there. I could only imagine how much worse it was for Liam, who had seen Alex lounge on the sofa in the family room and eat at the counter in the kitchen. By the time we left I couldn't decide whether I was grateful to run away from the reminders of the dead, or heartbroken to be leaving the only comfort and safety I had known in a long time.

Liam looked on the verge of tears when he hugged Miriam goodbye. Hank drove us out to a Wal-Mart on the outskirts of town and helped us load our bags into a pickup which had seen many better days. There was a tarp over the back, and I could just make out the shape of something that had to be a small boat underneath.

"Thank you," Liam said, shaking the older man's hand in a stiff and formal manner. "I owe you one."

Hank used the hand Liam was shaking to pull him into a hug. "You owe me nothing. I've told you time and again, I will always be here for you. *Always*." Liam merely nodded, his lips pressed together tightly. Then we got in the truck and watched Hank drive away.

And then we continued to sit there.

After three full minutes (I know because I clocked it), I turned to Liam. "Are we waiting for someone?"

He shook his head.

"So, we're... what? On a schedule? A sit here for a really long time schedule?"

Another shake of the head.

"Liam, seriously. Why are we sitting here?"

All of his air left his lungs in a rush as his chin hit his chest. "I don't..." He mumbled the rest of the sentence so quietly even with my super-hearing I couldn't discern a word.

147

"Care to try that again? This time try using your tongue, lips, and vocal chords."

His head snapped up and the oh-so-familiar Liam glare hit me full-on. "I said, 'I don't know how to drive a stick shift.' Happy?"

I probably shouldn't have laughed, and I certainly shouldn't have done so until tears streamed down my cheeks, but I couldn't help myself.

"I'm glad you're enjoying yourself," he groused once I calmed into giggles.

"What were you going to do? Just sit here until it magically turned into an automatic?" I knew he wouldn't answer, so I went ahead and got out of the car and walked around to the driver's seat. "Scoot," I said, opening the door.

"What?"

"Scoot." I made a shooing motion with my hand to illustrate the point. "Slide over to the passenger's seat."

Liam eyed me suspiciously, which just made me smile bigger. This was so much fun.

"I would try to tell you how to do it yourself, but I suck as a teacher. So, scoot over and let me drive."

"You know how to drive a stick shift?" He was still suspicious, but he did move on over.

I hoisted myself into the driver's seat and readjusted it so I could actually reach the gas and clutch. Stupid boy with his stupid ridiculously long legs. "Of course. I was raised in Kentucky, remember?"

"That merely necessitates that you know the basic rules of basketball and have an affinity for open-faced sandwiches."

"*And* know how to drive farm equipment." The truck started with a grumble. "I was driving a tractor when I was seven."

I didn't mention how I ran over my father's foot the first time, or how I took out an entire fence row on my second attempt. Things like that a girl should keep to herself.

"But your family doesn't live on a farm. You don't even have a garden, unless you count the two tomato plants your mom planted too late in the season and then forgot to water."

I started to ask him exactly how he knew about that, but then I remembered how he had been my personal secret bodyguard over the summer. It was one of those things I knew fundamentally, but when it came to realizing the actualities of it, I was ignorant. Like, I knew Liam had hung around our house in his wolf form, but I hadn't thought about how he would have seen my mom's sad attempt at going organic.

"My mom's parents have a big farm out in Livingston County," I said, referring to the mother who raised me instead of the one who died in child birth. "Jase and I spent a week with them every summer when we were little. I had to feed the pigs, gather eggs from the chickens, and work in the garden. I was quite the little country bumpkin." The truck jerked to a stop at the red light. "Which way? Or does the driver get to choose our adventure?"

"I thought you said you knew how to drive a stick." Liam braced one hand on the dashboard while the other clung desperately to the oh-crap handle.

"I do. There's an adjustment period."

"Can we get to the part where you're not trying to decapitate me with the seatbelt soon?"

"I can't promise anything," I said, jerking the gear shift back into first.

He led me through town and onto the highway, which went straight north. Since we were in Fargo, North Dakota, there was only one thing to the north.

"Liam, are you taking me to Canada?"

"You're the one driving, so I think that means you're taking me to Canada."

"Seriously?"

"Seriously."

"We're going to sneak into a foreign country?"

"We're going to use the world's longest undefended border to our advantage." I shot him a panicked look. "Hey, it worked just fine for Pamela Anderson."

"We don't have passports. Or legitimate driver's licenses." We were going to get arrested. And what was in the back of the truck? Yes, a boat, but what else? Was there a dead body under the boat? Or an arsenal of weapons? Would I go to jail for murder or treason or terrorism?

"Breathe." Liam's voice interrupted my visions of handcuffs and mug shots. "I've got it covered."

"And by 'I've got it covered' you mean...?"

"IDs. Passports. The works."

I'm not sure exactly what "the works" entailed, but it turned out we didn't really need them. At the border, Dudley Do-Right simply glanced at our IDs and asked us what we would be doing while in Canada. I wanted to answer, "Ingest as much maple syrup as humanly possible," but Liam, whose new ID sported the name Sam Newman, told him we were camping before I got the chance.

I was only mildly surprised to discover Canada looks just like North Dakota. Even the road signs looked the same, except for the whole kilometers thing. I entertained myself by converting everything into miles while Liam channel surfed the radio, only stopping for the occasional Guns n Roses or weather report.

Just outside of Winnipeg I stopped at a Mac's Convenient store. Liam filled a bag with trail mix and bottled water while I marveled at the way their Reese's came in packages of three instead of two. An hour later, Liam directed me off the main road and into the wilderness, which is saying something when you're talking about Canada.

We were only about 482 kilometers (or 300 miles) north of Fargo, but the air was much more frigid and a good inch of snow covered the ground. Liam, who was only wearing a lumberjack-worthy flannel, didn't seem to notice as he began untying the tarp from the bed of the truck.

"Are all Shifters impervious to the cold, or are you just so badass the cold avoids you out of fear of being Chuck Norrised?" I asked, grabbing the tie-down closest to me.

Liam pulled back half the tarp to reveal part of a canoe and a sled of some sort. "All Shifters are more tolerant of colder temperatures because of our metabolism, but gray wolves are native to northern climates. We tend to carry some of our animal's preferences for things like that in our human form." Without taking off the rest of the tarp, he started sliding the canoe out. "Like you. You're not cold, are you?"

"One, I can't believe you completely ignored my awesome Chuck Norris reference, and two, I'm actually a little chilly, so nah!" I said, sticking my tongue out.

"I was kind enough to not point out that 'Chuck Norris' isn't a verb and shouldn't be used as one." The act of dragging the canoe to the side of the truck closest to the water placed him just a few feet from me. He closed the distance by reaching out and grabbing the arm of the jacket I was wearing. "You're standing around in temperatures hovering right around zero degrees Celsius in nothing more than some jeans, a t-shirt, and a thin cotton jacket without shivering or turning blue. You're handling the cold just fine, Snowflake." And then he stuck out his tongue and repeated my "Nah!"

I giggled and knew I wasn't imagining the wolf-like cadence to the sound.

It didn't take long to load the canoe with the sled and our few bags. I stayed at the water's edge while Liam went to dispose of the truck, which I assumed meant just leaving it hidden somewhere, but revised my theory when I saw flames lick up towards the afternoon sky. Since there seemed to be more water than land in this part of Canada, I decided to only be mildly concerned he was going to burn down the entire country.

Jase, Talley and I got carted off to 4-H camp the summer we were ten, so I had a basic understanding of canoeing, but Liam was clearly the expert. He easily fell back into his role of Always in Charge Man, giving me an obnoxious amount of instruction as we made our way through the waters.

"This is beautiful," I said once we finally settled on a rhythm. "It looks so different from home."

A look of contentment settled onto Liam's features, and I realized this was home for him. After years of being away, roaming all over the United States, he finally returned to the familiar land of his childhood.

"It's really cool in the summer, but there are always tourists around then. It's better now. I like the quiet."

Later, as the sun began to slink towards the earth, I decided I wasn't quite so sold on the whole silence thing. Not that there weren't any noises - the water lapped at the boat and our paddles, birds screeched in the sky, and animals went about their normal, everyday lives in the woods - but it was nothing like the world I knew. No car engines. No music or TV or other background noise. Since I became a Shifter I had gotten used to all the various sounds and smells associated with humans, from the shuffling of their feet to the beating of their hearts. All that was absent, and I missed it. I felt isolated in a post-apocalyptic, dystopian future kind of way. It made me tense, as if I was going to have to fight to the death at any given moment.

I consider myself a fairly competent person - I can change the oil in my car, hook up pretty much any electrical piece of gadgetry I come across, and have decent skills when it comes to reading a road map, even without the aid of Google - but navigating water ways was completely unfamiliar to me. It wasn't shocking, however, to discover Liam excelled at it. Just when I was about to mention how sundown was coming soon and I wasn't really looking forward to Changing on a boat, he muttered, "There it is," to himself and began steering us towards the shore.

We worked quickly and without conversation as we unloaded our supplies. Several of the bags were ones we found in the back of the truck. I tried to peek inside one to see what they contained, but Liam barked at me about how we were running out of time and could take inventory later. Once the boat was empty, Liam pushed it back into the water and let it float away.

"What? No fire this time?" I asked in an attempt to tamp down the panic I felt at being stranded in God only knows where.

"No time." He quit arranging the various bags onto the sled and began to secure them as quickly as possible. Once everything was to his satisfaction, he unzipped one of the bags on top and withdrew a series of nylon straps. "This part goes over my head," he said, opening up a hole in the middle. "Put that on first, and then slide my front two legs in here," he opened another hole, "and here."

"I'm sorry, what?"

"We don't have time for this. I have to Change, and you have to get me harnessed and attached to the sled before your Change starts."

Whoa. Wait a minute. "You could have explained this all to me while we were floating up the river, you know."

He moved fast and was towering over me before I could back away. "Just do what you're told."

"Screw you!" I yelled, although in my fury I may have used a harsher word. "I thought we were past this. I thought we were going to work together, that this not telling me anything routine was over."

Liam looked ready to explode, and I braced myself for an attack, but it never came. Instead, he took a deep breath and rubbed the back of his head. "Sorry. I screwed up. Again. But please, Scout. We can only get to the cabin in our wolf forms, and we need these supplies. Work with me here."

I was still angry, and I knew this discussion wasn't over, but I'm not so selfish or stupid to not realize the importance of what he was saying. "Let's make sure I get it right," I said, taking the harness from his hands. "Show me one more time what goes where. And you'll have to tell me how to hook it to the sled."

We barely made it in time. Liam Changed in record time and was very agreeable with the whole harness situation, even in wolf form, but I was clumsy and uncertain, and by the end I was shaking from the effort of holding back the Change. Once I was sure everything was hooked up the way it was supposed to be, I barely got hidden and my clothes removed before I fell to the ground. Even without someone there to time me, I knew it was my fastest transformation yet, but it was also my most painful. When I was finally able to lift my head I found myself looking into a pair of familiar grey eyes.

Hey you, Wolf Scout thought at her friend. Liam's ears perked up and he tilted his head, as if he had caught a whisper of what I said and was straining to hear more. *Can you hear me?* I asked, hopeful, but when he continued to twitch his ears around, I realized it wasn't going to happen.

Since Liam had a sled attached to his back, I took on the responsibility of procuring us some dinner. The first track I found didn't smell like anything familiar, but I followed it all the same. Maybe if I had recognized the scent as a beaver I would have found something else knowing a dip in the freezing waters might be in my future. As it was, I was still shaking water off my fur when I returned to Liam. When he laughed at me, or the closest a wolf can get to laughing, I considered not sharing my kill with him.

The path Liam led me down was narrow and winding, and involved a whole lot of climbing up and over things. Wolf Scout loved it and wanted to run it as fast as she could to show off her strength and cunning. Fortunately, the beaver had been enough to let Human Scout have a say in the matter. Following Liam was frustrating, but when the sled started to topple or needed an extra hand (or nose), I was there. The trek took most of the night. It was nearing dawn when the trees began to thin and a small cottage appeared nestled at the base of a small hill.

Once we were close, Liam collapsed onto the ground, exhausted from having to haul a load over such rough terrain. There wasn't much moonlight left, but I went off in search of food anyway. Luckily, I was able to snag a small bunny rather quickly. It wasn't enough for the two of us, and Wolf Scout really thought she should have it since she caught it, but I gave it to Liam, who inhaled it with gratitude in his eyes.

When the sun's first rays started turning the snow into a field of diamonds, I trotted off to the far side of the cabin to Change. Somewhere around halfway through the transformation Human Scout took charge. Her first thought wasn't of pain or exhaustion, but the realization that she had no idea where her clothes were.

Chapter 17

Being outside in the snow completely naked is not something I would recommend to anyone, even if you're a Shifter who happens to Change into an arctic wolf. Even if the air temperature on your exposed flesh and the wet snow crunching beneath your bare feet doesn't bother you - which, by the way, it will - the frigid breeze whipping across your exposed naughty bits will have you shivering as if your life depends on it. Which, I suppose it might. My understanding of hypothermia is basic at best.

I stood hidden behind the corner of the cabin contemplating if shivering was a good thing or bad and at what point I should become concerned about losing appendages when a sad, frustrated whine reached my ears.

Liam was still in wolf form.

Of course he is, the part of my brain that was completely human and not obsessed with how cold I was said. *How can he Change when you've got him wrapped up in that harness?*

If I didn't have my hands shoved up in my underarms for warmth, I might have done a face palm. Liam was going to be trapped in wolf form until I could free him from the harness. Sure, he could *try* to Change back in that thing, but it would hurt, and if he couldn't break through it as he Changed... Well, I didn't really know what would happen. Would he be trapped in between forms? Would he just revert back to being a wolf?

There was no way I was going to make him find out, which left me with the whole conundrum of what to do about the naked situation.

"You're going to have to close your eyes," I called out. "I'm going to come out and find me some clothes, and then I'll let you out of that thing, but only if you promise to keep your eyes closed until I tell you to open them."

Liam yipped.

"Was that a yes or a no?"

His low growl told me I was being ridiculous. And, once I thought about it, a little presumptuous. Like Liam Cole wanted to see my boobs.

I darted the distance to the sled, horrified to realize the cabin had been blocking most of the wind. I couldn't locate my bag anywhere, but Liam's was on top. I found a long-sleeved t-shirt and threw it on. Luckily, it came nearly to my knees, since there was no way I could keep his pants on. If it had been Jase's or Charlie's clothes I was stealing I would have grabbed a pair of boxer shorts, but my many visits to laundromats had taught me Liam was a tighty-whitey kind of guy, and I was so not going there.

Liam had neglected to mention how to remove a harness from a wolf, but after a few mishaps, one of which had my favorite wolf snapping at me, I managed to break him free.

"Your clothes are there," I said pointing to where I piled an outfit on the ground next to him. "I know you're tired, so I'm going to wait on the other side of the cabin" *where the wind won't cut straight through my flesh and embed itself in my bones.*

He growled at me and gave me a look which obviously was supposed to mean something. Unfortunately, I misplaced my Wolf Liam to Human Scout dictionary, but took a stab as to the meaning. "Okay, okay," I called over my shoulder as I walked away. "I promise to not look."

As I waited for Liam to finish Changing, I tested various methods for staying warm. I rubbed each of my limbs vigorously. Did jumping jacks. I even attempted to Mr. Myagi some heat back into my flesh. I was trying to fold my body in as small of a ball as possible when a furious wolf in human skin barreled around the corner.

"Idiot," Liam muttered, lifting me off the ground as if I was an unruly pre-schooler. One arm was braced under my knees while the other secured my shoulders. I tried really hard not to think about how close either of those arms were to my bare bottom.

The door to the cabin gave with three hard pushes from Liam's shoulder. I tried to get a look at the inside, but Liam whipped me around so fast everything was a blur. He practically threw me in a wooden chair before dropping down in front of me and taking my foot in his hands.

"What the hell were you thinking?" He growled at me. "Is it so damn hard to grab some socks and shoes? And a t-shirt? *Just* a t-shirt? You think because you're a wolf you're invincible? Think again, Snowflake. Even you can lose a toe to frostbite. And it's not exactly like we've got a doctor out here to amputate it. You'll die from blood infection, and then what in the hell am I supposed to do?"

My lips pulled back over my teeth, Wolf Scout coming off the leash. "Yeah, I was letting myself turn into a Smurf because I think I'm a badass. That has to be it. Has nothing to do with the fact some asshole buried my clothes under a mountain of other bags."

Liam froze, and then, in a move I never would have expected in a million year, he exposed his throat to me.

158

"I'm sorry," he said. "I endangered your life. I accept whatever recompense you demand." And then he sat there, unmoving.

"Liam?"

He looked up at me, but didn't change positions.

"Is this one of those Shifter custom things I know nothing about?"

Still no movement, other than what could be interpreted as an eye roll. "You're supposed to punish me for leaving you in a situation where you could have died thanks to my idiocy."

"Oh." I thought about that. "What kind of punishment?"

"One that matches the crime."

I started to laugh, but his face told me he was serious. I didn't want any kind of compensation. He forgot to put my clothes where I could reach them. Big deal. My clothes and I have a long history of amnesia. I'm forever forgetting to put them in the laundry basket or take them out of the washing machine. But I could tell Liam wasn't going to let this go, and I couldn't really handle much more of this whole submission routine.

"Well, then, Liam Cole, I sentence you to one foot rub." Because my feet were really cold, and his hands were nice and warm. "Actually, make that two foot rubs. Don't leave out Lefty down there. She would be sad."

Not only did Liam rub the feeling back into my feet, he also bundled them up in two pairs of those super-expensive socks I bought from Spence's shop. Then, he started the task of cleaning out the chimney so he could start a fire. I offered to help, but he shot me a don't-be-stupid look, although I don't know if he was referring to my almost-hypothermia or his lack of faith in my ability to clean out a chimney.

While Liam worked, I took a survey of the cabin. It was a one room affair that probably covered no more than 200 square feet (or 61 meters, since we were in Canada). There was very little in the way of furniture and most of it looked homemade - the table, all four chairs, and the two large cabinets swallowing the far wall. The only thing that appeared to be bought instead of forged out of trees was the futon mattress sitting on the wooden bed frame.

When Liam moved outside where he couldn't yell at me for wandering about on the cold wooden floors, I got up and explored the inside of the cabinets. What I found there reminded me of this crazy show I saw one time about people whose hobby was to prepare for catastrophic events. Canned food was stacked as tightly as possible in the space, along with a First Aid kit, some blankets, a few knives, and several of those old oil lamps one of my grandmothers collects. Stacked in between the cabinets was several bottles of oil.

At first the amount of stuff in there seemed overwhelming, but then I made the mistake of calculating things in my head. It was October and already snow covered the ground. Most likely, we wouldn't be seeing grass until... when? April? May? Later than that? I wasn't up on my Canadian weather patterns. Even if we went with the conservative idea of leaving in April, we would be trapped here for more than six months. Thirty days times seven months was 210 days. Was this enough food to last that long?

I instantly regretted ever having read *Life As We Knew It*.

I tried to drum down the panic by reminding myself that several of the bags on the sled were filled with nonperishable food. Heck, one small bag was stuffed full of candy bars. We wouldn't starve if we had like a hundred candy bars, right?

God, I didn't want to die of starvation.

The sound of something slamming to the ground rescued me from my mini-meltdown. I spun around just in time to see two squirrels race out of the fireplace and around the cabin in a fury of movements. Being able to totally relate to their sense of despair, I took pity on them and opened the door. It took a few minutes, but they finally found their way outside.

"There was a nest of squirrels living in the chimney," Liam said as the two streaked past him towards freedom.

"You don't say." I leaned against the open door as he surveyed the mess sitting in the fireplace. "Don't suppose you have a broom?"

"Look under the bed."

I did, and to my surprise, indeed found a broom there. It was the old-fashioned made-by-hand kind that made me want to etch "Nimbus 3000" onto the handle. Instead of handing it over to Liam, I took on my good womanly role and did the sweeping myself.

"How are your feet?" he asked while gathering some wood from a pile stacked just outside the cabin door.

"All pins-and-needles. That's good right? No feeling is bad; pain is good?"

Liam shrugged. "Sounds good to me."

It took us the better part of two hours to get the fire going. We stopped just long enough to eat a few sticks of beef jerky and a can of applesauce to restore some of the calories we lost during the Change, although not nearly enough. Normally I gorge after a Change, eating at least 5,000 calories for breakfast alone, but knowing how little food we actually had, I rationed myself.

"Whose cabin is this?" I asked later as Liam took inventory of the firewood stacked against the wall.

"Mine," he said as he examined a piece of kindling. "My dad built most of the outside, but Alex and I finished it a few years ago."

"You did all this?" I looked around, taking in everything with new eyes. "Impressive," I said, and meant it. The cabin wasn't big, but it kept out the wind and snow. The furniture wasn't pretty, but it was functional and sturdy. If Jase and I attempted to build a cabin and furnish it there would have been nothing to show for our efforts other than a couple of trees chopped down in the middle of the forest. Actually, that's probably overly optimistic. If Jase and I managed to chop down a single tree it would have been a miracle.

"Alex is the one who figured out how to make it all work. I just put it together," he said as if building a cabin and piecing together furniture without the assistance of the home improvement professionals at Lowe's was a menial task.

Once we both thoroughly examined the inside of the cabin, we began unloading the sled. By the time we had everything inside and arranged in something that could pass as order, it was getting dark. After a dinner of cold beans and tuna, I found myself yawning on a regular basis.

And that is when I realized there was only one bed.

"So... ummm... it's... ummm... bedtime for Scout," I said in fashion which in no way hid my discomfort.

Liam rubbed the top of his head. "Yeah, there's some blankets and stuff." Which I already knew because I moved them from the cabinet to sit on top of the bed during our efforts to get all the food we brought with us in the cabinet.

I got up and walked over to my bag. "I guess I'll put on my pajamas now." My intention had been to go change in the outhouse - yes, we had an old-fashioned outhouse - but I wasn't looking forward to it. At all. Not only did it not have plumbing, it was completely without heat. Or lights. And was a really long way away from the cabin.

Thankfully, Liam saved me. "I'll just..." He jerked a thumb towards the door. I nodded a little too enthusiastically, eager to have some privacy, space, and warmth while I stripped.

I assumed Liam was going to the bathroom or some such thing when he left, but when I heard a scratch at the door later I realized what he had done.

"Hey, you," I said, opening the door for the wolf. "Do I need to go get his clothes?" Liam disappeared back around the corner for a moment, and when he came back there was a carefully tied bundle of clothes in his mouth.

I gave the wolf another can of food and brushed the snow and dirt out of his fur before we crawled in bed, me beneath the covers and him curled up on top, his head resting on the pillow beside mine. I thought it would take a long time for me to get used to his breathing right next to my ear, but it was mere moments before exhaustion overtook me, and I slid headlong into a dreamless sleep.

***

I woke up the next morning, fully rested and completely toasty. My nose was buried in the wolf's warm neck, my fingers wrapped in his fur. "You're like a heating pad," I muttered, only half-awake. "A nice, fuzzy heating pad. Or maybe an electric blanket." His nose came around and bumped my forehead, and I let out a tiny yelp. "Okay, so not all of you is nice and warm."

Liam's eyes shone with laughter as he stood up and leapt off the bed. He grabbed his clothes bundle, trotted over to the door, and waited impatiently for me to open it.

"Grow some opposable thumbs," I said from the bed. "I like these blankets and have no intention of leaving them until I absolutely have to." I was already starting to get cold without him. I couldn't be sure, since we didn't have a thermostat, but I thought the temperature had dropped significantly in the past twenty-four hours.

Liam didn't really care about my distaste for facing the cold, if his impatient growl was anything to go by. I tried to ignore it, but when the whining started up, I gave in. I made sure to call him a few choice names and wish for unmentionable body parts to get frostbite as I let him out.

My first few days as a Canadian were exhausting. The cabin had survived without anyone tending to it for years better than one could have reasonably hoped, but there were still lots of repairs to be done. Liam and I climbed on the roof to remove a limb and fix the damage underneath. We worked on sealing off all the cracks where air could get in. There was an ax hanging next to the fireplace, and Liam and I used it to chop down a tree.

Have you ever chopped down something with an ax? Not fun. I now have serious doubts regarding George Washington and his cherry tree.

Every night, Liam went outside and Changed before bed. Every morning, I woke up cuddled into the wolf's warmth. It was nice, but it couldn't continue.

"You can't keep doing this," I said on the fifth night when Liam made his way outside after sundown. "We don't have enough food to fuel your Change every night." He just stood there with his hand on the door. "You're not getting enough calories even now. There's no way you can do this all winter."

He came back into the cabin and grabbed the extra blanket I hadn't felt a need to use yet from beside the bed. It wasn't until he began folding it into a long rectangle that I realized his intention.

"You're not sleeping on the floor." The look he gave me made color rush to my cheeks. "Good grief, Liam. I'm not going to molest you. Just get in the freaking bed." I plopped back onto my pillow and then turned quickly to face the wall. There are very rare times when I get so embarrassed I cry, and if this was going to be one of them, I didn't want Liam to see my tears. It would only serve to piss me off, which often brings even more tears.

Sometimes being a girl is all sorts of awesome.

I thought he was going to be stubborn and sleep on the floor anyway. If he did, I decided, I wasn't going to feel sorry for him or guilty. And I wasn't going to take turns. I didn't have any problems sharing a bed, so I wasn't going to give it up.

I was about to share this realization when I felt the covers pull back and Liam slip into the bed.

***

The next morning started just as every other morning in Canada. I woke up slowly, my back slightly chilled, but the rest of me kept warm by the fur I had clutched in my fingers.

Except it wasn't fur.

I pried my eyes apart slowly and then had to tilt my head at an equally sluggish pace since my face was smashed against Liam's very human chest. With an exceptional amount of care, I unbent each individual finger, letting go of the sweatshirt Liam wore to bed. It took me no less than five minutes to fully disentangle myself from Liam, although even when I was finished his arm was still nestled underneath my waist. I wasn't quite sure how to move away without waking him up, and waking him up was the absolute last thing I wanted to do. I couldn't handle the horror on his face when he realized how I had cozied up to him in the night. My own horror was quite enough, thank you very much.

I weighed all the options and finally decided to just roll out of bed as quickly as possible. With any luck, I would be out and away from the bed before Liam woke up enough to figure out who had been where.

I counted to three and then made a leap for the floor. And find the floor I did. With my face.

"Scout?" Liam asked, his voice rough with sleep.

"I'm okay." Nothing wounded but my pride. "Blanket reached out and grabbed my foot."

"Beware the blankets," he intoned like a bad horror movie. I peeked up over the side of the bed to make sure he hadn't been spirited away by sprites and a Changeling left in his place, but he was already back asleep.

Chapter 18

Life in the cabin quickly took on a routine. Every morning Liam would head out to chop wood. It's truly amazing how much you need to heat a small space, and it's especially difficult to keep up with the demand when you're using an ax as opposed to a heavy duty chainsaw. Sometimes I helped with the chopping, but not for very long. I normally would say anything a boy can do, I can do better, but chopping wood is an exception to that rule. Especially when the boy in question is Liam I-may-actually-be-a-descendant-of-Paul-Bunyan Cole.

On our first day there I discovered an old, tattered edition of *The Foxfire Book* along with *War and Peace* and *Anna Karenina*. I promptly ignored the two giant tomes, despite not having read anything since Liam bought me a Nicholas Sparks book at a gas station outside Milwaukee and I paid him back by reading a few choice selections aloud. However, up against the magnitude and overwhelming literary-ness of *War and Peace* and *Anna Karenina*, even Nicholas Sparks sounded appealing.

The Foxfire Book, on the other hand, quickly became my new best friend. My dad's father had a full set of them on his bookshelf, and always liked to tell me how when my zombies came to overtake the earth I would need to remember where those books were so I could survive. Turns out, I did need the books to survive, although it was the wilds of Canada forcing me to live without modern amenities instead of the living dead.

We didn't have a gun, which would have made hunting a bit easier, but I made spears out of limbs from the trees Liam chopped down. Pairing my Shifter super-abilities with the hunting tips I got from *The Foxfire Book*, I was able to kill something one out of every three hunting trips. Then, once again using the book as a guide, I would dress and cook my kill.

The first time I served Liam something he could actually eat I couldn't stop smiling long enough to eat any myself. My heart hurt from wanting to call Jase, Charlie, and Talley and relay my many accomplishments, including my new mad cooking skills.

Every afternoon, just before the sun disappeared, we trained. I taught Liam martial arts, and he taught me to fight dirty. I taught him how to use a stick like a bokken, and he taught me how to stab someone with a knife. We both ended up bleeding onto the freshly fallen snow more often than not, and loved every single moment of it.

The only time our schedule changed was in December. I was making an impassioned speech about the injustice of using basket weaving as the go-to easy college major in my head while attempting to coax some splints I made into a hamper when Liam came stomping through the forest, a tiny evergreen tree trailing in his wake.

"What on earth are you doing?" It would have made more sense to hack it to bits where he chopped it down and bring it back piece by piece.

The smile stretched across his face made him look all of five years old. "It's December sixth!"

"Yes, I saw that on the calendar you insist on etching on the wall."

His boyish enthusiasm wasn't the least bit marred by my cynicism. "It's Saint Nicholas Day!"

"Of course. Saint Nicholas Day." Whatever that was. "You do remember I'm not Canadian, right?"

The temperature had dropped throughout November, and now we looked forward to days where the high was only three ice cubes below freezing. Rarely did we venture outside without the full regalia of hats, scarfs, and gloves, but Liam had shed his ubiquitous Trapper John hat, letting snow crystals decorate his chestnut and copper hair. His teeth were a brilliant white and his eyes almost silver against the redness of his cheeks.

"Saint Nicholas Day is a European thing, not Canadian," he said, smile still firmly in place. "My family always celebrated by putting up our Christmas tree and getting candy in our shoes."

Europeans are so weird.

"So, this is our Christmas tree?" It was a small affair, not nearly as filled out as the fake tree my mom put up every year, but I kept my mouth shut out of fear of sounding too much like *Peanuts'* Lucy. Not to mention, I would really hate for a dog - or wolf - to show me up by proving how a little love could make even the scrawniest of trees beautiful.

Our normal daily chores were suspended in favor of getting the tree inside and set up. Once it was firmly in place, I couldn't help myself.

"O come all ye faithful..." I began.

"Joyful and triumphant..."Liam joined in.

We made it through the first three words of the second verse, and then realized we didn't know any more.

"Liam?"

"Yeah?"

"We could be the two worst singers in the history of the entire world." I don't actually know anything about pitch or harmony or any of those things which signify good singing, but even my tone-deaf ears could hear how much of a train-wreck that was.

"Even worse than that girl who was really happy about it being Friday?"

"Yes. Even worse than Rebecca Black."

Liam sighed. "I guess that means no more Christmas carols then."

"What are you talking about? We're going to sing all the freaking time. Did you know no one else lets me sing? Angel says it hurts her ears, and Jase says I throw off his rhythm. But you..." I poked him in the chest. "You can't sing either. I can't screw you up any more than you can screw me up."

Liam's laugh was rich and deep, and I briefly wondered how anyone who could sound so good laughing managed to sound so awful when he tried to sing. "And we're out here in the middle of nowhere. No neighborhood dogs to upset."

"Exactly! We're going to become a freaking Disney movie, singing about anything and everything!"

And while that may have been a tiny bit of an exaggeration, we did sing every Christmas carol we knew over the next few weeks. We even decorated the tree. I folded soup labels into little stars and fashioned tinsel out of Pop-Tart wrappers. Liam cut a star out of a Cheerios box and stuck it on top. When Christmas finally rolled around it looked...

Well, it still looked like a really crappy tree covered in trash, but it was *our* really crappy tree covered in trash.

Christmas morning started like every other non-full moon morning. I woke up wrapped around Liam, burrowed into his warmth. That morning I sent up a silent prayer to Baby Jesus that Santa's gift to me would be getting to spend a few extra minutes enjoying Liam's body heat and smell without accidentally waking him up. In the end, though, I didn't risk it. Yes, the cold sucked, but not as much as having to own up to the fact Liam and I snuggled every night.

I snuck out of the bed and tip-toed across the cabin. From behind the cans on the third shelf of the left cabinet I gathered two wrapped packages. Liam started to stir at the crinkling of paper, and I raced across the room and threw them under the tree. Then, I turned around, gathered as much air as possible into my lungs, and yelled with all my might, "It's Christmas! It's Christmas! Santa came! It's Christmas!"

Liam threw the covers over his head, and I giggled. No wonder Angel did this every year. Torturing people with Christmas Cheer is fun.

Well, it would have been fun if I hadn't broken my own heart by thinking of the little sister I missed more than geeks miss *Firefly*.

No, I thought to myself. *You need this. Liam needs this. You will have a merry little Christmas, and not in the wrist-slitty Judy Garland way.*

I wiped the moisture from my eyelashes and dove onto the bed.

"Come on, Sleepyhead! It's *Christmas!*"

"Hey," came a voice from his cocoon. "Could someone maybe tell me what today is?"

"It's Chhhhrrrrriiiisssssttttmmmmaaassss!" I yelled, pulling back the covers.

Liam's glower would have been much more impressive without the twinkle in his eye. "You know, a perky Scout is not only wrong, it's really disturbing."

"Up and at 'em, Grinchy McGrinch. I was visited last night by the spirits of Christmas Past, Christmas Present, and Buddy the Elf, and now I want keep Christmas in my heart all year long. Wake up so I get a move on it."

Of course, mentioning being visited by spirits at night nearly made me cry again. I didn't know where Alex had gone, but I hadn't seen him since I fell asleep on the bus a million and a half years ago.

God, was Christmas always this depressing?

"Come on." The words came out sounding more like an actual desperate plea than barely contained excitement. I plastered an overly wide smile on my face to compensate. "It's time for Christmas breakfast."

If Liam noticed my slip in enthusiasm, he didn't show it. "Oh no, we're not having spaghetti and maple syrup, are we?"

"One, that's a dinner meal, not breakfast." I pulled him up into a sitting position, but only because he let me. "And two, we don't have any maple syrup because I'm living with the only Canadian in the world who doesn't know how to make it." I slid off the bed, only slightly wincing at the sharp sting of coldness on my feet. I had two pair of the super-expensive socks on, but that helps very little when you're in the middle of the frozen tundra with nothing more than a tiny fireplace to keep you warm. "I do have a special breakfast treat for us, though," I said, digging around in the cabinet, stretching on my tiptoes to reach behind the barrier of cans I constructed two weeks ago. My hand finally touched cardboard and I pulled it out with a flourish. "Pop-Tarts!"

Liam was across the room before I could even pry them open.

"You said we were out," he accused, jerking the box out of my hand.

"I lied," I said, grabbing the box back. "I was saving them for today." They weren't cinnamon toast, the traditional Christmas breakfast in the Donovan household, but brown sugar cinnamon Pop-Tarts was as close as I was going to get. When I realized we were down to only one box, I put them back so we would have a special Christmas morning treat. I knew Liam would have found it more of a treat if it had been some ridiculous non-breakfast flavor, like chocolate, but a Pop-Tart was a Pop-Tart, and any Pop-Tart was better than our normal breakfast of plain, no sugar or flavor added, oatmeal.

There was a strong chance I would never eat oatmeal or canned food again once I finally made it back to the real world.

And I would not think about how very little time I would have to eat anything before I would have to face off with Sarvarna and her Knife of Doom once we returned to civilization. It was Christmas. We were going to be festive, damn it.

We each ate a package of Pop-Tarts and agreed to split the last one on New Year's Day. When I couldn't stand it anymore, I sent Liam to the tree.

"You bought me presents?" Liam never showed much emotion, but over the months I began to pick up on the slightest change in tone and facial expression and was able to decipher the stronger emotion lying beneath each. The slight widening of the eyes and nearly imperceptible twitching on the right corner of his mouth was new, but I knew what it meant all the same. Liam was touched by my big-hearted kindness. I saw the potential for one of those deep bonding moments Sam and Dean have all the time on *Supernatural* and reacted quickly.

"Yes, Liam. I went to the mall and grabbed you something from The Gap, but I had to order the other one from Amazon."

The corners of Liam's eyes crinkled and there were lines down each of his cheeks were he suppressed a grin. I knew this look well. It meant he was laughing at my awesome wit. Sadly, it was a look I saw on the rarest of occasions, so I allowed myself a moment to bask in its glow before bringing the focus back.

"Open them," I demanded impatiently.

He tried to take his time. I imagine he is one of those people who carefully lift each corner of a wrapped gift, but since I only had empty potato chips bags to work with, it didn't take long for him to unwind the top.

He spent a long time looking down into the bag.

"Your socks."

Liam pulled them out of the bag. "I see."

"No you don't." I leaned over and examined the toe of each before flipping one up for his inspection. "This is the one you hooked on that board by the front door. I darned it for you."

"You darned my sock? You? Scout Donovan?" This time a full grin spread over his face. "Jase would be so proud to hear how domesticated you've become."

"I cook. I clean. I darn socks. I'm a regular June Cleaver." I clasped my hands together and batted my eyelashes. "Oh, Liam, do you think Santa brought me a vacuum cleaner? And maybe a new washer and dryer?"

Although, in truth, I would have loved a washer and dryer that would magically work in the forest without electricity. Breaking the ice at the creek where we got our water, hauling up a few buckets to the cabin, heating them in the washtub over our outdoor fire pit, and then scrubbing our clothes with one of the millions of bars of Safe Guard we had was the exact opposite of fun and easy.

"Actually," Liam said, reaching under the bed. "I think Santa might have brought you something useful."

When Liam pulled my gift out from under the bed I couldn't stop the single tear that snuck out of my eye and trailed down my cheek. I wasn't expecting any gifts from Liam, and the ones I wrapped for him - a darned sock and a bag full of nuts I gathered - hardly showed the same thoughtfulness and level of awesomeness as what he handed me.

"You made a bow?" I plucked the string. It was rustic, but it was a bow. A handful of homemade arrows were still clinched in his hand. "How did you know how to do this?"

You can't see a Cole man's embarrassment by looking at his cheeks, but if you pay close attention to the back of his neck, it's obvious. "I just messed around until I figured it out. It doesn't shoot exactly straight, and there's a good chance these arrows will just bounce off the side of whatever you're shooting instead of actually killing it."

"I'll never know if it's the shoddy workmanship or my complete lack of skill." I took an arrow, nocked it, shot it at the door, and watched it bounce off the wall, a full three feet away from my target. "I love it," I said, hugging it to my chest.

Since it was Christmas, we didn't do our normal chores. Instead, we spent the day eating nuts and taking turns with the bow. By nightfall, Liam could get it to stick into a tree, but not the one he was aiming at, and I could hit my target, but couldn't ever get it to actually stick.

"Our powers combined," Liam muttered after the third round ended with the exact same results.

That night we ate a stew Liam whipped up from a rabbit I trapped two days ago and some cans of vegetables. It was the best thing we had eaten in weeks, and had plenty left over for the next few days. Once the sun set, we sat around the fire and spouted lines from our favorite Christmas movies and belted out every holiday song known to man, including "Happy Birthday".

When we finally went to bed, we lay there like we always did in the beginning, back-to-back, pretending the other didn't exist. But unlike normal, I didn't almost immediately drift off to sleep. Instead, I waited until I was sure Liam was out before I finally let go. The tears were hot as fire as they streamed down my face, but cooled quickly on my cheeks in the freezing night air. My heart ached for my family and friends. I thought of the celebration at Gramma Hagan's house and wondered if Charlie was able to be there, or if he was still in the hospital. I wondered if my parents had gone over to Mrs. Matthews last night, as was our tradition, or if her hatred for all things Scout extended to my parents.

I missed the sound of my father's voice, the smell of my mother's perfume. I missed Angel's unbound enthusiasm and the way Jase knew what I was thinking without so much as a look in my direction. I missed my bed and the under-appreciated joy of central heat.

And then, because I was in the mood to feel sorry for myself, I let my mind wander to Christmas night a year ago. It was the night I found out about the secrets Jase and Charlie hid from me, and the night Alex told me the truth about Shifters. But those things paled in my mind to the memory of a kiss beneath the mistletoe.

I don't know how long I had been crying when the bed creaked as Liam turned over, but when his arm draped over me and pulled me towards him, I let the momentum roll me over, making a conscious decision to turn towards him for the first time. And while he continued to sleep, I let his shirt soak up all my tears until there were simply no more left inside me.

Chapter 19

After Christmas, the weather took a turn for the frigid. Even with our Shifter tolerance and layers upon layers of clothes, most days we couldn't venture from the fireplace more than thirty minutes before worrying about frost bite. And even if we could tolerate the freezing temperatures, the snow, which engulfed my entire calf in the smallest of drifts, was hard to navigate. Thanks to Liam, we had enough wood to make it a few months, but he still went out when he could to cut more. I think we both realized what our fate would be if the fire ever went out.

My training continued through those cold, dark months, but it was different. We didn't have room in the cabin to spar, so we focused on strength building and flexibility. We devised different routines for one another, combining our different styles of fighting to create what Liam referred to as the Mutt Method.

The majority of my training, however, wasn't physical. Liam knew Shifters from all over the world who had suffered loss at the hands of the Alphas, and he told me each of their stories. I heard about beautiful, laughing girls who went missing out of the blue. Girls with devoted parents and amazing talents who suffered sudden, tragic accidents. I even heard about boys like Spence who hadn't been able to suppress their powers and avoid unwanted attention. The list of sins the Alpha Pack committed was mind-boggling, and not limited to ridding itself of future competition. They eliminated potential threats wherever they saw them, using their absolute rule to cling to the power they abused most aggrievedly.

The point was clear: Horrible, evil crimes had occurred for decades, if not centuries. Justice needed to be served, and that meant killing the Alphas. After weeks of stories, I thought I was ready for it.

Then, Liam changed tactics.

"Do I really need visual aides?" I asked as he handed me a tattered sheet of paper. "I'm having enough bad dreams as it is." Which he probably knew from the noises I woke myself up making. Every day featured a new story, and every night I saw it unfold in my dreams. I had stared into the face of more dead little girls than I could handle. I really didn't need to add another to their number.

"Her name is Ananda," Liam said, taking the chair opposite me. I tilted the paper towards the lantern to see the image of a girl with big brown eyes and two thick black braids. She was sticking out her tongue and pulling up her nose to make it look like a pig's snout. The page was folded down the middle and I flipped it over to another picture. In this one she was wearing a pink feather boa, a giant green beaded necklace, and a giant, floppy purple hat.

"She was a Shifter?" Knowing the little girl who appeared so full of life in these pictures was murdered made my stomach hurt.

"Nope. She's a Seer."

Well, this was new and interesting.

"She's still alive?"

"Yep."

"And not a Shifter?"

"Nope."

Okay... "So, who is she?"

Liam handed me another piece of paper. There were several pictures on this one of the girl, people who were obviously her parents, and another familiar face.

"I don't understand."

"Ananda is Sarvarna's little sister. They adore one another despite, or maybe because of, their fifteen year age difference." He tapped on a picture which showed an Olan Mills-style family portrait. "When Sarvarna became Alpha, she insisted her family move into the Den. She eats dinner with them every night and makes time to either watch a movie or play board games with them at least once a week."

The Sarvarna in the pictures didn't look like a baby killer She looked like an average girl with an average family who she loved. I felt a heavy weight in my chest and told myself it was just frustration over Liam wasting my time with this.

"I'm assuming you have a point?"

"The point is for you to understand who Sarvarna is. She's a person, Scout, just like us. She has a family and friends. She feels happiness and pain and sadness. She'll bleed when you stab her, and cry when she's hurt."

In my head, I saw Talley's vision, but in reverse. The knife was in my hand, and I was sliding it into Sarvarna's gut. I saw the blood blossom across her shirt, heard her screams rip from her throat, and even smelled the tears rolling down her cheeks.

"Why are you telling me this?"

"Because you need to know. You need to understand how she truly, honestly thinks she's doing the right thing. You need to see her as something other than evil incarnate, and still want to kill her."

I scrubbed my hands against my face. Once upon a time I would have worried about smearing what little makeup I wore, but I hadn't worn any in so long I forgot what it felt like. Since July I had been living out of a single duffle bag. The selection of

179

clothes may have changed two or three times, but the maximum number of outfits I had to choose from at any one time was four, and that was matching different tops with different bottoms. I've never considered myself a girly girl, but I realized there was something about putting on a nice outfit and taking the time to make sure you looked as nice as possible that made you feel more human, more connected to society. Sitting in a cabin, God only knows how many miles from civilization, wearing the same flannel-lined jeans, thermal, and sweater I wore the day before, I found it hard to remember how the real world worked. Normal people didn't have blood stains on the cuffs of their sweater from dinner preparation. Normal people didn't train night and day to the point of obsession. And normal people didn't look at a picture of a smiling family and think about how easy it would be to kill one of them and leave the others to suffer.

"How do you do it?" My voice was muffled by my hands, which were still pressed against my face.

"How do I do what?"

I let my hands fall away and took a deep breath. "Push it all out of your head. How do you kill someone and not let it kill you?"

Liam's face went blank, and his tone was lifeless. "How many people do you think I've killed, Scout?"

"I don't know. How many people have you killed, Liam?"

He sat perfectly still, save the clenching of his right hand. "One."

"One?" But that would mean... "The first time you killed someone was that night by the lake? When you killed Hashim?"

"What? You thought I was a serial killer or something?"

I flinched at the anger in his voice and immediately felt horrible. Of course I hadn't thought he was a serial killer, but for some reason I assumed he had killed others. Why was that? And why did I suddenly feel as though I had been unfair to the boy sitting across the table?

Instead of addressing the issue of me being an assuming ass, I turned the conversation back to my original topic. "Do you still think about it? About what happened? About him?" When Liam didn't respond, I pushed on. "I can make it through most days without thinking about him now, but in the beginning, when we were doing nothing but driving around for days on end, I couldn't get Travis's face out of my head. I know I did what I had to do, but I still feel guilty." That didn't seem strong enough a word, or really encompass the chaos of emotions just uttering his name caused. "Sometimes I'll get this queasy feeling in my stomach and not know why. Then, I'll realize that I was thinking about something that reminded me of him. Like sometimes, right before a snow storm, the sky will turn the same color as his eyes. And even though I'm not actually thinking, 'Hey, that sky is the same color of Travis's eyes,' I get the achy, queasy feeling anyway and have to work out why it's there."

Liam's face still didn't betray any emotion, but his shoulders relaxed a fraction of an inch. "I can hear him scream. It was just a short burst of sound, but it's like the vibrations are trapped in my ear, constantly bouncing around, making it where I'm unable to escape the last noise he ever made."

The flickering light from the lamp caught a sheen of moisture on his eyes. I swallowed hard and dug my fingernails into my palm to keep from breaking apart.

"What if I can't do it?" I trailed a finger over the picture of Sarvarna and Ananda. "What if I do it, but I can't live with myself after?"

The silence stretched out forever. Just when I thought the conversation was over, Liam spoke.

"I keep thinking about his family. He was married. Had two kids." Unable to look at his face while he spoke, I watched the flickering shadow thrown on the wall by the lantern. "Maybe he deserved to die, maybe he didn't. But this is war, and he was a solider for the other team, so I killed him like I was supposed to. And I'm okay with that part, but his family..." The shadow rubbed the back of its head. "Those kids don't deserve to grow up without a dad. His wife doesn't deserve to be a widow. This isn't their war, but they're the ones who have to live with what I've done."

God, I had never even thought about whether or not Travis had a family. I didn't think he had kids or anything, but surely he had parents. It's not like he could have sprung fully formed from Stefan's head or anything.

"I can't do it." My hands were shaking, and I thought I might have to make a mad dash to the outhouse to regurgitate my tuna fish dinner. "I can't kill her, Liam. I just... I can't."

He moved around the table to stand in front of me. "Look at me." I stared at my shaking hands instead, certain I could see blood embedded in the fingernails. "Scout, look at me."

I felt the tears fall as I tilted my head up. "I can't, Liam. I can't."

Grey eyes held mine. "You can." He steadied my hands in his own. "You will. You have to."

"Why? Why me?" It wasn't fair. I didn't ask for any of this. "Why do I have to do it?"

His gaze was gentle, as was the squeezing of my hands. "Because no one else can."

"You're not going to give me some crappy line about it being my destiny or fate or whatever?"

The corner of Liam's lip turned up, but it wasn't a smile in the classic sense. "You've got the wrong brother. I'm not much for all that pre-destined crap. I'm more of a responsibility and greater good kind of guy."

"And killing Sarvarna is for the greater good?"

"Overthrowing the Alpha Pack is for the greater good. Killing her, and anyone else who opposes us, is the unfortunate way we achieve our goal."

"And the responsibility... It's all mine? I have to be the one to go all Thunderdome on Sarvarna? And then the rest of the Shifter world?" I remembered Jase's reasoning for Liam not taking on the task himself. Was I just a weapon, like Liam had said? "Where will you be while I'm bathing in the blood of our enemies... or getting myself good and dead? Watching from the sideline? Maybe waving a pom-pom, spelling out my name and trying to convince the world if I can't do it, then no one can?"

Liam's eyes narrowed to slits. "Gee, Scout. I'm going to get a big head with your high-as-the-sky opinion of me."

Refusing to let him intimidate me, I leaned forward. "I believe in the cause. I understand the necessity of fighting. What I want to know, is why do I have to do it alone?"

"Why the hell do you think you're going to be alone?"

"Why the hell would I think otherwise?"

He lunged, and my body reacted before my brain could even process the movement. By the time my mental faculties caught up, I was sitting on the table instead of the chair, my legs wrapped around Liam's waist. One hand was bunched in his sweater, while the other held his head to mine. Even then I entertained few thoughts other than the feel of his lips and the taste of his tongue. A growl rolled through the room, and I had no idea from which of our throats it originated, nor did I care.

His hands, whose span had been clinging to my outer-thighs, traveled up and around to my lower back to nudge me closer, as if it was possible. For the first time in months, I didn't feel the cold. All I could feel - all I could smell, taste, or see - was Liam.

Then, it ended just as it began - much too abruptly for me to realize what was happening. One minute he was there, pressed against me, sending tiny electrical storms of sensation all over my body, and the next he was striding out the door. I waited until I heard him moving through the trees, away from the cabin, before sliding off the table and onto the floor. I spent the rest of the night in that spot, my fingers trailing over my kiss-swollen lips, waiting to see if happiness, lust, embarrassment, guilt, or betrayal was going to win out as the dominant emotion.

Chapter 20

Liam didn't come back that night. Some time shortly before dawn, I crawled in the bed and dozed off. When I woke up, freezing cold from sleeping alone, Liam was sitting at our one and only table, a can of peaches by his elbow as he sketched something on one of the papers he gave me the night before.

I've been in many awkward and uncomfortable situations in my life, but sitting there, wondering how I was supposed to act around Liam after the most amazing kiss anyone ever kissed in the history of kisses, was by far the most awkward and uncomfortable. It might have helped if I managed to figure out exactly how I felt about the whole situation, but I was still filtering through about a million different emotions a second. Maybe if he was someone else, if I hadn't loved his brother first, it would have been different. Maybe I would have called after him last night, begged him to stay. Maybe I would have told him how much I missed him when he wasn't right beside me or how his smile could instantly make my day happier.

Then again, maybe not. Maybe I would have still wondered if it was actually *Liam* who made me feel all sorts of warm, fuzzy emotions, or if I was just reaching out to the only other person in my tiny, cabin-fevered world.

I was in one of those emotionally-wrought, my-soul-is-so-filled-with-angst-I-can't-breath places the emo kids are so fond of. I'm talking listen to bad country music and wail along in despair kind of thing. Would it have killed him to at least pretend he was feeling *something?*

"By my estimate," he said, apropos of nothing, "there are at least a half dozen men who will stand beside us, close to two dozen who might, and more than fifty who will support us once we've established new Alphas."

"Okay..."

I jammed my feet into my boots and got out of the bed, pulling on another sweater as I made my way across the room. I dropped into the chair opposite Liam in what I hoped was a clearly apathetic heap.

"A half dozen to the Alpha Pack's twenty-four? Good odds."

Liam rubbed the back of his head, still messing with the names on his list. He would scratch one off of one column, and put it in another. Then, he'd do it again. And again. And again. I sat on my hands to keep them from taking the pen away.

"It doesn't really matter," I said after he moved Silas Elliot's name around for the eighth time. "We're not prepping for a battle, Liam. I'm issuing a Challenge. It's not a a group effort."

Liam moved Kirk Cates to the "Maybe" category. "It does matter."

"Why?"

Serious grey eyes met mine. "Because no one should feel like they're all alone."

That day we trained harder than ever before. The next, even harder. We still only had a tiny space in which to work, but we got creative. Somewhere in amongst all the push-ups, drills, and attempts to Change when the moon wasn't full, the kiss went from the center of my thoughts to a faded memory. The first few nights after it happened, bedtime was a tense affair, with one of us making it a point to be asleep before the other crawled under the covers, but eventually we fell back into our old routine. And after a few weeks, I got so comfortable I started titillating conversations most good, sane girls knew better than to even think about. But snuggled up under the covers, the heat of Liam's back sinking into mine, under the disguise of darkness, I couldn't help myself. The desire was too strong.

"I would kill for a cheeseburger," I said into the night. "The kind with a really thick, juicy patty sitting on a fresh bun with crisp lettuce and a sweet tomato."

Liam's voice drifted across the bed. "I would assassinate the President of the United States for a steak, with a baked potato covered in butter and sour cream."

"I would take out the Queen of England for a salad. One of those huge restaurant affairs with chicken strips and honey mustard dressing."

"There is literally nothing on this earth I wouldn't do for a sandwich."

"French fries! French fries! My frozen Canadian kingdom for a single freaking French fry!"

"I want tacos."

"I want Mexican rice."

"Fajitas."

"Lasagna."

"Spaghetti."

"Pie."

"Cake."

One night I actually cried because I craved a Mello Yello with such a raging desire I thought I might die without it.

Every night we would talk about food until we drifted off to sleep, and every morning we would eat our ration of canned fruits and vegetables and wild game as if we were perfectly satisfied with what we had.

I told myself any parallel I noticed between our food situation and any other situation was completely in my head.

As the winter drug on, I found myself talking less and less. There were no more questions about the various Shifters who were aligning themselves against the Alphas, no random thoughts or insights, no clever quips to try to coax a smile out of Liam. Back home there was a commercial from a local mental health facility which provided a depression checklist. From what I could remember, I had them all.

There were times when it got exceptionally bad. The sun wouldn't shine for days, the snow would keep us imprisoned in the cabin, and there would be nothing to occupy my mind but fighting and blood and death. When it got to the point where I thought I would break, my lifeline would come from the great beyond while I was asleep. My meetings with Alex were never long, nor did anything significant happen, but for a few moments I would get to stretch out under the warm sun and laugh as Nicole tickled my hand or neck with her little puppy tongue while Alex talked about anything and everything just to keep the conversation going.

In March the weather started getting warmer. It wasn't like March down in Kentucky, which would herald in the wearing of flip-flops, but the temperature did transition from frozen-river-in-the-inner-ring-of-Hell cold to normal cold. Liam and I were able to be more active outside, which was great. However, we weren't the only ones.

The first time I realized we might have a problem I was crouched on the ground two nights before the full moon, cursing Liam and wishing for horrible ends for all his descendants. I was no closer to being able to Change at will than I had been in the fall, but he still had me spending ten minutes out in the cold without my knickers on just in case. To keep me from getting frost bite on my naughty bits, I was stationed by our outdoor fire pit, the giant flames keeping one half of my body a reasonably warm temperature. I was watching the shadows the fire created dance across the forest when I noticed something in the snow. Grabbing any excuse I could find to pull on my clothes, I found it necessary to investigate.

I didn't realize I knew exactly what both Liam's and my paw prints looked like until I was standing over the markings.

"Liam." It came out as little more than a breath. I pulled more air into my lungs and tried again. "Liam!"

I was shaking all over by the time he arrived, and not from the cold. I knew I was panicking, and I knew I really shouldn't, but I couldn't help it. Someone had found us already, and I wasn't ready. I needed more time to train and prepare. It couldn't start now. Not like this.

"What's wrong?" He came running up from behind the cabin. I had to throw out an arm to keep him from running over my evidence.

"We have company," I said, pointing to the tracks, not that they were incredibly hard to notice. The forepaw was at least five inches long and maybe four and a half inches across.

Liam squatted down and lowered his nose to the ground. Once he got the scent, he followed the trail, occasionally stopping to sniff a random tree or bush. Not wanting to get in the way, I stayed where I was. Eventually, he came back, concern etched on his face.

"It looks like there are at least four of them, maybe five," he said, plopping down on the fireside bench next to me. "And they're all huge. All of the prints were about the same size as the one you found."

"Four?" My heart pounded against the confines of my chest. Who would they have sent? A local Pack? The Taxiarho? The Stratego? Could Liam and I take on five and win? "What do we do?"

Liam kicked a chunk of ice off the leg of the bench. "Nothing, I guess."

"Nothing?"

"Yeah, wolves usually leave us alone. I'm surprised they got this close to the cabin."

"Wolves don't..." It finally clicked into place. I couldn't stop the laughter erupting from my chest. "Wolves. As in natural wolves, not Shifters."

The look I got suggested I might not be mentally stable, which was a pretty accurate accusation. "You thought they were Shifters?"

"No." Of course not. Nope. Not me. I didn't jump to ridiculous, outrageous conclusions and almost have a complete and total meltdown over them.

Proving he wasn't stupid, Liam didn't believe me. "If there was a Shifter nearby, we would both know it. I promise." He frowned as his eyes followed the trail the tracks left in the snow. "Actually, I can't believe we didn't notice these guys. It must have happened while we were asleep."

"Do you think their den is close?" Knowing I wasn't going to have to fight for my life, I became curious. I had never seen a natural wolf in the wild before and was eager to compare them with us.

"Doubt it. They were probably just passing through and caught our scent. We'll probably never see them again."

But he was wrong. We didn't see the wolves, but their tracks became a common sight in the area surrounding the cabin. They never again got as close as they did the first time, but they seemed to travel around it on all sides. I thought it was cool, but Liam seemed uneasy.

By April, we were able to spend longer stretches of time outdoors. Liam and I resumed our sparring sessions, taking an exorbitant amount of delight in throwing one another into trees and rolling across the semi-frozen ground. Our canned food supply was dwindling down to virtually nothing, but we were able to compensate with wild game. Liam and I were both out hunting - me with a spear since the bow and arrow, while cool and a sentimental favorite, wasn't exactly functional, and Liam with teeth and claws - when I heard the wolf pack for the first time.

The howl ripping through the afternoon sky was beautiful and terrifying at the same time. I stood in awe, listening for more. Then, I heard them. A second wolf growled. And then a third. A fourth.

A fifth.

My heart stalled as my nose confirmed what my ears already told me.

Liam was under attack.

I don't know which happened first - my starting to run or the wolves attacking - but in my head it was at the exact same moment. I flew across the ground, ears and nose trained on the fight Liam had no chance of winning. I don't know what I thought I would do, one girl in human form with a pointy stick, but I knew I had to get there and help him, or he would die. Liam was strong, his wolf one of the single most amazing creatures I've ever seen, but even he couldn't overcome five to one odds.

I was so attuned to Liam, I wasn't paying proper attention to where I was going. One second I was running at top speed through the trees, the next my face was speeding towards the ground.

No!

I knew something, or somethings, were going to break when I hit the ground. I would be no use to Liam, and I would most likely have to lie there until the next Change, if I made it that long before the wolves smelled weakened prey.

It happened without conscious thought. After all those Buddha-like attempts at mind over matter, it was instinct that had me smacking the ground in the form of a human and raising up as a wolf mere seconds later. Not having the time to marvel over my bout of awesomeness, I shook off tattered clothes still clinging to my body and started running at four times my human speed.

A battle was well underway when I arrived. The wolves in the pack were huge, although none of them were quite as big as Liam. They were all bigger than I was, but Wolf Scout didn't care.

She jumped into the fray, which was now down to three fully functional wolves and one injured wolf against the Shifter she considered hers.

I had never really practiced fighting in wolf form. Sure, Liam and I messed around and hunted, but never were there any lessons on how to best take advantage of my opponent or how to best employ my strengths. Human Scout took about half a second to worry about that before Wolf Scout shut her up and let instinct take over. I bit and ducked and lunged and jumped, not because it was the way I was taught, but because it was the way I was going to stay alive. I felt the teeth of others as they grabbed onto me, but the pain didn't stop me, and I was able to break their hold before too much damage was done. In fact, I thought I was doing a fairly marvelous job of taking on an entire wolf pack.

It was my overconfidence that kept me from noticing the alpha of the pack had quit paying attention to Liam and decided I needed to be dealt with. He slammed into my side, catching me off-guard. I tried to dig my claws into the ground for traction, but the melting snow left it too soft and muddy. He was on me before I fully hit the ground. The last thing I saw before his mouth clamped over my throat was Liam's panicked grey eyes.

Chapter 21

The temperature at the lake was perfect, as always.

"What's up, ketchup?" I linked my arm with Alex's and pulled him alongside me as I strolled up the beach. "It's been a while."

His answer was a succinct "yes" that sounded as flat as a nine year old girl's chest.

That wasn't right. Alex was always happy to see me. It was the way this whole dream thing worked.

"So, how is the afterlife been treating you?" I asked, hoping to pull him out of his funk.

"Fine."

No luck there. Maybe we needed a third party to distract us.

"Where is Nicole?"

Alex nodded up ahead at the same moment a little girl stepped out from behind a tree. Her hair was more red than brown, but her grey eyes gave her away.

"Oh wow," I breathed. "Look at you."

She waited with her hand stretched out until we got close enough for me to clasp it.

"Hey, Scout," she said, her little hand tucked comfortably into mine.

"Hey, you. What's with the girl suit?"

Her eyes flicked towards Alex's. "I didn't want you to go away without ever getting to talk to you."

"Sweetie, I'm not going to go away. I'll always come back here to see you guys. It's my very favorite place to be." I thought my words were of the reassuring variety, but they just made Nicole frown harder. I glanced over my shoulder and noticed Alex's mood wasn't faring any better. "I'm missing something here, aren't I?"

Alex took a deep breath through his nose. "Maybe we should sit down," he said, gesturing towards a patch of grass.

A patch of grass I had never seen before.

Here's the thing about my little piece of paradise by the lake - the scenery never changed. We stayed on the same stretch of beach. Always. We would walk for hours and hours, and always see the same fifty feet or so. It just kept looping over and over. At this point I knew every square inch of land, and this patch of grass was not part of it.

"Where are we?" I asked. "How did we get here?"

And then I remembered how I got there. I remembered the growls and fur, the teeth and blood. I remembered my throat being torn out.

My knees went rubbery, dumping me onto the ground.

"I'm dead." Oh God. I thought I was ready for this moment, but I was wrong. "I died."

A little hand touched my cheek. When I raised my head, it was to meet Nicole's calculating gaze. She had her head cocked to one side, her eyes narrowed in concentration.

"Not yet," she said. "Close, but not quite there."

"I thought it would be the Alphas. I thought I would die for a cause, for something important." My eyes stung, and I blinked back the tears threatening to fall. "I was going to be a martyr, but ended up being just a random victim."

Nicole continued her intense assessment, which was quickly becoming unsettling. Alex, however, didn't leave me to wallow in my misery alone. His arms wrapped around me in a strong embrace as his warm lips pressed against my temple.

At least there was one upside to this being dead thing.

"I get to stay here with you now, right?"

Alex leaned back so I could see his face. There was no hint of a smile on his lips, the graveness from before still etched in every line of his face. "Maybe. There are rules to the afterlife, but mostly we get to choose for ourselves."

Oh good. Cryptic Alex was back. "What kind of choices?"

"Lots," he shrugged. "Right now your most pressing one is whether or not to stay."

I felt a bit like I was being ripped in two. Here was comfortable. Here was safe and warm. Here was where Alex was. But there was so much I still wanted to do in life. I wanted to travel around, visit foreign lands and all that. I wanted to go to college, learn stuff, and make a few bad decisions, like getting a tattoo.

I wanted to see the Alphas overthrown.

And then there were all the people I would leave behind. Angel. Jase. My parents. Talley. Charlie. Liam...

"Liam!" My shout was so abrupt and loud Nicole jumped back in shock. "Alex, Liam was there. He was fighting, and he was hurt." I looked around, half expecting to see him walking up the shore to join us. "I don't know if he's okay." I grabbed onto Alex's arm, my fingernails biting into his skin. "Do you know? Do you know if he's okay?"

If it was possible, Alex looked even grimmer.

"Alex, damn it, is Liam okay?"

"No."

It was a good thing I was sitting. Otherwise, I would have collapsed. It felt as if everything inside of me had vanished, leaving a brittle shell, ready to crumble in upon itself.

"What's happened to him?" The image in my head kept flipping from a broken and battered Wolf Liam to a broken and battered Human Liam. It occurred to me he might be more than injured, but I quickly dismissed the idea. If Liam was dead, he would be with us. With me. "Alex, please. *Please*. You have to tell me."

He slid his knuckles along my jaw. "He needs you."

"So, that's my choice? I can die and stay here with you, or live and go back to Liam?"

A stiff, slow nod.

"I have to go." I forced the words out of my mouth, and even though I put all my strength into it, they were little more than a whisper.

"I know."

"I won't get to come back here again, will I?"

He replied with a small, heavyhearted shake of his head.

I had said goodbye to him so many times before, but it never got any easier. This time there was no melding of mouths or wracking sobs. As I clung onto him, my arms latched so tightly he would probably have bruises, I actually felt all the emotions battering through my heart instead of the numb emptiness which had accompanied his death. Maybe it was because this time the leaving was my choice, or maybe it was because I was filled with resolve and purpose. Whatever it was, my heart ached at the knowledge I would never see him again, but I was able to appreciate and be grateful for the time we had been given together.

"I will miss you every single day for the rest of my life, however long that may be."

His arms tightened around me. "You better make sure it's a long, long time."

"I did love you," I confessed into his chest. "I still do."

197

"And I have always and will always love you." He finally loosened his grip on me. When he pulled back to meet my eyes I could see a hint of dimples underneath the tears. "But you're going to keep doing the living thing, and I'm not." A kiss against my brow. "You've got a big heart, Scout. Don't be stingy with it."

Speaking of stingy... I pulled his face to mine and gave him a real kiss. "Goodbye, Alex Cole."

"Goodbye, Scout Donovan."

"Bye, Scout," came the small voice from around my hip. I knelt down and gathered her in my arms.

"I'm going to fight for you, kid," I said to the girl who should have been given the same choice, the choice to go back and make things right. "I'm going to make sure no more little girls have to come here too soon."

"We've been waiting a long time for you," she said.

"I won't let you down." It was a promise; one I had every intention of keeping.

"Okay," I said standing up. "Tell me how to go home."

Alex's smile was genuine, and I was glad since it would be the last time I saw him. "All you have to do is Change."

At first I was confused, but then I was staring up at him from a completely different angle. The pain came about the same time the smell of blood hit my nose. I reached down deep inside of myself, and began the process of making myself human once more.

Chapter 22

The transformation from Wolf Scout to Human Scout was long and arduous. There was no way to mark the time, but I know I laid there for what seemed like an eternity, feeling my body knit itself back together. Bones cracked. Skin ripped. Muscles tore. It was the same song and dance as any other Change, but the intensity had a whole new beat. It was like going from the Foxtrot to the Salsa. When I finally came through it - human, alive, and whole - I sent a silent prayer up to God, thanking him for the miracle. And then, because He was obviously pleased with my consideration, He let me pass out.

I didn't fully wake up again until I was in the bed, under a mountain of covers, but there was a hazy recollection of being carried in a pair of strong, familiar arms.

"Do you ever get tired of that?" I asked, although my mouth felt like it was full of glue.

Liam's face slowly came into focus. "Scout? Are you okay?"

"How many times have you carried my unconscious body now? Three times? Four?" Talk about your Damsel in Distress routine. I had it down pat. "It's got to get old after a while."

He sat down beside me on the bed, his hands sliding along my face and neck. "What I'm tired of is you almost getting dead. I swear, I'm going to lock you in a padded room if you don't stop all this stupid, life-threatening crap."

"Irony, thy name is Liam," I said, sitting up. As the covers started to slide down I realized I wasn't wearing clothes. Luckily, Liam was on top the situation, grabbing the sheet so my boobs stayed under wraps, although I suppose it was kind of pointless since he had to have seen them while he was carrying me back. Still, I was grateful for his quick hands. It's one thing to be exposed when you're unconscious, and something completely different and more embarrassing to be aware someone can see you naked.

I took over the burden of holding up the sheet, which allowed Liam to start waving a finger in front of my face in slow motion.

"Ummm... Whatcha doin'?"

"Testing for brain damage." His finger glided to the top of my nose and then pulled back. "Quit looking at me like that and follow my finger with your eyes."

To anyone else, including me a few months ago, his voice and abrupt manner would reek of annoyance and anger, but I knew better. Just as I had learned to read the tiny quirks of his face, I was now an expert in the various gruff tones Liam used on a daily basis. This one didn't say, *"I can't believe you're such an idiot and have inconvenienced me so,"* as much as, *"You scared me to death you stupid, stupid girl."* Maybe a minor difference, but an important one.

"I'm fine. I know it was touch-and-go there for a while, but..." I took a deep breath. It was supposed to be an attempt to gather my thoughts and decide how to word the whole almost-dying-and-deciding-to-stay episode, but that plan was cut short by the smell of blood. Some of it was mine, but not much. Nowhere close to most. "You're hurt!" Of course he was. Wasn't that why I came back to the Land of the Living in the first place?

"What happened?" I leaned towards him and caught the sheet just in time. "Where are you injured?"

"It's nothing--"

My eyelids snapped together in my own version of a Liam Cole glare. "Don't mess me right now. I'm having a really bad day."

"It's just some scratches along my side and on my arm."
When I didn't ease up on the death look, he let out a sigh of
defeat. It wasn't until he started to take if off that I noticed he
was only wearing a t-shirt, exposing his arms to the cold. Of
course, I couldn't exactly lecture him on it since I wasn't wearing
anything but a sheet.

"Holy crap! They attacked you *after* you Changed?" The
markings along his side and up his arm were vicious, and
obviously the work of a wolf.

Liam didn't look at me as he replaced the shirt. "It was an
accident."

"A wolf *accidentally* clawed..." Apparently the trauma of
almost dying was making my brain work a little slower than
normal. "I did that?" It had to have been me. Anything the other
wolves had done would have healed during the Change, and he
wouldn't have been able to Change in the first place if they all
hadn't been killed or ran off. "Oh God, Liam. I'm sorry. I'm so, so
sorry."

It looked awful. The cuts weren't life-threateningly deep, but
they weren't exactly tiny scrapes either. I knew first hand how
much being clawed up hurt. And I knew how hard it was to
forgive the one who did it.

Liam was exhausted and in pain. I was certain because there
was no other way he would have curled up on his good side
beside me on the bed, his hand resting on my out-stretched leg.
It was a pose of familiarity and submission, neither things Liam
showed willingly.

"My fault," he said, his words muffled with weariness. "I
know better than to stay so close to a Shifter when they're
Changing. I wasn't thinking. You had been laying there so long,
barely breathing. I thought you were gone once there in the
night, but I could still hear your heart, and then, finally, your
breaths." His hand did this absent-minded rub/squeeze thing on

my leg. "When you finally started Changing this morning I tried to help, like there was really anything I could do. I was stupid, and got these nice parting gifts to show for it."

"Last night...?" I looked out the window. The sun was just starting to set. I thought I had been out for an hour, maybe two max, but... "How long was I unconscious?"

"Just a day."

Just a day? A *whole* day?

Something else was wrong. Alex had said Liam needed me, and I knew he was right looking into Liam's eyes. Whatever it was, I knew I would move heaven and earth - or at least leave heaven for earth - to ease whatever pain it was lurking in their depths.

"You can't do it," he said. "You can't fight her. You've got to keep hiding."

I would do anything except that.

"Someone has to fight for all those lost little girls and the ones who haven't been born, Liam."

"We'll find another way."

"There isn't another way," I said. "At least not a better way. I've got to do this."

"No." The rub/squeeze thing turned into a just plain old squeeze, and a somewhat painful one at that.

"I promised Nicole. I have to do this."

"You can't." It wasn't a command, but a plea. "I can't lose you, too. You can't leave me like they did." He was shaking. Hands, arms, and lips trembled. "Please, Scout. Please don't leave me."

In that moment all the confusion over what I felt melted away. Human Scout saw things with Wolf Scout's clarity. Liam needed me. As I leaned down, he rose up to meet me. And when the sheet started to fall, neither of us reached out to stop it.

***

While Liam caught up on his much needed sleep, I began to close up the cabin. I put anything we hadn't used, which wasn't much, in one of the cabinets, stored all our tools, and had a bonfire with all the left-over garbage. I swept out the cabin, covered the smoldering embers with snow, and rounded up all my animal traps. And then I waited. And waited. And when I got bored with that, I had nothing to do but wait some more.

More than once I checked to make sure he was still breathing.

"I've got everything ready to go," I said once he was finally awake and dressed.

All the tenderness and vulnerability was gone from his face when he said, "Go where?"

"America?"

His eyes narrowed. "This is America."

"This is Canada."

"Which is in North America."

Silly Canadians wanting to be part of the Cool Kids Club. "Fine. The States. The good ol' USA. The land of the free and home of the brave."

"No."

"Excuse me?" While Prince Not-Always-So-Charming got his beauty sleep, I worried about how I would be able to face him without dying of embarrassment and shame after what transpired before he escaped to Dreamland. That worry quickly turned to anger at his superior, condescending tone.

"We're not going to the United States."

"Yes, we are. It's time. I'm as ready as I'm ever going to be. And we're going to do this on my terms. Not theirs. Not hers. Not yours." I pushed into his personal space. "We're returning to civilization so I can rebuild my strength and put on a little more muscle." We hadn't starved over the winter, but we hadn't been eating well enough to keep our weight up with all the training we were doing. Both of us fought a constant battle to keep our clothes from falling off our shrinking bodies. "When I'm back to a hundred percent, I'll make my Challenge." I jerked my chin up, putting the force of my conviction into my words. "I'm ready."

A muscle jumped in Liam's jaw. "And if I say no?"

"You can't stop me, so don't even try. It'll be a waste of breath."

I've heard people talk about the air being charged before, but I didn't really get it until that moment. Liam and I stood face to face... or face to chest if you want to be technical. But even though I had to crane my neck to look him in the eye, I didn't feel small or disadvantaged. In fact, I felt powerful, as if the Dominance I had seen on other Shifters, like the Stratego, was pouring off of me in waves. And that Dominance? It was colliding up against the Dominance Liam was throwing off just as strongly. If I could have broken eye contact without yielding I would've looked around to see if it was actually happening, but I didn't really have to. I felt it in every cell of my body.

Just when I thought we were going to have to solve this with a fury of fists, Liam dropped his eyes, sighed, and ran his hand over the back of his head.

"We don't have a canoe," he said, all aggression bled from his voice. "There's another path back to civilization, but it's going to take more than a night to get there, and there won't be anything fit for our human forms between here and there."

"What are our other options?"

"There will be a boat waiting for us after June first. We wait until then and go back the way we came."

No way was I sitting around here and waiting until then. "I can hold my wolf form long enough to get us wherever we're going. We'll leave today."

Instead of arguing, Liam asked, "When today?"

I looked around the cabin that had been my home for half a year and knew there was nothing left for me here. "How about right now?"

Chapter 23

"Everyone is staring at us."

Liam glanced up from his All-Star Special. "If by 'everyone' you mean a nearly comatose drunk man and the homeless woman having a conversation with the salt shaker, than yes. Everyone is staring at us."

We were in Ely, Minnesota. I think Liam may have been aiming for Fargo, but we got a little off course somewhere.

"The waitress keeps cutting her eyes over here," I muttered without moving my lips. I tugged on the XXL Harley Davidson hoodie engulfing me. "What if she recognizes the clothes and calls the cops?"

Liam grabbed a piece of toast off my plate. "She doesn't recognize your clothes," he said, not even attempting to be discreet. "And even if she did, she's not going to call 9-1-1 over some stolen pajama bottoms and a sweatshirt when I'm pretty sure her co-worker is cooking up a side of meth to go with everyone's waffles."

I tugged on the hoodie again. It felt wrong against my skin, all scratchy and sinful as if I was having an allergic reaction to immorally obtained clothing.

I had never stolen anything before in my life. When we were kids, Jase took a Snickers from the Five Star when Mom wouldn't buy him one. I ate one bite, and it felt like a lump of lead sitting in my stomach. It was my last brush with thievery until Liam and I assumed human form again for the first time in several days. I hid in the bushes while he broke into the house and procured something to cover our nudity and enough money for a Waffle House smorgasbord.

Maybe I would have felt differently if he thought to grab me something other than a pair of four inch too-short pink jogging pants and a hoodie big enough for two Scouts to fit in.

Liam, meanwhile, was sporting a pair of snug fitting jeans and an almost-too-tight black shirt, which might have been the true reason for our waitress's frequent glances.

A bell jingled as a couple of men in matching work shirts came through the door.

"We're going to have to get out of here soon." Liam mumbled around his coffee cup.

I nodded, noticing an old SUV and beat-up station wagon pulling into the parking lot. "Yeah, it looks like the breakfast crew is arriving. Any ideas about where we should go?"

"I can get my hands on a phone and call Miriam and have her send us some money, but it'll take an hour or two before she can get it, and then we'll have to find a Wal-Mart or something with a Western Union."

I nodded at the building that held my attention through much of the evening. "Let's go there," I said. "They'll probably let you use a phone, and there are some books I want to look at again."

Liam turned so he could see what I was talking about. "A library? Seriously?"

"There is nothing wrong with being smart." I started to slide out of the booth. "Brains and the ability to Change at will. Honestly, Liam, what more could you want in a woman?" I realized what I was implying as it slipped out of my mouth. I continued on to the bathroom just as I had begun to do, not looking back so I wouldn't see the panicked horror I knew was etched on his face.

***

There weren't any hours posted on the library's entrance. It was too early in the morning for it to be open, but I tried the doors anyway. Amazingly, they were unlocked.

It was a small library, probably the same size as the one I frequented in Timber. But where our library was housed in an old church and was filled with dark wood, stained glass windows, and an air of reverence, this was one of those completely modern affairs with lots of gleaming metal, taupe colored furniture, and glaring lights. I did a quick sweep of my surroundings - which were completely deserted with the exception of Liam and me - and headed off towards the stacks with purpose.

Although I had never visited the Ely Special Collections Library in person before, I was familiar with part of its collection. When I first found out what Alex was, I requested a ton of books on werewolves through Inter-Library Loan in my uber-nerdy research attempt. The most informative books came from this library.

I thought I would be able to walk straight to what I was looking for, but I was wrong. Unlike the Lake County Public Library, there weren't just a handful of books on aliens, vampires, and werewolves hanging out at the beginning of the non-fiction section. No, their selection went on for aisles and aisles. I wandered the rows, my fingers trailing over the spines, most of which were simply stapled together or had one of those cheap ringed bindings. I came seeking one of the books I borrowed forever ago, but what I discovered was even more interesting. To heck with a few hours, I could spend days here.

Unfortunately, I wasn't going to have even a single hour, let alone the endless ones I craved.

I sensed the buzz of power in the air at the same time Liam did. He was silently following me, but as soon as a tickle creeped across our skin letting us know another powerful Shifter or Seer was nearby, he jumped to attention, attempting to push me behind his tense body.

It might have worked better if I hadn't been trying to shove *him* behind *me* at the same time.

Here's the thing, at this point I should have known that you couldn't predict the amount of power a Shifter or Seer yielded by their physical appearance. Toby is nowhere near the biggest or scariest looking Hagan, yet he's the Pack Leader. Talley is chubby and quiet and smiles more often than not. To the casual observer she looks as harmless as a butterfly, but she's the strongest Seer I've ever encountered, including Sarvarna. So, I shouldn't have had any expectations as to who was stepping into the end of the aisle, but apparently I did, because I was completely shocked to see a wizened old lady, her white hair bundled on top of her head while she supported her weight with a walker. I took comfort in knowing I wasn't the only one in shock. Liam froze as the little old lady came into view, and the woman herself looked as if she saw a ghost. And then a wide smile that looked vaguely familiar spread across her face.

"Bryce Allen Burkett." Her voice carried a faint British accent. "You finally got around to visiting your old aunt. Now, come, and give me a hug."

Chapter 24

"You have an aunt?"

"Of course he has an aunt," the old lady said. "Did you think he was born into a pack of wolves?" She started down the aisle, and although it obviously took a great deal of effort on her part, there was no doubt of the challenge in her movement.

"No, I don't." Liam took advantage of my shock and deftly maneuvered me behind him with a well placed elbow and hip. "I don't know who you are--"

"Rachel Frye-Bettany, sister of Judith Frye-Mitchell, the mother of Alexandria Mitchell-Burkett, the mother of Bryce, Christopher, and Nicole Burkett." She smiled and I saw dimples hiding in the landscape of wrinkles. "I've looked forward to seeing you again for a very long time."

Liam was so tense I thought he might crumble into a million little Liam pieces. I could feel his back muscles straining beneath my hand, which is how I realized my hand was resting on his lower back in a completely unacceptable fashion. I jerked it back quickly, but then had to face the task of figuring out where to put it. I stuffed it into my pocket, propped it on my hip, and let it hang down to my side.

Having appendages had never been so perplexing.

"Bryce Burkett is dead," Liam said, oblivious to my Hokey-Pokey dance.

"Yes, my records indicate he died alongside his parents and brother in a house fire over five years ago." Liam tensed even more at her arch tone. It didn't show on his face, and my hands were both stuffed dutifully into the kangaroo pouch of my stolen hoodie, but still I knew. I could feel his tension and unease like a ghost with his scent residing quietly beside my own emotions.

"Three years later the Alpha Pack made it known they were seeking two rogue Shifters. Teenagers. Grey eyes. Brown hair with a hint of ginger. Later, they identified them as Liam and Alex Cole." The old lady's hands clenched on the walker, her fragile skin stretched tight over misshapen knuckles, and leaned over until she was in Liam's personal space. "Bryce Burkett was a four year old who picked me wildflowers and peppered my face with kisses. Liam Cole is a dangerous man, a threat to the very structure of our society."

A flash of recognition in Liam's eyes.

"Will you give us a head start?"

"No."

Crap. I really didn't want to have to hurt an old lady, especially one with purple tennis balls stuck on the feet of her walker.

"You're not leaving," she said, and I began thinking of a way to disable her without breaking her hip. "You will stay at the Safe House for at least one week. After a week, you can run off and save the world if you must, but first you will give me a week." When neither Liam nor I responded - me because I was still trying to figure out if punching an elderly person would cause them to have a stroke - she gave us an Alex smile. "I'm an old lady. All I have left are memories and family. Please. One week to get to know you again is all I ask. Marie and Michelle are probably prepping the Safe House as I speak."

I was a little misty-eyed. Liam? Not so much.

"How do I know this isn't a trap?"

"Liam!" I smacked his arm with the hand which had yet again found its way to his back. "Of course it isn't a trap. She's your aunt!" *And really, really old,* I added mentally. I mean, seriously, old ladies were nice, unless, of course, they were like evil witches or whatever, but I wasn't getting that vibe off this lady at all.

"She's the Bibliothecary. Her loyalty is to the Alphas."

"My loyalty is to my family."

Maybe I'm a sentimental idiot, but I believed her.

"We'll go," I said. Liam started to argue, but I held up a finger. "But know this, you betray us, and we'll react accordingly. We won't care whose blood you share or how long you've been alive."

She flashed her dimples again. "Oh, I like her," she said. "You picked a good mate, Bryce."

On that she turned herself around, which was a multi-step process. "Come on," she said, ambling up the aisle. "The girls will be anxious, and it takes me a while to get moving. My legs aren't quite what they used to be." She chuckled, as if her inability to walk without assistance was some sort of joke.

I looked at Liam and raised my eyebrows. He shrugged. With a deep breath, Liam started after her, me at his heels. We were both aware there was someone walking up to the library before the front door opened, but Rachel didn't notice him until he strode up to the Circulation Desk.

"We're closed," she snapped to the man who looked as ancient as she did. "Go away, Carl."

"It's Friday, Rachel, and you're open to the public on Fridays. The lights are on. The door was unlocked." He slapped a hand down on the desk. "Now, I have a reference question."

Rachel huffed. "Unless that question pertains to where you can find the nearest exit, I don't want to hear it. Go away. Shoo."

"Did she just 'shoo' that man?" I asked Liam out of the corner of my mouth.

He nodded ever so slightly, his attention never leaving his long-lost aunt who had transformed from lonely old lady to spitfire in an instant.

"It's Friday."

"We're closed."

The man leaned a little harder against the desk, though whether it was to show his resistance or because he needed the support, I couldn't tell. "You kicking those two out, too?"

"We're all leaving," she said, hobbling past him without a glance. "Gas leak. Stay if you want. I'm sure Randi will be glad to finally get her inheritance."

The old man muttered some choice phrases about crotchety librarians and ungrateful children, but he followed us out of the building and to Rachel's gigantic luxury car which cost roughly the same amount as my parents' house.

"You open the Archives to the public?" Liam asked from the passenger's seat once Rachel safely maneuvered us onto the road. And by *"safely"* I mean *"I can't believe that semi-truck didn't hit us and send us to our graves."*

"We're open twice a week. All the important information is kept behind a locked door, but the harmless stuff is made available to anyone willing to get a library card. It makes it easier to operate. No one looks too closely at a tiny special collections library, and we get tax money."

"So, that place is some sort of Shifter library?" Which would explain all the crazy books on werewolf mythology. It didn't really explain why there was a whole shelf devoted to Stephenie Meyer books, though.

As we barreled down the street, Rachel and Liam gave me the rundown on the whole Archives thing. Instead of being a single library, it's like a whole library system, with one branch on every continent except Antarctica. The main purpose of the Archives is to keep a record of the whole of Seer and Shifter history (although I somehow doubt the part about killing baby girl Shifters made it in), along with every book, scholarly paper, journal article, etc. that can be linked to Seers or Shifters in any way, including all those sexy paranormal books I like so much.

What really interested me was Rachel's role in The Archives. As the Bibliothecary (which is just a fancy word for librarian) she no longer exists within the normal Shifter and Seer social structure. Her job requires her to be an impartial party, collecting and recording what happens in our world without bias. Rachel said it was so the information would always be accurate and complete, no matter who served as Alpha. Liam suggested we not be so naive and asserted the Bibliothecaries were nothing more than the Alphas' lapdogs, especially since they were once in line to be Alphas themselves.

Yeah. That's right. Sweet little old Aunt Rachel could have been the Queen of Evil. No wonder Liam still looked like he was ready to bolt at the first hint of an ambush.

After fifteen minutes in the Car of Doom we found ourselves parking behind a big southern style house with all the wrap-around, screened-in porches and such. Even though it looked completely out of place against the Minnesota backdrop, it made me feel like I was home in Kentucky.

"That's the Safe House?" I would certainly feel safe there. Safe and very comfortable.

"Yes, this is where I raised my daughter, but once she was gone it was simply too much house for one woman. I moved into an apartment in town and make this place available to any Seer or Shifter needing shelter," Rachel said, opening her car door. I quickly grabbed the walker and dashed out of the car. She smiled as she accepted my assistance. "You sure are a sweet girl, Scout. I'm half tempted to keep you."

"Ummm... Thanks?" Knowing she was a potential Alpha I worried about what "keeping me" might entail. Probably chains. And whips. And maybe a dog collar.

And now I was going to have to live with scary *Fifty Shades* Aunt Rachel pictures living in my head for all time.

It took more than a few minutes to get Rachel up the steps. The whole way I could smell a potpourri of different Shifters imbedded in the wood of the porch and wafting out from the open windows. None of the smells were current, but some were fresh enough to have been there in the past two or three months. Others were old and faint, barely a whisper of scent.

"How many Shifters have you housed here?" I couldn't pull out each individual scent, but there were a lot.

"Not as many as I thought would come," she said, throwing open the door. The smell of garlic and Italian seasonings made my mouth water instantly. "But even one is too many. No one should live in fear or be shut out from what is known and safe."

She was so freaking sincere it hurt.

"You would have made a wonderful Alpha," I told her.

"Oh no, dear, I am far too tender hearted for such a task, which is why I am here, and not in Romania with the other Matrons."

The step to get into the actual house was both steep and narrow. When it became obvious Rachel couldn't navigate it on her own, Liam swooped her into his arms and carried her across the threshold.

"Oh my!" Rachel clutched onto his shoulders, her dimples flashing. "I haven't done that since my honeymoon."

Liam's face turned shades of red I didn't know existed. "Sorry. I should have asked first."

"It was perfectly wonderful." She gave me an apologetic look as he sat her down. "Although I do suppose we should have asked you if it was okay first. I know how mates are in the beginning.

The whole touching other people thing can be grounds for a fight, even if it's their old aunt."

"She's not my mate," Liam said before I could.

Rachel clucked her tongue. "Don't be silly. Of course you are."

Now my face was attempting to match the color of Liam's. "No, really. No Declarations. No ceremony. We've never even..." We got close. Very, very, *very* close, but then, when things started getting really serious, Liam bolted. He was there one minute, all lips and hands and tongues, and the next he was walking out the door. Once I finally got my wits about me, and some clothes on, I went outside to search for him. I found the wolf instead. Neither of us had spoken of it since, although from the look on Liam's face, we were both thinking about it now.

Rachel kindly ignored both of our shame-filled faces. "Declarations and ceremonies are bureaucratic nonsense based on human customs. Mating is something more primitive and magical." She narrowed her eyes and laid a hand on each of our cheeks. I felt the power of her Sight crashing through my body. "Yes, I'm quite right." Her face lit up as she patted the cheeks she had been holding on to. "You have chosen each other. It's done. You're mates."

While I stood there in dumb shock, two girls rounded the corner from the direction of the heavenly smell. "We thought we heard voices," said the one with a riot of curls bouncing around her face. "Hey, Grandmother." She turned to Liam and me. "Tall scary man. Girl whose face I know from somewhere but can't remember where," she said to us in acknowledgement.

"Chick in a Super-Man shirt and cardigan," I acknowledged back.

The other girl, the one who looked almost identical to the first but sported decidedly more adult-like attire and had tamed her hair with a twisty-ponytail thing, held out a hand. "I'm

Michelle," she said. "Please ignore Marie. No one ever bothered to teach her manners."

"Scout," I said, my hand still down at my side. "Sorry, but I don't shake hands with Seers whose powers I don't know." Speaking of Seers whose powers I didn't know, I really needed to find out what Rachel was packing. I hoped it was something like the right answers to those word quizzes in the *Reader's Digest* or how to put a computer together. Anything other than whether or not two people were mates.

"Don't worry about her," Rachel said. "Michelle is latent."

"And I See need, which doesn't require contact." Marie tilted her head to the side and pursed her lips. "Scout... Scout..." Her eyebrows shot up. "The senator's granddaughter! I knew I knew you from somewhere!"

Of all the things for me to forget, why did it have to be that whole long lost senator's granddaughter thing? *How* could it have been that whole long lost senator's granddaughter thing? I mean, I know I had this whole Challenging the Alpha Female thing going on, and I spent half a year playing Survival of the Fittest in the Canadian wilderness, but you would think I could remember I was one of America's Most Wanted Amber Alerts or whatever.

"I'm not really--"

"You know, you're much more attractive in person than that picture they kept flashing on MSNBC. I think someone there must hate you." Marie turned and started back down the hall. Since it was towards the direction of food, I followed. "So, you like killed some Stratego and almost killed the Alpha Male?"

My heart skipped a beat, but Liam replied in his normal bored tone. "It was a group effort."

I wasn't sure what to make of Marie. If Rachel had spouted off knowledge of what went down at the lake last summer I would have been uncomfortable, but it would have made sense.

But having this girl who had a Post-It note stuck to her butt casually mention something which marked us as her enemy bothered me.

"You can relax," Michelle said from behind me. "We're not exactly Team Alpha around here. I think Marie did a little cheer and dance when we got the call that Stefan was in the hospital and not expected to live through the night."

"What have you got against our supreme rulers?" Liam asked.

Michelle looked up into his hard face and didn't even flinch. "They kill female Shifters."

I stopped so quickly Rachel clipped my leg with her walker. "You know?"

"Of course I know," Rachel said, clomping around me. "Why do you think I left the Den?"

"You know, but you don't do anything?"

This time it was Rachel who stopped abruptly. "I'm a seventy-nine year old woman with two fake knees and a bad hip. What exactly is it you think I can do, Miss Donovan?"

"I don't know, but something. Something other than just sit here and let it happen." I could feel Wolf Scout pushing to the surface as my anger level rose. How on earth could someone let that happen? How could Rachel? Nicole was her *niece*.

Rachel straightened her back as much as she could. "I have done something. I've given those who oppose the Alpha Pack a place to stay when they need it. I keep records of things they would rather be hidden. And I've waited here for her return, for the day..." A surge of Seer power so strong it almost knocked me off my feet. "I've waited for you. Now, the question is, what are you going to do, Lilith?"

***

I couldn't believe we were back to this again.

"Listen, I really appreciate your opinion and all, but I'm not the first Seer or whatever it is you think I am." I sat at a dainty looking table while Michelle filled my plate with a ginormous heaping mound of the best smelling spaghetti my nose ever encountered. The bread, whose timer had beeped just as Rachel was throwing out the L-name, smelled even better.

"What I believe is the truth," Rachel said, her British accent making it sound extra haughty. "It's all I am allowed to believe."

Since my mouth was stuffed full of noodles and meat sauce, I raised my eyebrows at Liam, requesting a translation.

"Aunt Rachel Sees truth," he explained around a mouth full of bread.

Truth Seer. I knew there had to be one of those out there.

Of course, that didn't mean she wasn't full-on crazy, which I quickly started to suspect.

"And the truth as I See it is this: You, Harper Lee 'Scout' Donovan are Lilith, the first Shifter." Didn't she mean Seer? "The Daughter of the Creator. Artemis. The moon, sent to watch over the night." I started to protest, but she cut me off with a look that said there would be sever repercussions should I open my mouth. "Do you wish to hear the truth of your story?"

I wished to hear her say she was just kidding.

"Scout is the moon." Liam's tone said he also found Rachel's mental stability suspect.

"And God's daughter," I added helpfully.

Rachel didn't seem fazed by our sarcasm. "He goes by many names. God is merely the most popular."

"I'm Southern Baptist. Let's stick with 'God'."

"Well, then, when *God* created the earth, he left its care to his children. His son resided over the day, bringing brightness and warmth to all those who lived beneath. Later, that son would go on to make his own choices which would lead to the Thaumaturgics and Immortals, but in the early days, he was nothing more than a light unto his people. His sister, on the other hand, protected the creatures of the night, looking after each of them with warmth and compassion."

"Especially a wolf," I said, figuring this was how her story matched up with the one I already knew.

"Yes," Rachel said. "Every thirty days she would leave her heavenly home and walk amongst her people upon the earth. Wolf, the first of his kind and the most fierce of the night's creatures, walked with her on each visit. Over the years, their affection for one another grew, until they could no longer bear to be apart those other twenty-nine days. That is when they petitioned The Creator, your God, for a chance to be together forever."

"Oh wait. I do know this story." Marie gestured with a whisk she was using to make some sort of batter. "The Creator said they could be together, but there was a price to pay. Lilith could never return to her place in heaven, giving up the care of the night to her brother. Both of them were made humans, except on the one night when her brother was allowed to rest. On that night, they Changed into wolves so they could watch over the land." Marie spooned a bite of batter into her mouth and broke into a huge grin, obviously pleased with both her knowledge and whatever it was she was making.

"You forgot the part where they both became mortal," Michelle added. "But their spirit was supposed to live on. They would be reborn over and over again, becoming the eternal leaders of a new race of people."

This was so not the story Talley told me.

"That's great and all, but I'm not Lilith. And anyway, I thought she was the first Seer. What is this crazy first Shifter business?"

"What sense would it make to have a woman become the first Shifter if no female Shifters exist?" The way she asked made me feel like I was being taken to task by a stern British headmaster who believed strongly in corporal punishment.

"They changed it? Turned the first Shifter into the first Seer to keep the power tipped in the Alpha Female's direction?"

"What do you think?"

I thought it would take a lot of effort to change a hand-me-down story. "If Lilith was the first Shifter, where did Seers come from? Are they dusk and dawn personified?"

"The servants of the night, which shone on high with the Moon, were sent to Earth to keep her company and protect her."

The servants of the night, which shone on high... "So, you're a star?"

Rachel smiled. "Yes, or I suppose you and your fellow Southern Baptists might call us fallen angels."

A pair of grey eyes met mine from across the table. I expected to see more of this-lady-is-batshit-crazy, but it was replaced with thoughtfulness and...

Crap.

"You don't seriously buy into all of this, do you?"

"It makes sense."

"In what crazy, topsy-turvy world does this make sense? Bizzaro-Shifterland?"

"The one where a girl who shouldn't be a Shifter, is. The crazy world where that girl Shifter can Change at will and hold her wolf form for an infinite amount of time."

I wanted to pound my head against the table. Why was I the only one to realize how stupid this all sounded? I wasn't the reincarnated anything, let alone God's daughter. I mean, God doesn't even have a daughter.

"I suppose there is no use in me pointing out that you can also Change at will and hold your wolf form for an infinite amount of time?"

"Of course he can," Rachel answered. "He is Wolf. He bares the mark on his hip."

"The only thing on his hip is that stupid paw print tattoo."

Rachel's face was smug. "It's not a tattoo."

"Yes, it is." I looked at Liam. "Tell her."

His non-response said everything.

"You told me it was a tattoo."

Liam put down his fork and leaned onto his elbows. Most people would have looked comfortable and compliant in the same pose, but not Liam. Maybe it was muscles which had always been massive, but became more clearly defined over the winter as he chopped down half the forest and trained with unwavering focus. Maybe it was the set of his jaw or firmness of his mouth. Or maybe it was the intensity of his stare. Whatever it was, there was no doubt Liam was the exact opposite of comfortable and compliant. "I never said that. You assumed, and I let you."

"So... what? You've always known you were going to grow up to be the Alpha Male some day?"

"What I've always known is my life isn't mine to live." He dismissed me and my million questions by turning to his elderly aunt. "You know what we intend to do?" he asked her.

There was absolutely no apprehension coming from the old lady who once could have been an Alpha herself. "You're going to right what has been wrong for far too many years."

That sounded so much better than "kill them".

Liam nodded. "There may be others coming here in the coming weeks. Can you promise their location and identities are kept from The Den?"

"I will continue as I always have, providing shelter and safety for those who seek it."

Something in my chest clenched at the realization that this was it. This was where we would make our last stand and fight for the future of Shifters and Seers the world over against unbeatable odds.

This is where I would sacrifice my life so no one else would have to pointlessly die.

Liam's thoughts must have gone to the same place. "Will we win?"

"Fate is on your side," Rachel said. "How could you not?"

Chapter 25

There were no mirrors in Canada. Well, of course there are mirrors in the country of Canada, but there weren't any in our tiny cabin. Maybe if there had been, if I had seen the changes come over me slowly, I wouldn't have quite so frightened by the person looking back at me from above the sink in one of the Safe House's many bathrooms.

The basics of what make Scout Scout were still there - the silvery blond hair (which had grown out into a rather wretched Friar Tuck hairstyle); the pale skin (although the forty-five minute shower had managed to put a little color in my cheeks); and the ice blue (bloodshot) eyes - but the rest of me was different. The lack of proper nutrition left me sharp and angular while the nonstop training corded my arms and legs with muscles. I never considered myself soft and feminine before, but compared to the hard and hungry warrior in the mirror, high school Scout was a Disney Princess.

I leaned in closer, fascinated by the dark circles under my eyes. How did they get there? What was the dark stuff? Skin discoloration? Bruises? The dark parts of my soul coming to the surface?

I kept tilting forward until my forehead tapped against the glass and closed my eyes. I thought about just staying like that for the rest of ever, but despite the desire to collapse on the linoleum and take a little nap, I went in search of Liam. Again I got a hint of emotion, one that somehow felt like Liam instead of me, telling me he wanted to be left alone. It made me hesitate, but not for long. There was too much for us to discuss before I could actually go to sleep. I followed his scent up to the second floor. He didn't answer when I tapped on his door, and a test of the knob proved it to be locked.

"He's sleeping," a female voice said from my left. I swung around, already crouched down to pounce.

"Whoa. Sorry." Michelle stood with her hands raised in the air in the classic surrender pose. "I thought you knew I was here."

I ran a hand through my very wet, very ugly hair. "I should have." Crap. I was so focused on Liam and all the stuff happening inside my head I didn't take the time to adequately survey my surroundings. Stupid mistake. Sure, this place was supposed to be a Shifter Sanctuary or whatever, but if there was one thing I learned over the past year and a half is that I should take nothing for granted. There were always surprises. Things always went wrong.

People I trusted always locked me out.

I glared at the door, weighing the advantages of ripping the damn thing off its hinges.

"I thought you were going back to the library." Better to leave the door in one piece for now. There was no doubt Michelle would report the incident to Rachel. It wasn't like I was *scared* of a little old lady or anything...

Okay. Fine. I'm a little bit afraid of one particular old lady.

"Went and came back already." She grabbed the messenger bag she had strapped over her shoulder. "I have something for you."

I accepted the bag, which was weighed down with books and papers. "What's this?"

"Research." Michelle nodded towards a window seat at the end of the hall. I thought it might be a ploy to get away from Liam, but there was no way a few feet were going to make a difference. He wouldn't even have to try to overhear our conversation from that distance, but I didn't bother telling Michelle. I did accept the invitation to sit down, though. Actually, I wasn't opposed to having the conversation with me curled up on the gigantic cushion, even though it would mean that I would fall asleep after the first two sentences were uttered.

Liam was probably just as exhausted as I was. And he probably knew there was a chance one of them would come back. That's why he locked the door. It wasn't like he was trying to avoid me or anything.

And I was going to keep telling myself that until I believed it.

"I'm guessing this isn't the new JR Ward novel," I said, taking out a large book with an old fabric covering. "*Armstrong Line* doesn't really sound like one of her titles. Maybe *Strong Armed Lover*, but that's not quite the same."

Michelle's eyes narrowed from where she stood above me. "Aren't you a little young to be reading JR Ward?"

"Aren't I a little young to be attempting to overthrow a centuries old government?"

"Touché." Michelle didn't melt down into the cushions like I did. No, she perched rather smartly on the edge, her back straight and shoulders back. I took a moment to wonder if she had attended Catholic school. I always imagined the nuns made their students sit like that. "That's why I'm here, actually. Do you know who Reginald Armstrong was?"

"Should I?"

Michelle took the book from my hands and flipped through until she was just a few pages from the end. "Here," she said, handing the book back. The pages were set up ledger style, all the writing done by hand. She pointed to the top of a page where the name "Reginald Armstrong" was written in red ink.

"Ooookay..."

"The names written below are those of his children."

I scanned the list. Lois. Evelyn. Gladys.

Wait.

"Gladys Armstrong. I know that name." How did I know that name?

"Her family's information is on..." she checked a notation beside the name, "page 173."

I flipped over, and immediately knew where I heard that name before. "Gladys Armstrong became Gladys Minter. She was my great-grandmother." I remembered seeing the name on the family tree Gramma Hagan gave me as a birthday present last year. I didn't really make it far past the great-grandparent line, but that name stuck out because I sent up a secret prayer of thanks that my mom hadn't followed Take County tradition and named me after her grandmother. Gladys Donovan. Ick. "Why do you have a book with my great-grandmother's name in it?"

"We have a book for each of the Shifter family lines. This one just happens to be yours."

All the Shifter family lines...

I flipped through the pages, noting how several of the names were written in red ink, many with a "PL" beside them. All those names were male.

"My great-great-grandfather was a Shifter?"

Michelle nodded.

Holy crap. This was big. Huge. And something I really wish I had known a year ago.

"This is why I'm a Shifter then, right? I'm a real one, not some crazy reincarnated moon posing as a Shifter."

Michelle's eyes darted down the hall to Liam's room. When she spoke, her voice was lowered. "I knew you weren't buying the whole magical voodoo stuff either, so when I went back to pick up the other information I did a quick search of our databases. I was lucky, really. Someone just sent in an update of the Armstrong line last summer."

Last summer was the same time I got my very own copy of the family tree. Coincidence? Doubtful. Gramma Hagan has always been a smart lady.

"My best theory," Michelle continued, "is that something prodded you to Change last spring. Maybe the trauma of your accident, or your closeness to other Shifters, or--"

"Or getting a blood transfusion from a Shifter?"

Finally something broke through her perfectly-manicured appearance. "You got a blood transfusion from a Shifter?"

"You know about the accident?"

"The one where you were attacked by a 'wild coyote' and almost died?" She added air quotes around "wild coyote".

"Yeah, after that I needed a lot of blood. Our local hospital is small and was running low, so my step-brother Jase gave me some."

"Jase Donovan of the Hagan Pack? A coyote Shifter?"

Yeah, I totally saw the same flaw in my logic, and God knows Jase would have been all over it if he was there. "But a Shifter is a Shifter, right?" I thought out loud. "Like, whatever it is that makes a person Change is the same, the only difference is the animal they Change into."

"And whatever activates the Change might be the same in both wolfs and coyotes."

"And maybe wake up dormant Shifter tendencies in the great-great-granddaughter of a Shifter."

Michelle's smile was wide and sported those ubiquitous dimples. "I knew it! I knew there had to be a scientific explanation!"

I was really starting to like this girl.

"So, you're not into the whole magical voodoo either?"

I had pegged Michelle as one of those always-serious, super-together chicks who walked such a narrow line of "rightness" that black and white offered too many color options. So when she snorted and prefaced her "no" with the most forbidden of all four-letter words I almost fell off the window seat.

"In case you haven't heard, I'm latent."

As if someone would have missed her grandmother's somewhat rude announcement. "What does that have to do with anything?"

Michelle sighed and leaned back against the wall. I wondered if this was the real Michelle, the one few people got to see. Had we bonded? Were we friends now? I've never had many of those and most of the ones I have are either by default or accident. I wasn't sure how this worked, but I thought maybe this was it.

"Imagine spending your whole life surrounded by unexplained things and hearing that it's magic, but never getting to experience that magic for yourself."

"I guess you would get a little bitter..."

"No, not bitter," she spat out. I raised my eyebrows in the beat that followed. "Okay, maybe a little bitter, but more than that, you start to think of reasons, real reasons, it works for some people, but not you."

"You look for science and logic." I could certainly understand the appeal. "Is that what these papers are? Is this the science behind who we are?"

"I wish. Unfortunately, everyone besides you and me are satisfied with the magic explanation. I try to learn as much as I can about genetics and stuff like that, but I'm usually so busy helping Grandmother with the library--" She shrugged as if her inability to follow through was nothing, but I could see the frustration written all over her face. "Last week Marie told me we needed to start researching history of the Alpha Female. Since she can See what's needed but doesn't have the research skills it took some time for me to find what she was being pulled towards, but eventually we came up with all this. I thought it might help."

"Thanks." I flipped through the first few pages and already things were catching my eye. "Seriously, I'm really grateful."

"Pay special attention to the stuff in the manila envelope. It was really hard to get my hands on, which probably means no one is actually supposed to ever see it."

When I was finally able to pry my eyes away from my new treasures, Michelle was at the top of the stairs.

"I don't know anything about magic or fates, but I know people," she said. "And I know that you're the good kind. I may not be able to See or Change, but my daddy made sure I know how to fire a rifle. If you need me, just say the word."

***

I doubted I would ever call on Michelle to fight, but I moved her to the top of my "people to call when I need information" list. The stuff she gathered on the Alpha Females was amazing. I was so tired I could barely keep my eyes open, but I sat in the bed I claimed as my own and read for a long time. I started with the stuff in the manilla envelope. At first glance, I couldn't figure out what was significant about it other than it was a translation of some records from nearly two thousand years ago. Then, finally, I saw it. Alpha Female after Alpha Female was listed, and each was a Shifter. Their daughters were Shifters. Two thousand years ago female Shifters lived and flourished. Of course the current regime wouldn't want this information easily accessible. Who would believe that whole "girls are too weak to Change" propaganda then?

The translation wasn't complete, which I suppose is bound to happen when the original manuscript was written on parchment scrolls or whatever, but something happened right around the time they were nailing God's son (or Sun, depending on your beliefs) to the cross. The files were annoyingly short on details, but the Alphas both died suddenly at a young age with no children. In fact, from what I could understand, a large portion of Shifters died around that time, leaving only a few male Shifters and a Seer in the Alpha Pack. After that change of leadership there was a period of about five years that a very young Female Shifter took the Alpha position, but then the daughter of the Seer who originally filled the role was listed as Alpha. From then on, it was all Seers all the time, and the number of female Shifters listed in the records dropped dramatically.

Two thousand years. It was a span of time I couldn't really wrap my head around. How many had to know what was going on? How many turned a blind eye? How many willingly participated?

I wanted to think the number was small. I needed to. I may not be the fountain of happy thoughts and kumbaya Talley is, but I had to believe in humanity at least enough to think most people wouldn't allow this sort of thing to happen over and over again for so long.

I grabbed the phone Michelle left tucked into the bag and scrolled through the pre-programmed numbers.

"Hello?"

"Mrs. Rachel, it's Scout."

I heard the sound of footsteps, and then a door closing. "What is it? Has something happened?"

"No, nothing has happened. I'm fine. I just..." How to ask? "I was wondering how you found out about what was happening with the female Shifters."

"I see." There was scraping noise, probably a chair being pulled out. "You're wondering how they pulled it off for so long. How deep the corruption runs."

"Yes."

"It is not as bad nor as good as you think." I didn't bother telling her she had no idea what I was thinking. "It is not as if everyone in the Den knows what is going on, and I believe most of the Alpha Males, if not all, have been kept in the dark."

"So, Stefan could actually be innocent in all this?"

"Stefan killed my niece and her husband, and then spent a considerable amount of effort tracking down my nephews so he could do the same to them. And, if I'm not mistaken, he tried to cut your head off."

"Okay, maybe 'innocent' was a bit generous."

"You meant to say that he is not involved with the genocide of female Shifters, which I believe may or may not be the case. I simply know that he was not among those aware when I left the Den."

"Who was aware?"

"The Alpha Female and the girl she was grooming to be her replacement, Alexandria."

Wait. Alex and Liam's mom was going to be the Alpha? "I thought you were the potential Alpha."

A soft chuckle. "That was many, many years ago. I had already been passed over and was beginning to train as a Bibliothecary, although I hadn't really planned on moving off and using the knowledge. It was simply a way to fill my days. But then Alexandria came to me. She said the Alpha Female took her aside and told her the story of Lilith, the demon who seeks to eliminate Seers from the face of the earth. According to her, every generation Lilith is born into the form of a female Shifter, who are in and of themselves an abomination. In order to protect Seers, and the world, the Alpha Female must ensure no female Shifter is allowed to come of age. It was a compelling story, one I'm almost positive she believed, but Alexandria struggled. She came to me, asked me to See the truth in what was being said." There was a brief stretch of silence on the line. "She and I both left the Den by the end of the month. By the end of the year,

Alexandria had begun to put things into motion that would become this insurgence you have joined."

My chest was tight, and my stomach queasy. I felt like curling up into a little ball and crying, but I couldn't figure out what was causing this almost-panic-attack. Something wasn't sitting right with my subconscious, but for the life of my consciousness, I couldn't figure out what it was. Luckily, Rachel knew.

"You're questioning what you're going to do. You worry you're going to be spilling innocent blood."

Yes. That was it exactly.

"Liam said Sarvarna believes she's doing the right thing. This is what he meant, isn't it? She honestly thinks I'm an evil being bent on Seer genocide."

"Does that change what she has done? The deaths she has condoned?" I laid my head on the pillow. It suddenly seemed too heavy. "You've spoken with her, seen how she treats others. Do you really think the truth will change her actions? Do you honestly believe she will allow anyone who might take her power away from her to live?"

"What about the Stratego and Taxiarho? They're not evil." I knew from all those hours I spent locked in a basement with them. Sure, they held guns to my head and led me to death, and I did have to kill one just to stay alive, but they were just people. In any other circumstance, I might have considered some of them friends. Was it their fault they worked for a corrupted system? Did they even know? "Some of them will die, some of them already have, because of me."

"No, they will die because this is a war, and innocents always die in war."

Chapter 26

Liam was standing in front of the stove when I finally came out of my exhaustion-induced hibernation and ventured out of my room.

"I know it's technically supper time, but breakfast just sounded better," he said without turning towards me.

"Sounds great." And it smelled even better. I walked past the toaster just as two pieces of bread jumped out. I grabbed a butter knife and tub of margarine and started in on one of the few culinary tasks I was ever allowed to do at home. "Liam, we need to talk."

I was expecting an exasperated sigh or annoyed glare, but instead I got no response.

Zero.

None.

Nada.

"I'm not this Lilith person."

"Rachel said you are, and she Sees truth." Stoic Liam was stoic.

"My great-great-grandfather was Reginald Armstrong, a Shifter." Still nothing. "I think I was born with Shifter genes, but they didn't become active until Jase gave me blood after the accident." And still nothing. "See? There is an actual reason I can Change. No personification of the moon or offspring of deity. I'm just a normal girl with some abnormal genetics."

Finally, he looked at me. "What makes you think one cancels out the other?"

"Liam, you can't seriously believe I'm some destined leader sent to save the race or whatever. That's crap, and you know it."

And there was the annoyance and anger I was looking for. "Why? Why is it crap?"

"Because it is! There isn't any such thing as fated paths and destined leaders."

"And if I believe there is?"

I sagged against the counter. "Come on, Liam. You said it yourself. You don't believe in fate. You're not Alex."

"No, I'm not." He turned back to the stove and stabbed the eggs with excessive force. "Too bad you didn't remember that sooner."

"And what's that supposed to mean?"

More egg stabbing. I considered doing a little stabbing of my own.

"You are so pissing me off." Although, to be perfectly honest, I wasn't sure if it was the fact he was being a giant pain in the ass, or if it was because I could feel the force of his anger pulsing through me. It was probably a combination of both. "Will you just turn the Hades around and talk to me?"

He slammed the skillet onto the counter, his shoulders caving in as he dragged in a breath. "This is wrong," he told the eggs.

"Is this about the mating thing?" I could be brave and bring this up, right? "Listen, Liam, I think our wolves somehow made the choice for us, and--"

"This is wrong!" He wheeled from the counter. The moment his eyes met mine, he dropped them. "You're Alex's mate. He chose you. *He* loved you."

"In case you've forgotten, Alex is dead." I don't know who was more shocked and appalled by the callous way the words fell

235

from my mouth, Liam or me. I do know the sword of pain stabbing my heart had two edges, one for each of us. And I know that when he walked out of the kitchen and away from me, I had to let him.

***

I don't deal well with straight-forward rejection. The whole rejection en masse thing? Eh. No big. People, in general, suck. I don't really give a crap what they think about me. But I did care what Liam thought. A lot. A whole, whole lot. The more I thought about it, the more I cared, and the more it hurt.

For three days we avoided one another as much as possible. In the rare instances when we found ourselves forced to be in the same room together, like when his Aunt Rachel came to check on us, we adopted façades of apathy. My wandering eyes and carefully blank express didn't betray my wounded ego any more than Liam's bored scowl showed his true anger.

I don't know how or why he ended up in the living room where I was immersed in a *Downton Abbey* marathon. Maybe he wasn't paying attention, or maybe it was intentional. Whatever the case, one minute I was watching Professor McGonagall snip at some poor lady, and the next I couldn't tell you if there was a naked Jensen Ackles on the screen or not because Liam was standing in the doorway.

"Couldn't sleep?" I said without turning around, certain he would disappear like a ghost. "Me either." I remembered sleep. I wanted sleep. It just wasn't happening.

Without saying anything, he left. I knew he would. What I didn't expect was for him to come back.

"Liam?" I turned to find a wolf peering over the arm of the chair. "Oh. Hey you." I rubbed my hand over his head, and then dipped down to press a kiss there. "You know this is cheating, right?"

The wolf barked and backed up a couple of steps. Fully understanding his intent, because I was like Dr. Doolittle or something, I got up and followed him. We ended up back in my room. That night, for the first time since our little discussion in the kitchen, I got a full night of deep sleep. He was gone the next morning, but his scent still clung to my pillows.

***

"If you put your weight on your right foot in the second turn, you would get more force behind the kick."

I used the bottom of my shirt to wipe the sweat off my forehead. Well, mostly to get the sweat off my forehead. It also did a great job of hiding my face long enough for me to school my expression.

"I don't have time," I said, turning towards him with a perfectly bland face. "I'm coming off the roundhouse. I'll lose my balance."

Liam rubbed the back of his head, the first slip in his own carefully constructed mask.

"Make it a part of the same move. The momentum will keep you going. Here..." He walked up behind me and placed his hands on my hips. "Start the roundhouse..." I brought my leg up with exaggerated slowness. "...And as you bring this foot down..." Liam shifted my hips with his hands, which I wasn't expecting at all. As a result, I toppled right into him, catching myself by grabbing onto his shoulders.

He looked down. I looked up. Our faces were only inches apart. I could feel his breath sliding against my lips--

A knock pounded on the front door.

I didn't know if I wanted to kill or kiss whoever it was for interrupting. I saw the merit in both as I trailed behind Liam down the hallway. We were only a few feet away when I caught their scent.

"We come in peace," said a voice I knew as well as my own.

237

Liam had enough good sense to move out of the way as I flung myself through the door. Jase caught me around the waist, our momentum driving us straight into Toby.

"Whoa, calm down. Someone might think you're happy to see me," he said as I sobbed against his shoulder, unable to catch my breath the tears were coming so hard. "Scout, those are happy tears, right?"

"I missed you," was my garbled reply.

"Hey, I missed you, too." He squeezed me harder, and then I felt another arm slung across my back as the smell of Talley's shampoo tickled my nose. Someone rubbed a hand over my hair, and another squeezed my shoulder. And then there was another pair of arms joining into our group hug and I finally found a reason to pull back from my brother.

I tried to say his name, but only some sort of embarrassing bleating noise came out. It didn't matter. Charlie always knew what I meant anyway and had seen me a complete sobbing mess many times over the past eighteen years.

"Hey, shhhhh...." He pressed a soft kiss against my forehead. "It's okay. We're here. It's okay."

It took me longer than I care to admit to pull it together. I almost had it at one point, but then I made the mistake of noticing how Toby's eyes weren't one hundred percent dry, and lost it again. By the time I could form real words, everyone had shed at least a tear or two.

"I can't believe you're all here." Toby, Jase, Charlie, Talley, and a handful of other Hagans, including a guy my age I'd never seen before, stood on the front porch of the Safe House.

"We heard some crazy kid was Challenging the Alphas and wanted to get in on it," Toby said, pulling himself up onto the railing of the porch. Sitting up there he was above everyone else, just like a Pack Leader is supposed to be.

I hopped up to sit beside him.

"Sensei."

"Scout."

"It's been a while." I hadn't seen Charlie's older brother since he basically offered his life in exchange for mine at the trial back in July.

"It has," he agreed. His eyes trailed critically over me. "You look like crap, kid. And that hair... not the best look for you."

Because it was Toby who always made me feel like a five year old, I stuck out my tongue while pulling up my nose so it would resemble a pig's snout.

"That's very mature and classy, Scout. I hope you use it during your Challenge to the Alpha Female."

"Yeah, about that," I said. "How did you know we were here getting ready for that?"

Toby raised his eyebrows and looked at Liam, who was leaning against the door frame. So much for mine and Toby's play for Dominance. Liam was the uncontested winner even when he was slouching.

"I thought it was time to start gathering the troops," Liam said.

God, I loved him at that moment.

Not that I *loved* loved him.

Or maybe I did.

Crap. This was so not the time to be doing the angsty teenage boy problems thing.

"I thought we were going to wait until we were ready?"

"You are ready," Liam said.

Did I say "love"? I think I meant "hate".

"Ummm... No. I'm not."

"Ummm... Yeah. You are." For someone who hadn't been able to look at me since Friday, he sure wasn't having trouble maintaining eye contact now. "You're lifting 200 pounds twice a day, running five miles, and can do more push-ups in under a minute than most Americans can in an hour. You're fine."

Jase laughed, although I'm not sure what he found so funny. "Good to see you two worked out all your differences over the past few months."

"She's who we want to be our new Alpha?" That shining endorsement came from Makya, Jase's cousin who was ranked somewhere below foot fungus in Things Scout Finds Awesome. Not only had the annoying brat from childhood grown into an even brattier teenager, but he was also turning into a total skeeze ball. I always felt the need to shower after all of our run-ins over the past year. "Someone remind me why."

"It probably has something to do with that whole Scout being Jesus's sister thing," Liam said ever-so-helpfully.

"I'm Jesus?"

"Jase!" Talley smacked his arm, eyes wide. "Don't be sacrilegious."

"Hey, he started it!"

"I didn't know Jesus had a sister." Charlie was propped up against the banister. I pretended I didn't see the cane he was trying to hide behind the post.

"He doesn't," I said. "Liam and his family just happen to be suffering from a case of inherited delusion."

"What, pray tell, does this delusion include?" Charlie asked.

"Oh, the usual. I'm the actual child of God, who used to be the moon but got turned into the first Shifter, and have now been reincarnated to lead my people out of bondage and set up heaven on earth, or some such nonsense."

"Heaven on earth. Would that be anything like an all-you-can-eat pizza buffet?"

"I was thinking more like Disney Land without the lines."

"I would've gone with Universal," the new-to-me guy said. "They have that cool Spider-Man ride *and* Butterbeer."

I actually took the time to look at him and realized he wasn't a part of the Hagan Pack. Hagan men are on the short side of average height, solid without the word heavy ever crossing your mind, and green eyed. This guy was like a six foot tall bean pole with big brown eyes bugging out of his narrow face. I decided he had to be from another Pack, although part of me rejected the idea of him being a Shifter at all. There was something off about him that I couldn't quite put my finger on.

"Who are you?" It wasn't the most polite introduction ever. My grandmothers, all four of them, would have been appalled.

"Joshua," he said, holding out a huge bony hand. "I'm Jase's roommate."

Surely I heard that wrong...

"Jase's roommate? From college?"

"Yes, ma'am."

"Jase somehow magically got paired with a Shifter roommate?"

"Me? A Shifter?" Joshua snorted.

I wheeled on my brother. "I know I said you needed to be more honest about all this Shifter stuff, but I was talking about with me, the sister you've known your whole life. Not some guy you met in August. And I certainly didn't mean to bring him to my cage match with Sarvarna."

Jase leaned back against the glider he and Talley were sitting in front of and pulled his mate against his chest. "Liam said we needed people."

"Shifter people. Not human people."

"Oh, well, if it helps, I'm not human." *Crazy not-a-Shifter say what?* "Maybe I should retry that introduction." He stuck out his hand again. "Hi, I'm Joshua, an Immortal."

I waited, but no one laughed.

"There are no such things as Immortals."

Joshua reached up and tugged on his ear. "Am I supposed to pinch you, or are you supposed to pinch me to prove my existence?"

"Either of those will only prove you're corporeal." I pulled out the pocket knife I had found in the kangaroo pouch of the Harley hoodie. Using a move Liam drilled into my head over the winter, I pinned Joshua to one of the porch posts and aimed the knife at his jugular. "That isn't what I need to know. Now, do I stab you, or do you stab yourself?" I pushed the tip a little further into his neck, but not enough to even nick him. I may be prepared to take on the entire Alpha Pack if I have to, but there was no way I could really stab a guy who looked like a Muppet. But I could scare him a little, especially if it would end whatever stupid joke he and Jase were having at my expense.

His hand grabbed my wrist, wrenching it around until I dropped the knife.

"No stabbing."

"But I thought Immortals were, you know, *immortal*."

"I am. If you stab me, I'll live, but it's still going to feel like someone shoved a knife into my neck."

I eyed the knife. It had been days since I had a proper sparring session, and anyone strong enough to disarm me was worth playing with. I trusted the Hagans not to bring someone who couldn't handle a little hand-to-hand for the fun of it. "You know, they say that which does not kill you makes you stronger." I lunged for the knife, but it was kicked away before my fingers could close on the hilt. And then a kick caught me in my ribs, not hard enough to break anything, but enough to knock the breath out of me. I flew back, not stopping until the house caught me.

"Thanks, but I'm strong enough already."

I would have agreed with him, but first I had to remember how to breathe.

"By the way," Jase said, "I brought my friend Joshua along. He's an Immortal. Don't pick a fight with him. Apparently those guys are like crazy strong."

"Thanks." I stood up and stretched. My ribs were tender, but not broken. I could feel a bruise forming on my left shoulder where it got up close and intimate with the brick wall. "Your timing is, as always, impeccable."

"Oh, and I already did the Touch-and-See thing to confirm it," Talley added with an impish smile.

"Great. You've turned Talley evil." I rotated my wrist, which seemed to be in perfect working order. "And don't think I can't see you trying not to laugh, Charlie Hagan. You're on my list now, too."

Charlie tried to swallow his smile and failed. "We thought about telling you right off the bat, but decided this would be way more fun."

Joshua seemed to be just as amused as the others. "I suppose you were in on the ambush plot?"

"I've always wanted to see how I'd fare against a Shifter." He shrugged those thin shoulders which should not have been able to hold so much freakish strength. "This seemed like a good practice round."

As I hobbled over to the glider next to where Liam was holding up a wall, I gave Joshua another perusal, this time doing nothing to hide my assessment. Yes, those arms were long and thin, but not lacking in muscle. His posture was supposed to appear relaxed, but once I took the time to actually look, I could see the warrior's stance. From the way he responded to my aggression, I would say he was trained. Extremely trained. Like Jason Bourne trained.

"Immortals are real?"

"As real as Shifters and Seers," he said.

"And Thaumaturgics?"

"I've met a few."

"How does that work? And how did you end up sharing a room with my brother?"

"How it works isn't for you to know, and Jase just happened to get the luck of the draw."

Right. Sure. That didn't sound way too convenient at all.

I folded myself onto the glider. "Tell me, Joshua the Immortal, why is it you're here?"

"Same as everyone else here. The Alphas took someone I loved. Since I can't get them back, I'll have to settle for a little vengeance."

"Funny, I thought we were all here to get ourselves killed so Scout can feel oh-so-special." Makya was sprawled across the glider facing me, making it impossible for me to miss the disdain oozing in my direction. "I mean, is she really so good in bed you're willing to die just to tap that again?" His question was aimed at Liam and Charlie. "If so, I need to be getting me some of that before we throw down with the Alphas."

Shifters are all fast, but Liam made the rest of us look like slugs when he crossed the porch and jerked Makya up by his throat.

You know those moments when the right thing is crazy obvious, and you know you're supposed to do the right thing, but you just can't seem to bring yourself to do it? This was one of those moments for me. I knew I was supposed to make Liam stop. Makya was turning blue, for the love of Pete. Of course he should stop. And I knew I should be the one to say, "Liam, put the idiot down," but I didn't. I watched Makya struggle, his feet a good two inches off the ground. I watched Liam, who could have been a statue for as much as he moved. I heard Jase say, "Dude, he can't breathe," and Charlie mention something about it not being worth it, but I did nothing. I suppose if Toby hadn't stepped in, I might have just sat there and watch Liam kill him, although I doubt Liam would have let it go that far.

"He's a coward and a traitor." Liam dropped him back onto the glider. In the first intelligent move of his entire life, Makya stayed down and didn't say a word. Although, I guess it's kind of hard to talk when you're gasping for breath. "I want him gone before morning," Liam said as he walked back into the house without sparing the rest of us a glance.

"He's crazy," Makya wheezed once he had enough air to accomplish it.

Finally propelled to do something, I went to stand over the sorry sack of loser. There were lots of people to blame for what went down last summer, and most likely it would have happened without anyone's help, but at that moment all I could think of was how Makya set off a chain of events which ended with me standing in front of a guillotine.

"Because of you, three men died, one is in a coma, and your cousin can't walk without a freaking cane. You've earned whatever bad crap happens to you, Makya. It's called karma, and it really is a bitch to those who deserve it." I leaned in and showed him my teeth. "Ironically, so am I."

"What did I do? None of that was my fault! That was your doing, you psycho!"

"We all know who made the call to The Matthews Pack which led the Alphas to us, so just shut up." I leaned in even further so he could feel my breath on his face. "Liam wasn't kidding. You better be gone by morning, but feel free to use my phone before you go to make your call. Be sure and send Sarvarna my loathing."

It was a stab in the dark, but his face proved I was right. "You'll get them all killed," he said. "My family. My father. They're all going to die just because you think you're so freaking special. Scout Donovan, the high and the mighty. I've been putting up with you and your holier-than-thou crap since we were kids." Pure hatred seared through his gaze. "I can't wait until they put you in your place."

"New deadline." I leaned back on my heels. "Either you're off this property in fifteen minutes, or I finish what Liam started."

I expected a lot of things, but a gun wasn't one of them. I darted to the left, grabbed Makya's arm, and used his momentum to throw him over my head... and directly into the outdoor fireplace Liam had lit earlier in the evening.

"You might want to stop, drop, and roll there, buddy," Jase said when a flaming Makya jerked himself back onto the porch.

Toby tossed a throw around Makya's shoulders and threw him to the ground.

"Fourteen minutes." My voice sounded cold and firm despite the adrenaline pumping through my veins.

Makya threw off the blanket, and I could see burns all down his left arm and across his back where his shirt had been charred off. They looked painful, but not life threatening. With one final declaration that we could all perform sex acts on ourselves, he jumped off the porch and started walking in a ridiculously leisurely fashion towards the road.

Chapter 27

"How are you *really* doing?" I asked Charlie, flopping down next to him on the two person glider. The adults had all found their way to various beds and inflatable mattresses, leaving the under twenty crowd to hang on the porch.

"I'm fine?" He looked genuinely confused. "Why?"

I grabbed his cane and twirled it like one of those wooden rifle things the marching band chicks have. "No reason."

Jase, who was once again snuggled up with Talley, reached over and took the cane, which never stopped spinning as it passed from my hand to his. "His left leg and back are jacked up. The back was broken, and the leg is from the gunshot wound. He was supposed to shoot his inner-thigh. He missed."

I made my hand into the shape of a gun and pointed at my leg. And then I tried a different angle. And then another.

"Okay, I give up. How did you miss?"

Charlie scooted down in the chair and then kicked up with his good leg. The cane went flying. He caught it before it smacked into his head without even looking up.

"Guess I'm just clumsy."

I laughed, because that was what I was supposed to do, but it didn't feel right. I hooked my arm with his and laid my head on his shoulder. At one time, sitting like that with Charlie would have sent my heart into spasms of excitement, but now it did the opposite. Being able to touch him, to know he was okay, calmed me. "You know I'm really mad at you, right? What kind of moronic move was that anyway? What were you thinking trying

247

to take on the Alpha Male and three members of The Alpha Pack on your own?"

"I was thinking, 'I'm not going to let them kill one of my best friends,' at first; and then I was thinking, 'I'm not going to let them kill me'; and by the end I was thinking about how the cake is a lie, but I'm pretty sure that was the brain injury taking over."

"First, *the cake is a lie*? Thanks for that vote of confidence. And secondly, a brain injury? Seriously?"

Joshua, who was about three-quarters of the way asleep, allowed a single eyelid to slit open. "Did someone say cake?"

"It wasn't so much a brain injury as a concussion," said Jase.

"A concussion is a brain injury, genius."

Jase looked at Talley, who confirmed my facts.

"Well, he's no longer brain injured, so unwind your knickers."

Again Joshua's eye slit open. "Did someone say Snickers?" And then he snored.

"Is it an eating disorder or sleeping disorder?" The guy seemed nice enough, and I was all for an enemy of my enemy being my friend, but Joshua was about three steps to the Russell Brand side of weird.

"It's a circadian rhythm issue," Joshua said without opening his eyes. "This staying awake all day is killing me."

"To be fair, it's also an incurable sweet tooth issue," Talley said. "Apparently living forever means you can live off a steady diet of sugar and starch without having to worry about diabetes."

"You're just jealous."

"And you're somehow snoring and talking at the same time. Go to bed."

"Talley Matthews, I am old enough to be your grandfather. Do not tell me what to do."

We all just sat there and watched Talley stare him down.

"Fine," he finally relented not thirty seconds later.

Not long after Joshua shuffled into the house, everyone else began succumbing to exhaustion. I was tired, too, but I just couldn't bring myself to go inside. With the influx of people, Michelle redid all the sleeping arrangements, throwing Liam and me in the same room. That was not a situation I wanted to walk into. So, instead I stayed on the porch, watching the stars from a cocoon of blankets.

"Got room in there for me?"

I opened up one side of my blankets. "There's always room for Talley-O."

My best friend snuggled in beside me, resting her head on my shoulder. "Go ahead," I said when I felt the gentle push of her Sight. Since she was touching me, I knew each emotion she felt: surprise, sympathy, and finally, exasperation.

"I did it again."

"Did what again?" she asked.

"I screwed up with this whole mating thing." I rubbed a hand over my face. "God, I hate this aspect of Shifter life. Aren't relationships hard enough without adding in some supernatural life-long binding crap?"

"Talk to me about it."

"Why? Didn't you already grab it out of my head?"

She burrowed in closer, the fragrance of her baby shampoo overpowering every other scent. The smell brought back so many memories I felt choked by them all.

"Maybe I need you to explain it to me."

"Maybe you're trying some sort of psycho-analytical bull crap."

A silent chuckle. "Maybe, but tell me about it anyway."

I sighed. "Rachel says Liam and I are mates, and since I get the same sort of snippets of emotions off of him that I do when you're projecting to me, I tend to believe her." Because, let's face it, that's what all those phantom emotions were. I wasn't fooling anyone, myself included, by pretending otherwise.

"And you don't want to be Liam's mate?"

A star shot across the sky, and like a little kid, I made a silent wish.

"Did you know Rachel says you're a star? All Seers are. You're stars, and I'm the moon. I'm not sure what Joshua is supposed to be. Maybe a cloud."

"Scout, you're avoiding the question."

Yes. Yes, I am.

"He's not the person I thought he was."

"And is that a good thing or a bad thing?"

"He's not angry," I said. "Well, he is angry, but he's also sad. And guilty. And overwhelmingly burdened with the weight of the entire world."

"Reminds me of this blond chick I used to know."

"He's so Dominant and bossy you want to strangle him half the time, but when no one's looking, he's kind and thoughtful. He even has a sense of humor."

"Sounds like a pretty good guy."

"He's a great guy."

"Not to mention incredibly attractive."

"Ridiculously so."

"Do you think you could love him?"

"I know I do."

Good God. I said it out loud. That made it real, right?

"So, what's the problem?"

"Take your pick. He thinks I'm betraying Alex. His wolf chose me as his mate, and he resents it. We're in the middle of picking a fight with the most powerful Shifters on the planet, which isn't exactly the ideal time to get involved in a relationship." When I tasted blood, I removed the inside of my cheek from my teeth. "And let's not leave out the whole 'Scout is a love whore' issue."

Talley tilted her face up. "What is a love whore exactly?"

"You know, some reckless person who goes around falling in love with every attractive guy she comes across. Charlie. Alex. Liam. I'm all, 'Oh! Pretty boy!' and the next thing you know I'm ruining everyone's lives because I want to curl up inside them and live there forever."

"That is quite possibly the most bizarre and creepy description of what it feels like to fall in love I've ever heard."

"Falling in love *is* bizarre and creepy."

"And awesomtastically, amazingly wonderful." A huge smile. "I know you think you made a mistake when you forced Jase to declare me his mate, but you didn't. You did us both the biggest favor anyone has done for someone else ever."

You couldn't argue against the joy radiating from her. "You're going to have to tell me how exactly you two became the world's happiest couple."

"I will. After."

"After what?"

"After you become Alpha."

I couldn't stop a chuckle from squeaking out of my throat. "Are you bribing me to stay alive, Talley Anne Matthews?"

"And accept the position once you earn it."

"Jase really has been a bad influence on you."

"He says the same thing about you." Her voice was laced with humor, but when she sat up, it was gone. "You're going to survive this."

"Of course I am." I tried for a smile. "Me and Death, we keep going at each other, and I keep coming out on top. Why would this time be any different?"

"This time, you have the hope of an entire species and the heart of a mate depending on your survival."

I glowered. "Thank you. Like I needed more stress."

"I'm just 'keeping it real,' as the kids like to say."

"What kids?"

"The ones from 1990."

We sat in silence for a while after that. I was thinking about being "the hope of an entire species" while Talley might have dozed off a bit.

"You realize the fault in your logic, don't you?"

Or maybe she was just staying super-quiet so she could scare the pee out of me when she finally decided to speak again.

"My logic is always sound, but which particular logical explanation are you having trouble understanding?"

"Liam's *wolf* chose you to be his mate?"

"Our wolves... they mesh. They always have." He was the first thing Wolf Scout knew in this world, and her trust of him has never wavered. She considered him hers, and he didn't seemed to have any problems with her claim. Their bond was undeniable. "Wolf Liam took the choice away from Human Liam."

It ripped my heart in two to admit such a thing, so it ticked me off a little that Talley found it so freaking hysterical.

"Wolf Liam? Human Liam? You act like they're two different people."

"They are."

"Are Wolf Scout and Human Scout different?"

"Of course."

"How?"

Why was she asking me? Wasn't she the one who explained it all to me in the first place?

"Wolf Scout is all instinct and acts without thought. I over think what I'm having for breakfast."

"But the base things - your beliefs, hopes, fears, and *loves* - do those change? Or is Scout always Scout, no matter how she may look?"

I could see where this was going.

"It's different..."

"And even if Liam's wolf was the one to make the choice to take you as his mate - which I don't believe for one minute - you're ignoring the fact that if ever there was a wolf who sometimes took human form instead of the other way around, it's Liam Cole."

This is why every girl needs a best friend. Sometimes you have to have someone to pull your head out of the sand and show you the stuff you're too stubborn or stupid to see.

"You think he does want to be with me?"

"Seriously? You have to ask?"

I collapsed against the back of the glider, relief and frustration vying for the top spot. "Then why is he being so difficult about the whole situation? Couldn't he just kiss me and say, 'Yay. We like each other and get to spend the rest of our lives together'? Is that really so hard?"

"I didn't say you guys don't have baggage."

"Alex?"

"Alex."

And back into a little ball I went. "I know he's not Alex, Tal. Seriously, I do."

"I know that, but does Liam?"

"Ummm...."

"And what about Charlie?"

"Confusing Charlie with Liam has never been a problem."

"You know that isn't what I meant."

"Charlie and me..." How to explain it? "Until the day I die I'm going to feel responsible for Charlie's emotional well being, and he's going to keep doing stupid stuff like shooting himself in the leg to try to protect me. We'll love each other forever, but like family. Any chance we ever had at a romance died along with Alex. We've both accepted that." And while it still made my heart ache, I really had accepted it fully. "One day he's going to meet someone I deem worthy, and their kids will call me 'Aunt Scout'. Every time they get in trouble, I'll tell them a story of something equally horrific we did as children."

"Remind me to keep your actual nieces and nephews far, far away from you."

"Not a chance, future sister-in-law."

Talley's hand stroked through my hair. "I'm going to go out on a limb here and say Liam doesn't know any of this either."

"Stories about our energy-filled, misguided youth?"

A classic Talley/Mom look. "That you and Charlie aren't *you and Charlie.*"

"It's never come up."

"You have to talk to him, Scout. You can't just go around hoping things will work themselves out. You have to do some of the heavy lifting."

"You know, he's probably overheard this entire conversation, so I don't really--"

"Talk to him."

"How about after?"

"How about now?"

I growled, but not because Talley was pushing me. It was because she was right and I knew it. I looked up to the second story as if Shifterdom came with X-ray vision.

Talley stood and stretched. "I can see my work here is done." She grabbed my hand, hauling me to my feet. "Now, get up there and claim your mate, Scout Donovan, Donovan-Hagan-Matthews Pack Leader and future Alpha Female."

***

There was a wolf in my bed.

No. Not "a wolf". I had to quit thinking of it like that. Liam. Liam was in wolf form in my bed.

And if he could cheat, then so could I.

"It was the day we fought the wolf pack," I said, sitting down on the side of the bed. "I know I didn't tell you before, but the only reason I was able to Change so fast in the daylight was because I knew if I didn't, you would die, and I couldn't let that happen. I couldn't lose you." I buried a hand in his fur, and he laid his head on my leg. "I almost died myself. I know that you know it was bad, but I'm telling you I was there, in that In Between place with Alex, and I was given the choice. I could go quietly into that gentle night and be with him forever, or I could come back and rage against the dying of the light to be with you." I looked into his eyes, eyes that were one hundred percent human. "I chose you, Liam. I didn't even have to think about it."

I brought my hand up to rub the fur on top of his head and tried to ignore the way it was shaking. "I know you don't want this whole mating thing, and honestly, I think we're way too young to be making lifelong commitments, but it's over and done with now. Maybe it's not what either of us planned on happening, and maybe it's not the ideal situation, but it's the one we've been given. And it may be selfish, but I can't help but be happy that I'm going to get to spend the rest of my life getting to know you. I mean, I know it's not going to be easy, and we'll probably have such epic fights there will have to be an entire volume devoted to them in The Repository, but I want to be there for all of it."

Liam stood up. My heart clenched, certain he was going to go Change, but instead, he repositioned himself on the bed. At first I thought it was another rejection, but then he lifted his head and stared at my pillow to say, *"What are you waiting for?"* Knowing I wasn't getting anything else from him, I crawled onto the bed, eschewing the covers for his warmth.

Chapter 28

"They're coming."

I landed in a heap at Talley's feet, thanks to Joshua the Freakishly Strong Immortal.

"They who?" I panted out. I held onto my ribs as I leaned to the right, and...

Yep. Some of them were definitely broken. It was a good thing I was becoming an old pro at Changing whenever I wanted, since everyone was using training as an excuse to play the Beat the Crap Out of Scout game. In forty-eight hours, I had to heal a sprained ankle, two broken fingers, and a dislocated shoulder.

"The Alphas," Talley said. "Mischa just sent me a text."

While Jase was sucking up to Sarvarna, Talley had been getting closer to the Seers of the Alpha Pack. In many ways, it was the riskier endeavor. No one knew for sure what Sarvarna Saw - the most popular rumors pegged it as either opportunity or what a person desires most - but everyone in our camp agreed it was something which allowed her to manipulate those around her. Works pretty well when you're playing politics, but it doesn't really help you identify a spy. On the other hand, Talley was dealing with Seers able to pull thoughts from her head. One misstep and it would have been game over. Fortunately, she soon discovered two of the more powerful Alpha Pack Seers - Mischa and Lizzie - were already on Team Scout. Apparently Mischa Saw something very convincing when she touched me last summer, so over the winter they began passing along helpful information to Talley when they could.

"And by 'coming' you mean...?"

Talley twirled a piece of hair around her finger. "Here. They're coming here."

"Do we know when?"

Talley shook her head as Charlie swore from the corner where he and Jase had been lifting weights.

"It was Makya," Toby said. "Damn it, how could he do that? What the hell was he thinking?"

I bit my tongue to keep from commenting on Makya's ability to think. His slimy weaselness was hitting Toby hard. The Pack Leader felt as if he had failed us both. I'm not exactly sure what it was he thought he could have done for Makya, other than possibly removing his vocal cords.

Liam appeared in the door of the sitting-room-turned-training-room as if summoned. "He'll have to be dealt with eventually."

"I'll take care of it." It was a statement, but one seeking permission. Liam gave it to Toby with a manly slap to the shoulder.

While the Makya the Backstabber issue certainly needed addressing, I felt we had more pressing matters to discuss. I pulled myself up into a sitting position, careful not to jar my ribs. "What is she up to, Jase? What will her game plan be once she gets here?"

Jase snagged a water bottle and dropped down beside me. "Why are you asking me? You're the brains of the operation. I'm mostly here as eye candy and the occasional witty retort, much like Thor in *The Avengers*."

"First, Thor is a god--"

"You're the one who said I'm Jesus."

"--Secondly, if you're Thor, then I'm Loki. I don't really approve of this comparison."

"Nah. You're not Loki. Your horns are too small. I'm thinking that role goes to Angel. Can't you see her trying to take over the world just because she can?"

"The difference between Loki and Angel is Angel would succeed, and probably have three quarters of the world happy she did." I could already see her sitting on a giant pink throne, issuing out orders. Most of them would have to do with making the world as pretty as possible. As far as absolute rulers go, the world could do a lot worse. "And third, you're the one who has been getting all buddy-buddy with her over the past nine months. Surely you've got a better idea of how her brain works than any of the rest of us."

"Scout, I've known you since I was eight weeks old, and I have no idea how your brain works. What makes you think I figured out Sarvarna's already?"

I started to put my head on my knees, but then my ribs reminded me why that was a bad idea.

"You know," Jase said, "I could just call her and ask."

"That's quite possibly the worst idea I've ever heard," Charlie said, saving me the trouble.

"No, think about it." Jase tilted forward with excitement. "We can do like those cop shows. Set up a tap. Let the smart people analyze everything she says and the background noise. Trace the call."

"We don't have phone tapping equipment, or a team of analysts," Toby pointed out.

"We're Shifters, and the full moon is tomorrow night. We don't need actual phone taps. And Joshua can handle the phone trace, right?"

"I could do it in my sleep."

"Toby's a cop," Talley noted. "He could probably pick up something from a conversation."

"Hey, I'm not a--"

"And don't forget about you and Scout and your complete nerdiness." Jase was literally rubbing his hands together.

"This idea sucks." I looked to Liam for support. "Tell him he's being stupid. He never actually listens to me."

Liam, the traitorous jerk, just shrugged. "I don't know. I think it's worth a try."

I kept up a running argument against what Jase was calling Operation: Phone Call until the moment we were sitting around the dining room table, a phone in Jase's hand.

Even knowing Sarvarna possessed normal human hearing, I was afraid to so much as swallow.

"Good afternoon, your majesty." Jase leaned back in his chair, his posture reflecting the same casual ease as his voice. Beside him, Talley sat stiffly, her hand in his. It was a condition he insisted on, wanting to make certain Talley always knew which part was a show for Sarvarna, and which part was real.

"Jase, dear, I've been trying to call you for days. I was starting to think you were avoiding me."

I fought to control my breathing. It was bad enough everyone in the room could hear the way my heart kicked up at the sound of her voice. I relaxed my face, hoping they would interpret the increased heart rate as excitement instead of the fear creeping up my spine.

"How have you been, Sari? How is the renovation of The Den going? Got my room done yet?"

I listened intently to the background noises. She wasn't alone, although those around her were taking as much care as we were to be quiet. I tried to count how many hearts I could hear, but it was impossible over a loud droning noise.

"The noise in the background, what is it?" I mouthed to Liam.

He cocked his head, listening. Then a hint of panic shot through me. *"Airplane,"* he mouthed back.

"Your room is very near finished. It makes me sad you will never see it."

So she wasn't playing dumb. Good.

"Yeah, well, I guess my priorities have shifted."

And neither was Jase. Thank goodness. I can only handle so much lying and subterfuge before my head starts hurting.

"I don't understand," Sarvarna said. "You could have had so much, yet you align yourself with those who want to destroy our entire society. Why would you do that?"

Toby, who was sitting on the opposite side of the table, held up six fingers. Liam shook his head and jerked his thumb up. More than six people on the plane. It was the general impression I was getting, too. Eight was my conservative estimate, though there could have been more, too far away from the phone to be heard.

"The system is broken, Sari. We've got to fix it."

"By declaring war on your race?"

Joshua spun a laptop around. The page looked like some sort of official Homeland Security type thing I did *not* want to know how he accessed. On it, there was a list of flights. He pointed to two, both of which were private planes taking off from Romania with final destination in the northern part of the United States. One landed in two hours, the other in six. He highlighted the one landing in two hours and wrote "80% probability" on a piece of paper.

"We're not declaring war. We're simply seeking a regime change. You could end this all by stepping down and handing over the leadership to someone who deserves it."

"And whatever makes you think I don't deserve it?"

You're an evil, hateful witch?

"You tried to kill my sister."

Oh, yeah. There's that, too.

"You know this will end badly for you all, don't you, Jase?"

"I don't know about that." Jase met my eyes and smiled. "I've got Lilith and Wolf on my side. Something tells me, you're the one looking at a not-so-happily-ever-after." And with that, he disconnected the call.

***

"They've got eight or more on the plane," I said as soon as Jase sat the phone on the table.

"And if the Immortal is right…"

"I generally am."

"…She's landing in Odom Pack Territory. I don't think that's a coincidence," Liam said.

Toby looked at the map Joshua pulled up on the laptop. "The Miller Pack isn't too far from there, either. And don't discount the Bowens. They might be all the way over in Utah, but they're the biggest and most Dominant Pack in America."

Talley's gaze flicked from one face to another. "I don't understand…"

"She's building an army," I said. "She's going to try to take us out before I can issue a Challenge." I closed my eyes, an attempt to focus through the panic. "Someone give me a number."

"Twenty-five, conservatively," Liam's voice answered.

"Talley," I said.

"Scout," she answered.

"I want you on the next plane out of here." I turned to Joshua. "Can you handle that? Get her back to Kentucky, but not to Timber. Send her to the Matthews Pack. If they decide to go after her, they won't immediately look there."

"No, I'm staying here."

"Tal..."

"I'm staying."

"You're going."

"No."

"Talley, you're not a fighter. You're a Seer. This is could get painful and messy. You don't need to be here."

Instead of arguing, Talley stood up, pulled a Baby Glock from underneath her bulky cardigan, and aimed it at my head. I dove as she squeezed off two shots.

The guys in the room uttered a chorus of profanities as I came out from under the table in a rage. "What the heck is wrong with you? Are you crazy? Were you trying to kill me?"

Charlie pointed to the window beside me, which Talley had shattered. "You're not the only one who has been keeping up with training," he said. "Talley goes to the range almost every single day. She's become quite the legend."

Rachel was one of those old ladies with a penchant for ugly yard decorations. There were metal owls nailed to trees, a variety of wind chimes making a racket, and ceramic creatures littering the lawn. Now there were two less, since Talley killed a ceramic squirrel and stained glass frog.

"You're like Samuel L. Jackson! What the crap?"

Talley slipped the gun back in its holster. "I need to stand up for what I believe in. I won't be in the direct line of combat, but if I need to, I can protect myself and those I love. Wasn't that the whole point of making me learn self defense? I mean, it was your idea, Scout."

Fine, if I couldn't talk Talley into leaving, maybe I could make our injured list see logic.

"I don't suppose there is any way I could talk you into leaving," I said to Charlie.

"Not a chance." I started to make my argument, but he cut me off. "I'm not planning on fighting, but I'm not leaving either."

Not a complete victory, but it was better than nothing.

"You'll stay with Talley?"

"And protect her with my life."

Of course he would. Protecting his friends, no matter what it cost him personally, is what Charlie does.

Within minutes the dining room became a war room. The guys talked defenses and perimeters, most of their plans sounding like video game strategies. While they talked, I Googled bloodless coups. The results weren't what I would call optimistic, but I still held on to hope.

The next night was the full moon. At Toby's request, Marie and Michelle moved into the Safe House. The Hagans were keeping watch over them while Liam and I went to guard over Rachel, who refused to be "bullied by a little girl with delusions of grandeur." Luckily, her apartment complex was on the edge of town, which meant there was a nice big field less than half a mile away where Liam and I could stand sentury.

"One of these days, I would like to wander up on a spot where I know something fantastically wonderful is going to happen," I said. "Like, 'Oh, look at this dirt path. This is where someone is going to give me a new car and a lifetime supply of ice cream.'"

Liam dropped his bag. "Talley's vision?"

"Talley's vision," I confirmed. "If you want a front row seat, I think the big showdown is going to happen right over there." I pointed back towards the little stream cutting through the field.

Liam turned in a slow circle, finally stopping once he faced the direction of the town. "We'll go that direction once we Change instead of sticking around here."

"No. We'll stay. No use in trying to run away from it."

"I thought you didn't believe in fate."

I dropped my bag beside his, then knelt down to dig out our food. "I don't, but I do believe in Talley."

We continued to get our things in order in silence. I was heading towards a patch of trees where I could Change in privacy, when Liam said, "It was when they were holding you captive." I stopped walking, but didn't turn around. "It was perfect. They were cautious the first few days, but once the Hagans started falling in line, they let up, thinking they were free of threats. I had everything I needed. I could have rigged it up and gotten Jase, Talley, and Charlie out of the way before it actually blew, but I knew there was no way to save you. I told myself it was because of Alex, that I couldn't let you die because he would never forgive me, but it was a lie. It had nothing to do with Alex, and everything to do with me." He was behind me then. I turned to meet his gaze. "Sometime, and I don't know when it was, you ceased to be Alex's obsession and became mine. The way you reacted to everything happening around you... It was strange and unsettling. But the stranger and more unsettling you got, the more intrigued I was. I wanted to know why you were like that. What made you so... *Scout*. And I knew if I did what I was supposed to do, if I blew up that cabin with you inside it, I would never get to know you." His hand trailed over my cheek, resting at the crook of my neck. "That was when I chose you, Scout. And even knowing what's to come, I would have done it again." And then, he kissed me.

There is something to be said for being kissed on purpose. Sure, out-of-control passionate kisses are all sorts of breathtakingly sexy, but knowing someone has actively made a decision to put their lips against yours is even better, especially when that person is as focused and thorough about the whole matter as Liam. He didn't pull back until my knees were weak from it.

"We're going to win," I said, hands clenched in his t-shirt so I wouldn't slide onto the ground into a puddle of properly kissed goo.

"Damn straight."

"And then, we're going to figure this out."

A slight lifting of the corners of his mouth in a classic Liam smile. "I look forward to it."

This time, I kissed him on purpose.

Chapter 29

"Surrender now, and I will let the others live." It was nearing daylight when I heard Sarvarna's voice echo through my head.

"I haven't issued a formal Challenge yet, your majesty. Don't you think you're jumping the gun a little bit?"

"You've gathered a group of Shifters together with the express purpose of overthrowing the Alpha Pack. Your brother has already admitted to it. As per our laws and customs, you are guilty of treason and subject to death."

I finally caught her scent, and not just hers. Liam was right, there had to be at least twenty of them, and they were close. Too close. They stayed downwind, which was the only reason we hadn't noticed them before.

"I thought I was supposed to die because I was a Thaumaturgic and an abomination. Come on. Make up your mind."

"There are many reasons I will kill you, but now you won't have to die alone. For your cowardice, your friends will now die alongside you."

Liam slinked through the grass in the general direction of the Alpha Pack.

"Cowardice is sending in a legion of Shifters to fight your battles, Sarvarna. Call them off, and we'll do this. Just you and me." I trailed behind Liam, veering off slightly to the left.

"A leader doesn't deal with such petty skirmishes. She delegates."

And then they were upon us. It was like a wave of wolves bursting from the tree line. The acidic taste of fear flooded my mouth, but I didn't let my terror control me. I sprinted across the grass and lunged at the first wolf I came to. The power he radiated marked him as a true member of the Alpha Pack, so I didn't hesitate as I sank my teeth into the soft part of his neck and yanked. I moved on to the next in line before he even hit the ground.

Or maybe I should say the next two in line, since I was tag-teamed. While one distracted me from the front, the other sunk his teeth into my right hip. The pain was excruciating, but not debilitating. I slung the wolf in front of me into a red wolf who was charging towards Liam, and then spun around to face the coward who had my blood staining his muzzle. My teeth ripped into his front leg. The injury wouldn't kill him, but he wouldn't be walking again until the sun rose either.

Liam and I were good, and even better as a team, but no one can expect to win when the odds are two against twenty. The fight would have been over before it started if a second wave of Shifters hadn't burst from the tree line, my brother's small body in the lead. I barely processed there were more than a handful of Hagans when a black wolf landed in front of me.

I was confused, unsure if this was a friend or enemy until his smell registered. Warm baked cookies and Miriam's favorite laundry detergent.

Hank. I wasn't surprised. He said he would always come when Liam needed him.

One of the Alpha Pack lunged, and Hank ducked low before coming up in a fury of teeth and claws. Convinced he could take care of himself, I turned to face my next attacker.

"Excellent timing, Tal." Just a few minutes more, and the army we had scraped together at the last minute would have been avenging our death instead of fighting by our sides.

"Most of them just got in before the sun set, and then we had to get all the way across town in animal form," came her reply. "You honestly didn't think to inspect the field you would be Changing in before you got there? If you would have told me yesterday where the battle was going down, this would have gone much more smoothly."

I would have defended myself, but I was too busy fighting for my life. I don't know what human war is like. I've never been crouched down in some Middle Eastern hole in the wall while gunfire and explosions echo around me, but I can't imagine the sound is any more horrifying than what I heard throughout our battle. Snarls and howls. Whimpers and whines. I constantly sought out the voices I knew, listening for sounds of triumph or harm.

Liam and I focused our initial energies on the the Stratego and Taxiarho. I tried to exert Dominance with them, to force them into submission, but it wasn't happening. I knew it wouldn't, but I still tried. I didn't keep up with how many I killed, although I knew their individual faces would come back to haunt me in my dreams. The others, the ones who had simply come to defend their Queen, were easier. Some of them would actually submit to me, which meant I could let them live. It didn't always happen, but it did happen. Maybe it was only the allies I had mistaken for the enemy, but I like to think otherwise.

Occasionally I would catch a glimpse of the others. Liam was, as always, magnificent. Like me, he was trying to force submission or merely injure as many as possible, but when there was no other choice, he killed quickly and without hesitation. Jase was paired up with Joshua, who was swinging a sword around like a gladiator. Once I even saw a coyote I was certain was Makya. He wasn't in the middle of the fray, but instead another Hagan purposefully kept him corralled to the sideline.

The battle seemed to wage on forever, but I know it couldn't have been more than half an hour before the sun started to rise in the sky. The less Dominant ones were the first to fall to the ground, the tremors of the Change wracking through their body. Liam and I stayed in wolf form until the very end, guarding over the others along with Joshua, who was still carrying around his sword. I don't know if there are actual Rules of Engagement for Shifters, but I felt strongly one of them should be not attacking someone mid-Change.

The field looked exactly as it had in Talley's vision. Blood was everywhere. Even though most every wound would heal during the Change, their skin would still be stained with the blood spilled. But not everyone would heal. I made my way through the mass of writhing bodies. Hank was one of the first I ran across. I could tell the fight had been particularly hard for him, but he was Changing quickly. I was happy for him, but more so that Liam didn't have to lose another father figure.

Jase was a bit harder to find. The relief at seeing him mid-Change almost outweighed the weirdness and grossness of seeing him mid-Change.

"Scout?" Talley's voice was tearstained, even in my head.

"Jase is okay."

"I know, but Toby--"

I took off at a full run, using my nose to find him. I leapt over bodies that were part human, part animal, only paying enough attention so I didn't accidentally step on anyone. I found him far away from the others. He was in human form, and had been for some time. Yet again a Shifter's last ditch effort to survive had failed.

Another Shifter lay crumbled in front of the body. Still mostly coyote, he growled and snapped his teeth as I approached.

"Talley, can you talk to Makya?"

269

"He didn't do it, Scout."

I already knew that. Not only could Makya not take Toby, but the grief rolling off of him was palatable.

"Tell him that no matter what happens, he's to stay here. If he lets anyone other than a Hagan touch the body, he'll wish he was the one who died."

"Scout--"

"Tell him."

"Is that an order from my Alpha?"

My eyes couldn't break away from the body crumbled on the ground. Memories flashed through my head: Toby talking Charlie, Jase, and me into stealing Grampa Hagan's prized watermelon out of the garden when we were kids. Toby walking out of the delivery room, a huge grin on his face as he cuddled Layne against his chest. Toby getting off the plane after nine months in Iraq, tears streaming down his cheeks as he ran towards his family. Toby standing in front of the Alpha Pack, asking them to let me go.

Brave, strong, chauvinistic Toby. I would be damned if I let him die for nothing

"Yes. Let's end this."

***

Speaking of Alphas, it was time for me and Sarvarna to have a little face-to-face time. I Changed back next to my clothes. It felt a bit like cheating with everyone else having to go naked, but there was no way I was confronting her with my boobs on display in front of a bunch of guys. Liam, who was wearing a pair of jeans, was waiting for me once I was fully human and dressed.

"Toby's dead." As far as greetings went, it sucked big time, but I couldn't help it. It was this rotten, horrible thing I had to get out of me. "They killed Toby."

Liam brushed the tears from my cheek with the back of his hand. "I am so sorry. He was a good man."

"How do I tell Charlie? Oh God. How do I tell Layne?" My heart was broken. I knew because it hurt so much.

"Scout, you need to breathe."

Couldn't he see I was trying?

"Who else? Who else did we lose?"

"We've lost about five. Joshua's arm looks like hamburger, but he assures me it'll heal. Everyone else should be okay once they finish Changing."

"Which is my one and only mercy." I didn't flinch, which probably pissed her off. She tried to sneak up on us, but not even the smell of blood could block her scent from me. "Surrender now, and I will merely Banish the others."

I thought I wouldn't be ready for this moment, that when it came I would see too much humanity in her to follow through. Toby's death changed that. I didn't care if she loved her parents or was adored by her little sister. And if she thought I was a demon, it was because she made me become one.

"If I don't?"

"We'll start all this again, but this time the wounds won't heal so quickly."

I looked across the field, even though this scene had been etched in my brain for almost a year. "That might not be the best idea, Sarvarna. As you might have noticed, most of your Alpha Pack is dead." And I would carry the guilt of it for the rest of my life. "Are you prepared to lose more?"

"I believe I'm more prepared to lose soldiers than you are, Scout." Her upper lip curled. "Maybe it's because we both know all this blood and death is on your hands, not mine."

"I can't tell if you're crazy enough to actually believe that or not."

"Surely you know none of this would have happened if you weren't a power hungry abomination."

"I'm sorry. Are you talking to yourself here? I can give you some privacy, if you need it."

Hatred lit her eyes. "You think this is a joke?"

"Actually, I think this is a Challenge." Shoulders back. Voice loud and clear. No one could be in doubt of what was happening. "Sarvarna, I officially Challenge you for the position of Alpha Female."

"You can't do that!"

"I can, and I did."

"Submit," I said to her through the brain-to-brain network. *"You know you can't beat me, and I don't want to kill you. Please. Submit."*

Sarvarna stood there debating her options for a second before releasing a breath. "Okay," she said, her head dipping down. She walked slowly towards me, her shoulders bent forward. Then, when she was standing directly in front of me, her head whipped up. "I accept your Challenge."

At first, I didn't understand. I saw her hand clutched around the knife sticking out of my stomach, but it seemed like a stage prop or something. Then, the pain hit and I knew it was real.

Pull it out. Pull it out. Pull it out...

There was a scream piercing the air, but it wasn't mine. I wanted to tell Liam it was okay, and maybe mention that I loved him, but I couldn't talk. I couldn't do much of anything. If only she would pull out the freaking knife...

"I told you I wouldn't let you take what's mine." She rotated her wrist and my vision wavered. "You should have just died like you were supposed to in July." Another twist. I wasn't going to make it. "In fact, you never should have existed."

"And you should have never been Al--" The world started going black. My body went slack, and Sarvarna pulled the knife from my stomach.

Finally.

272

With the absolute last of my consciousness, I yanked energy from the ground beneath me. Two heartbeats later, Sarvarna found herself pinned to the ground by a very angry arctic wolf.

Submit.

Sarvarna bared her teeth as if she was a wolf herself. It was the last thing she ever did.

Chapter 30

Death has many smells. The sulfuric bite of gunpowder. The metallic tang of blood. The harsh burn of hospital antiseptic.

"Would you like a few moments?"

The bright yellow and purple flowers on the nurse's scrubs offended me with their cheeriness. This wasn't a cheerful moment. It wasn't a cheerful place. The only part of a hospital where someone should be allowed to wear such blinding colors is the maternity ward. Everywhere else is filled with people in their darkest moments. When you're going through hell, the last thing you want to see is your nurse in something so bright it glows in the daylight.

"No," Liam said. "We're good."

Those ridiculous scrubs moved towards the IV pole. Just as her finger was posed in front of the touch screen I yelled, "No!"

"Leslie?" Liam asked, using the name we gave the hospital staff when we presented ourselves as Stefan's son and soon-to-be daughter-in-law.

I tucked a piece of the strawberry blond wig behind my ear. "I think I need some time with him first." Some time before they stopped all the drips and machines that were keeping Stefan alive and cemented Liam's and my positions as the new Alphas.

Before running off to fill out paper work or whatever it is nurses do while they're waiting to end a life, she grabbed a box of tissues from the shelf. "Here you go, sweetie," she said, handing them to me. "You take all the time you need." There was no door to shut in this unit, but she slid the curtain closed behind her as she left.

Stefan looked nothing like his former self. The man I knew was strong and proud, radiating so much power even normal humans instinctively knew to stay out of his way. The man on the hospital bed was shriveled up, except for the odd places he was bloated out like a Macy's Thanksgiving Day balloon. His dark skin had turned a sickly yellow, the color a cross between a bruise and a stain. The Stratego who kept watch over him had taken care of his hair as best as they could, but still it hung off his head in dull clumps. The scar which ran down the side of his face no longer screamed menace. Instead, it whimpered pain and defeat.

I blinked against the stinging in my eyes.

"The doctors say you're still in there," I said to Stefan. "They showed us graphs with wiggly lines and said it was your brain activity. And then they told us you may never wake up, and if you do, you will never be able to function like you once did. You won't be able to walk or talk or even swallow. You will spend the rest of your life hooked up to these machines." I took a deep breath. "Someone once told me I wouldn't be able to do this. They said I wouldn't be able to stand here and kill you while you're defenseless, but they were wrong. Of all the things I've had to do these last few months, this is the easiest, because I'm not killing you, Stefan. I'm setting you free." I squeezed Liam's hand even tighter. "*We're* sitting you free."

I moved closer to the bed. I thought about reaching out and grabbing onto his hand to give him some comfort in these final moments, but I couldn't do it. Yes, I felt sorry for him, but not so much that I could forget all the pain he caused others.

"You should know this is an official Challenge. Liam declared it to the Stratego, and they allowed it without protest. Of course, that was probably because there aren't many of them left, and with Sarvarna dead, they aren't willing to die for you."

The monitor lit up as his heart rate spiked, setting off a few bells and whistles.

"So, they were right. You are still in there. Good. I need to you to hear this," I said as Liam walked around to fiddle with the monitor, which surprisingly went quiet. I hoped it was because he somehow knew what he was doing, and not because he had unplugged it a few minutes too early.

"I didn't want this. It's not like I woke up one day and thought, *I'm going to take over the Alpha Pack.*' I know many people, including you, don't believe that, but it's true.

"I don't know where it all went wrong. You're probably as much a victim of circumstance as I am. The difference is, once we were in the middle of it, you chose power over basic human decency. I know the world is an imperfect place - that peace, love, and harmony are pipe dreams - but I need to believe it can be better than this." I looked across the bed into Liam's eyes. "I need to believe we can make it better." My voice cracked. I took a deep breath, and before I could release it, Liam was there, gathering me into his arms.

"I'm done," I said into his chest, letting his warmth seep through my clothes and flesh to warm the chill inside. "It's time. Let's get this over with."

Liam's lips pressed against the corner of my eye, absorbing the liquid gathered there. A rush of heat shot straight to my heart, and then he was moving away from me and towards the bed. He looked huge leaning over Stefan's withered form. His aura of power blanketed the former Alpha Male, and I could have sworn I saw is body shudder under the weight of it.

"For the record," he said, his finger hovering above the Call Button, "this is for my family, you selfish bastard."

I barely had enough time to be shocked before a flock of scrubs descended upon the room.

"Are you ready?" Cheery Scrub Nurse asked.

I nodded, afraid of what would come out should I try to speak. A middle-aged man with a paunchy gut and receding hair line also gave a nod of the head, which was apparently the call to action. Cheery Scrub Nurse started pushing buttons on the IV pole. It took both longer and less time than I expected. We all stood there - the doctor, nurses, Liam, and me - watching the monitor as Stefan's heart rate slowed. When it finally flatlined, someone turned off the screen, but I couldn't see who through the tears in my eyes.

***

I wanted nothing more than to escape the sterile sadness of the hospital, but it wasn't happening. In the thirty-six hours since Sarvarna's death, a lot of plans were made, including one to reintroduce Scout Donovan to the real world.

"Unless you want to see my butt, you better close your eyes," I called out the door before traipsing into a hospital room of my very own. Liam was sitting on the corner of the bed, his eyes very much open as he leaned to the side. "What are you doing?"

"Trying to get a glimpse of your butt, but you're ruining all my fun."

My face burst into flames as I double-checked to make sure I was holding my gown together in the right place.

"What is wrong with you?" I hissed, very much aware that the FBI agents standing outside my door had Shifter hearing as I crawled up onto the bed and immediately threw a sheet over my legs.

Liam shrugged. "It's a nice butt."

He was flying to Romania in a matter of hours and *now* he wants to get all cute and flirty? That was so not fair.

Once I was settled with all my nearly naked parts tucked away, Liam climbed up next to me. There was no awkward shifting or limb organizing. After half a year of sleeping side-by-side, we knew how our bodies fit together.

"You doing okay?"

I took a cue from him and thought before I responded. "It had to be done."

"That doesn't answer my question, Scout."

No, it didn't, but it answered the more important one.

"I'm going to miss you," I said, oh-so-cleverly switching topics.

"You could come with me. You're the Alpha Female now. Your place is at the Den."

"No, my place is with my family." He already knew my answer just as well as I knew his argument. This wasn't a new discussion. "I miss them so much it hurts."

"You could be putting them in danger if you stay."

"And I could be leaving them to face the danger alone if I don't." Not everyone was onboard with our little regime change, and I wasn't naive enough to believe those who wanted retribution would play by the rules. "I've not been very fair to my parents this past year. I need to make it up to them."

This is where our discussion ended. It always did, because there was nothing Liam could say to refute that. It didn't mean we wouldn't say the exact same things two or three more times before he left.

"I want you to relinquish your position as Alpha Female."

Then again, maybe we wouldn't.

"Excuse me?"

"I had Rachel do a little research, and it's possible. All you have to do--"

"You want me to *relinquish* my position as *Alpha Female?*" It was a good thing I wasn't hooked up to any monitors. Every freaking alarm would have been blaring. "The position I just got by ripping the throats out of anyone who would oppose me? The position you've been training me to take for months? You want me to just... *relinquish* it?"

"You don't want to go to the Den--"

"Because it's in *Romania*. Do you know how far Romania is from Kentucky? Fifty-five hundred miles. That's nearly 9000 kilometers, in case your Canadian brain can't do the math."

Liam had been reclined alongside me, but now he was sitting up, his scowl back where it belonged. "Scout, calm down."

"Calm down? You're asking me to give up after everything I've been through. What was the point?" A horrible, sickening thought occurred to me. "Was this your plan all along? Was I really nothing more than a pawn to you?" I was shaking with fury. "Did I do a good job, Liam? Did I kill them all dead enough for you? Did I save your hands from enough blood that you'll be able to live with yourself?"

"You're not being fair."

"*I'm* not being fair?!?!"

One of the Shifters/FBI agents outside the door discreetly coughed, pointing out that even people without super-senses could hear us.

When Liam spoke again, his voice was decidedly quieter. "I thought this is what you would want."

"You thought wrong."

"Obviously."

He didn't elaborate, so I did. "I made a commitment, and I'm going to stick to it. This is important. I might not believe in destiny or fate or any of that other crap, but I do believe I'm supposed to do this."

Liam picked up one of my hands. The knuckles were covered with scrapes and bruises from an encounter with one of the Odom Pack. More bruises stretched down the right side of my body, and if I wasn't mistaken, my wrist was broken. Again. I could have healed everything by Changing, but the bruised and battered look added more credibility to the "held hostage by terrorists" story. One of my first acts as Alpha Female had been to make sure the United States government recognized Toby Hagan for dying during the rescue mission.

"I can't protect you if you're Alpha," he said, his fingers gently tracing the damage on my hand. "This isn't going to stop any time soon. The entire Shifter world is in chaos, and you're at the center. You'll be safer if you just disappear."

"And what message would that send?" I shook my head. "No, I can't run and hide anymore. I'm going to stand up for what I believe in, even if it means I have to take a few hits every now and then."

A kiss against a knuckle missing all of its skin. "I don't like seeing you hit."

"Well, to be quite honest, I don't like being hit unless it's by you." As soon as it was out of my mouth, I realized what I had said. "That sounded all sorts of wrong."

"Insanely so, actually."

"To be clear," I said to any overhearing ears, "I hit him back--"

"Hard."

"It's a very give-and-take, non-abuse type hitting situation..."

The sides of Liam's mouth folded up like an accordion. "You should probably stop now."

"I'm trying. My mouth keeps moving of its own accord."

I felt the vibrations of Liam's laugh as he pulled me once again into his arms. "Go with me," he whispered against the top of my head.

"Stay," I countered.

"I can't."

Tears threatened, but I blinked them back. "Neither can I."

280

Chapter 31

"Banana splits are too health food. It's dairy and fruit and nuts. Dairy and fruit and nuts are good for you." Angel spooned up more sugary goodness from the bowl that was as big as she was. "Tell him, Scout."

"The kid is right. Dairy, fruits, and nuts are indeed good for you. We know. Our mom is a nurse."

The Strip was crowded, which was pretty much standard operating procedure for the summer. Tourists and locals swarmed to the only place in Lake County with anything that could pass as entertainment. I liked it well enough on rainy days and at the end of the season when the temperature dropped and everyone else had grown weary of its charm, but being there on a sun-shiny July Saturday was akin to torture, especially after the complete circus of the last three months. We had only been there for fifteen minutes and already three people had come over to either ask if I was *that* Scout (like there are five or six of us running around) or express their sympathies over those long months I had spent as a hostage of God's Army of Defenders. It was the same every single time I went out in public. For some reason people thought I would want to tell them all about "my personal tragedy" (CNN's wording) when I refused to grant an interview to every single media outlet in the world.

"Milk is good for you. Ice cream is not," Joshua, who was living with us for the summer, countered.

"Ice cream is made of milk," Jase added helpfully.

"So is the whipped cream," Charlie chimed in.

"She wasn't lying about the fruit either. Bananas, pineapple, *and* strawberries. It's like a vitamin explosion."

"And that would be the final nail in your argument's coffin," I said. "Talley is, as always, the deciding vote. You lose."

"Loser, loser, loser," Angel chanted. "Joshua is a big, fat L-O-S-E-R!" The second, third, and fourth verse were the exact same as the first.

It was good to be home.

I took a deep breath, delighting in the humidity laden air. Sure, it smelled of fish guts and sweaty children, but it was Timber air. At moments like this, when I was surrounded by the familiar, I could almost convince myself things were back to normal. It was hard to remember all the death threats (which had slowed from daily to weekly), Really Important Decisions (which I had to make with alarming frequency), or blood I had spilled when the teacher's aide from my kindergarten class was munching on a hamburger ten feet away from where my little sister was being slung over the shoulder of an 80 year old teenager.

Okay, maybe "normal" was pushing it.

"But you said we could ride go karts," Angel wailed, bringing my thoughts back to the here and now.

"They were full. We had to get a reservation," Jase explained for perhaps the twentieth time.

"When's our reserve?"

"Reservation," I said. "And it's at two o'clock."

Angel pushed a stray curl out of her face. "What time is it now?"

"Fifteen minutes until two," I said. *Which means it's 9:45 in Romania.*

Not that I kept up with what time it was in Romania and thought about what a person there might be doing at any given time of the day. Nope. Not me. I wasn't one of those crazy kind-of-not-really girlfriends. I mean, it wasn't like I constantly thought about him and sometimes, like when I was hanging with my favorite people on earth at The Strip, swore I smelled him on the breeze or anything.

God, I was a sad, pathetic excuse for a human being.

"Fifteen minutes? It'll take us an hour to walk there!"

Joshua, who had released Angel only when she agreed to hand over her banana split, pointed with the long, red spoon. "Those go-karts over there? It'll take us an hour to walk across the street?"

"Yes!"

I couldn't decide if she really didn't have a firm grasp of time and space, or if she was being overly dramatic. Either way, it was kind of hysterical, especially since it seemed to really bug Joshua. Don't get me wrong, I like the guy, but he's really fun to annoy.

"We probably need to go anyway," I said, peeling myself off the plastic picnic bench. "There will be a line--"

The world ceased to exist around me as I became entangled in a stare. He didn't smile or give any other indication that he was happy to see me, but I knew.

You always know with your mate.

I started to cross the street, but then had a better idea. "Go on without me," I said over my shoulder as I headed back towards the lake. There was a moment of indecision when I wasn't sure which tree was *the* tree, but eventually I found it and made myself comfortable. I didn't have to wait long.

"So, the guy sitting on the next bench down from me--"

"He smells like Play-Doh." I threw up a hand to shield my eyes from the glaring sun.

"Why?"

"It's one of life's greatest mysteries. I don't think we will ever know."

Liam sat down across from me. I wanted to reach out and touch him to verify his existence, but I didn't. A part of me knew he wouldn't mind, that he would want me to. Unfortunately, that wasn't the part of my brain controlling my motor functions. That part imagined how much it would hurt if he pulled away or looked uncomfortable at the contact. So, I sat there, hands in my lap, and tried to appease myself by looking at him.

"We could ask him."

"Don't be ridiculous." The urge to touch wasn't fading, so I leaned back against the trunk, putting more distance between us. "I don't know where you come up with these crazy ideas."

It wasn't like we hadn't talked over the last few months. We sent emails (social networking sites weren't really a great place for me to be, so we had to kick it old school), called, texted, and even had a weekly Skype check-in. Still, it was different to see him in person, to be able to see each of the folds in his cheeks when he smiled.

"Any new Challenges?" I asked to divert my attention.

"Just two since Wednesday; one backed down as soon as I walked into the room."

"And the other?"

Liam plucked a blade of grass from the ground. "Dead."

Which brought the total up to four. With each failed Challenge, I hoped it would be the last. It wasn't that I doubted Liam's ability to always prevail, but I worried about the scars it was leaving on his soul. We had already revoked the fight-to-the-death clause of Challenges, but there were some who refused to submit, no matter how badly they were beaten. I couldn't decide if I found those men audacious or stupid.

"I had a Challenger from the Logsdon Pack show up this morning."

Liam froze mid-pluck. "At your house?"

"Yeah, but he never got around to actually issuing the Challenge. Apparently he was one of Talley's former suitors, so Jase answered the door with Joshua's sword. I think the poor guy may have cried a little."

Liam went back to ridding the earth of grass one blade at a time with a chuckle. I was about to ask him if he had heard any more about the pack of Siberian Husky Shifters someone was rumored to know when he looked up with a frown.

"Why are you wearing that face?" he asked.

I touched my cheek. Thanks to my mom and Gramma Hagan, I was starting to gain weight, but my cheekbone still stuck out a bit too far.

"This is the face God gave me," I said, trying to hide the hurt in my voice. "I can't exactly take it off and put it on a shelf."

"I'm talking about this." A finger brushed against my mouth. "And this." He tapped the corner of each eye.

"Those came with the face. It was a package deal."

"Did they come all scrunched up like that? Because, in my experience, you only look like that when you're stressed or frustrated." He huffed out a breath and rubbed the back of his head. "Is it because I'm here? I should have called you first. Sorry. I just wanted to surprise you."

Something in my chest felt warm, probably the last little piece of my heart melting for him.

"I'm frustrated because I want to touch you so bad I'm literally hurting my hand to prevent it, and I'm stressed because I don't know how you'll react when I lose control."

Liam looked at me like I was an alien for about half a second before crawling over me, one hand finding the back of my head to drag my lips to his. He was enthusiastic in his kiss, and I responded in kind. I didn't realize how much I missed the taste and feel of him until he was in my arms.

Nearly two years had passed since Liam and I first met at this very spot. So much had happened; so much had changed. I wasn't sure what brought us to this point - fate, destiny, or merely the choices we made - but I wasn't sorry for it. I regretted the pain I caused others and mourned the lives lost, but I knew I was where I was supposed to be. It wasn't a happily ever after. We had more than our fair share of challenges and Challenges ahead of us, but we were heading in the right direction. Liam and I are going to make the world a better place. Together. And for us, it's enough.

Scout's journey may be
over, but the world of
Shifters & Seers
lives on...

New series
coming in 2013!

Acknowledgements

I'm just starting to accept the fact that Scout's journey began in the first place, so I can't even begin to comprehend the fact it's over. This entire process has been beyond my dreams and expectations. I sincerely thank each and every person who has walked this path with me. Thank you for taking a chance on a self-published book, for loving the characters like I do, and for encouraging me to keep going, even when it wasn't easy.

Thanks are also owed to...

My early readers, Crystal Blackwell and Jennifer Noffsinger, who push me to keep coming up with more words. These have been my go-to girls from the very beginning, believing I could do it even when I wasn't so sure I could finish a chapter, let alone a whole trilogy.

Alyson Beecher and Erin Lowery, who have looked at messy first drafts and helped me find the story hidden within. Scout (and I) owe you a lot.

Victoria Faye, the best cover illustrator in the business, for making me look good.

Dr. Joe Lowery, who answers all my uneducated science questions with patience and in a way I can actually understand.

The Beta Fish. Scout wouldn't have existed without you, and you've helped her find her way time and time again. Each of you will always hold a very special place in my heart.

Jennifer Sanders and Lydia Powell for being such awesome new beta-readers. Your guidance was greatly appreciated!

Leslie Mitchell, for letting me be her test-run as a freelance editor. If there are errors in here, it means I changed something after she looked at it.

Sarah Pace-McGowan, who finds all my lost commas and only asks for a free meal in return. This time, we're eating steak!

Everyone at the Marshall County Public Library. Life would be much less bearable if I didn't love my day job so much.

Holli Powell at Thrive Consulting for not only taking care of my finances, but also being an awesome friend who makes awesome playlists.

Samantha Young, my first "fellow writer" friend. You are awesome. One day I'm going to visit Scotland and buy you a drink.

All the UtopYA girls, especially Abbi Glines, for being fantabulous.

My friends - Becky, Dusty, Jason, Shauna, Matthew, Jennifer, Robby, Kelly, and Crystal - for dealing with my constant distraction and whining. If I've forgotten an important event or date in your life over the past two years, my sincerest apologies.

Haley, for being the best kid in the world. I love you more than I'll ever be able to say.

My parents, who made me the person I am today. I would be nowhere without their love and support. My greatest regret is that my father didn't live long enough to see me become a published writer. I know, without a doubt, he would have been my biggest and most vocal fan.

To all the people who have blogged about my books; wrote a review on Amazon, Goodreads, or another site; or simply told a friend about Scout, I will forever be indebted to you. Thank you for helping me live my dream.

About the Author

Tammy Blackwell is a Young Adult Services Coordinator for a public library system in Kentucky. When she's not reading, writing, cataloging, or talking about YA books, she's sleeping. You can follow her on Twitter (@Miss_Tammy), write to her at Miss_Tammy@misstammywrites.com or visit her at www.misstammywrites.com.

CPSIA information can be obtained at www.ICGtesting.com
Printed in the USA
LVOW081647220313

325631LV00013B/187/P